B.J. DANIELS

STROKE of LUCK

HQN™

This book is dedicated to my husband, Parker William Heinlein,
who puts love into everything he cooks for me.

CHAPTER ONE

"Bad luck always comes in threes."

Standing in the large kitchen of the Sterling Montana Guest Ranch, Will Sterling shot the woman an impatient look. "I don't have time for this right now, Dorothea."

"Just sayin'," Dorothea Brand muttered under her breath. The fifty-year-old housekeeper was short and stout with a helmet of dark hair and piercing dark eyes. She'd been part of the fixtures on the ranch since Will and his brothers were kids, which made her invaluable, but also as bossy as an old mother hen.

After the Sterling boys had lost their mother, Dorothea had stepped in. Their father, Wyatt, had continued to run the guest ranch alone and then with the help of his sons until his death last year. For the first time, Will would finally be running the guest ranch without his father calling all the shots. He'd been looking forward to the challenge and to carry on the family business.

But now his cook was laid up with a broken leg? He definitely didn't like the way the season was starting, Will thought as the housekeeper leaned against the counter, giving him one of her you're-going-to-regret-this looks as he considered who he could call.

As his brother Garrett brought in a box of supplies from town, Will asked, "Do you know anyone who can cook?"

"What about Poppy Carmichael?" Garrett suggested as he pulled a bottle of water from the refrigerator, opened it and took a long drink. "She's a caterer now."

Will frowned. "Poppy?" An image appeared of a girl with freckles, braces, skinned knees and reddish brown hair in pigtails. "I haven't thought of Poppy in years. I thought she moved away."

"She did, but she came back about six months ago and started a catering business in Whitefish," Garrett said. "I only know because I ran into her at a party recently. The food was really good, if that helps."

"Wait, I remember her. Cute kid. Didn't her father work for the forest service?" their younger brother, Shade, asked as he also came into the kitchen with a box of supplies. He deposited the box inside the large pantry just off the kitchen. "Last box," he announced, dusting off his hands.

"You remember, Will. Poppy and her dad lived in the old forest service cabin a mile or so from here," Garrett said, grinning at him. "She used to ride her bike over here and help us with our chores. At least, that was her excuse."

Will avoided his brother's gaze. It wasn't like he'd ever forgotten.

"I just remember the day she decided to ride Lightning," Shade said. "She climbed up on the corral, and as the horse ran by, she jumped on it!" He shook his head, clearly filled with admiration. "I can't imagine what she thought she was going to do, riding him bareback." He laughed. "She stayed on a lot longer than I thought she would. But it's a wonder she didn't kill herself. The girl had grit. But I always wondered what had possessed her to do that."

Garrett laughed and shot another look at Will. "She was trying to impress our brother."

"That poor little girl was smitten," Dorothea agreed as she narrowed her dark gaze at Will. "And you, being fifteen and full of yourself, often didn't give her the time of day. So what could possibly go wrong hiring her to cook for you?"

He groaned. "You aren't making this any easier." He was already short-staffed. Normally the guest ranch didn't take guests this early in the season. Late spring and summer were the guest ranch's busiest times, with a fall season for hunters. But a friend of their father's had made a special request for Will to open for four days in March.

Big Jack Hanson owned a small fly-fishing vest company outside of La Quinta, California, called On the Fly. Big Jack wanted to hold a retreat for some of his employees at Sterling Montana Guest Ranch, a place from his youth. He'd been uncompromising on when.

Although anxious to get his first season running the guest ranch alone started, Will had tried to talk him out of it, reminding him what the weather could be like this time of the year in the mountains of Montana. Also that they would be short-staffed. Which meant that the guests would be making their own beds each day and taking care of the housekeeping in their cabins. Dorothea would be helping in the kitchen and making sure their guests had everything they needed from daily treats in their cabins to clean towels.

"Sounds perfect," Big Jack had said. "Won't hurt them a bit to do for themselves for what time we're there."

A charismatic, large man with red hair like a fireplug, blue eyes and a talent for hyperbole, Big Jack had offered to pay extra. "My crew needs this. I need this. You don't have to roll out the red carpet or go to any trouble." Spoken like a man who knew nothing about hosting guests. But Will had given in since, at one time, Big Jack had been like family.

He knew his father would have wanted him to do whatever was necessary to accommodate Big Jack and his employees.

At the sound of the shuttle van arriving from the airport down in the valley, Will knew he couldn't be choosy about a cook. His guests would be expecting dinner tonight and since neither he nor Dorothea could do more than boil water…

He called information for Poppy Carmichael's number and was put right through. The moment she answered, he hesitated, reminding himself of why this was a bad idea on so many levels. He and Poppy had a history—and not a good one. True, it was twenty years ago, but still…

Through the front window, he saw his guests begin to pile out of the van. They were all wearing what appeared to be new matching navy winter jackets with an On the Fly logo on the back and matching stocking caps. They looked tired from the long trek from the airport up into the mountains outside of Whitefish, Montana. They also already looked hungry.

"Poppy?" He cleared his voice. "It's Will. Will Sterling. Up at the Sterling guest ranch."

"Will."

The sound of her voice threw him for a moment. It was soft, refined, his name spoken on almost an amused breath.

He plunged on. "My cook, Buckshot Brewster, broke his leg and I'm desperate, as I have guests arriving as we speak. Is there any way—" Dorothea was shaking her head and mumbling again about bad luck and this whole retreat already being cursed.

"How long?" Poppy said on the other end of the line.

"Four days starting today, Sunday. The guests leave Wednesday afternoon. If there is any way you can fit it into your schedule…"

A soft laugh. "So you need me." There was a small hesitation before she said, "Right away."

"Yes! I have nine guests that have to be fed tonight. I'm

sorry for such short notice. If you can swing it, I'll pay your going rate and a bonus at the end of the four days. What do you say? Buckshot brought most of the supplies up already and my brothers just delivered the rest, so I think we have everything you'll need to cook up here. We have our own supply of beef, bison and elk, and plenty of canned goods. We just need a…cook."

An amused chuckle. "I see."

"I would be in your debt." He squeezed the receiver of the landline in the kitchen. To say that the guest ranch was remote was putting it mildly. There was no TV, no internet, no cell phone service. The lodge had three landline phones with outside access, one of them large and black and possibly original to the ranch. It was located in the lodge lounge. Guests always got a kick out of it since anyone under about thirty had never used a phone with a dial.

"Seriously, I apologize for calling at such late notice," he said, closing his eyes as he made a wish that this would work out. "I'll understand if you really can't do it." There was no reason this woman would agree to this given the way he'd treated her when they were young.

Another bemused chuckle. "How about I pick up a few things and see you in a couple of hours."

Will couldn't believe it, telling himself that no matter what Dorothea said, their luck had changed. He let out a relieved breath. At the back of his mind, though, there remained a sliver of unease about hiring Poppy given their history. He hoped he wasn't making a mistake.

He watched his younger brother leave the kitchen to go outside to welcome the guests. Shade was more of a natural at this than either Garrett or himself, Will thought. But it was late March, calving season, so both of his brothers would be returning to the ranch down in the valley today. They'd

only stopped up to bring him the supplies Buckshot hadn't
been able to finish delivering himself after he'd broken his leg.

"You're saving my life," Will said into the phone.

"What are old friends for?" Poppy replied and disconnected.

He stood for a moment holding the phone, repeating her
words in his head and trying to decide if her tone was cause
for concern. They had definitely not been old friends—at
least, not at the end.

"What's wrong?" Garrett asked as he finished his water and
deposited the plastic bottle in the recycling bin.

Will shook his head. "Poppy. It's just that I don't remember leaving things on the best of terms with her before she
moved away."

His brother laughed. "That was twenty years ago! I'm sure
she doesn't remember. She was just a kid."

He nodded. "A kid with a crush on me. I'm betting I could
have handled it better."

"Seriously?" Garrett said as he placed a hand on his shoulder. "You were fifteen and what was she, twelve?" He shook
his head. "It will be fine." Then he laughed. "Of course, if
I'm wrong you just hired a cook who might poison you." He
seemed to think that was a lot more humorous than it was as
he left laughing.

Will turned to see Dorothea shaking her head.

"Everything is going to be fine," he tried to assure her and
himself. He'd waited years for his father to step aside and let
him run the guest ranch. After his father's fatal heart attack,
he wanted to make him proud. They might have butted heads,
but he loved his father and knew that the man only wanted
the best for him and his brothers—and the guest ranch. Now,
it was up to Will to take over the legacy he'd been left and
not screw it up. "I have everything under control."

"Just keep telling yourself that," the housekeeper said. "First

Buckshot breaks his leg. Now you've hired a woman with a grudge against you to cook for us? Can't wait to see what the third batch of bad luck is going to be. Should be a humdinger." She glanced out front as if expecting doom to be knocking at the door at any moment.

"Are the cabins ready for our guests?" he asked pointedly.

She sighed as if the weight of the world rested on her shoulders. He'd made sure that the guest ranch's two wranglers, Slim and Huck, had helped her get the rooms ready. But he didn't need her telling him about any bad vibes she felt right now. He had enough apprehension over hiring Poppy Carmichael.

"Why don't I go check the cabins?" she said haughtily.

"Why don't you?" He headed into the massive living room of the guest ranch. Through the front window, he watched the small group of men and women his age or younger drag their luggage and backpacks from the back of the van.

Near the front of the van, Big Jack Hanson stood talking to his brother Shade. Jack, too, wore the coat and hat with the fly-fishing company logo like the rest of his crew. Will shook his head. Big Jack never did anything halfway, he thought, and was reminded of his own father. Big Jack and Wyatt Sterling had that in common. He bet the man had bought the gear as a surprise for his employees to wear on this trip and that wearing it had been mandatory. It was something his father would have done.

He pushed thoughts of his father away, feeling guilty. The two of them had disagreed about most everything, but especially running the ranch. It had been like pulling teeth to get his father to make any changes over the years.

"It's always worked fine doing it this way," Wyatt Sterling would say. "Worked for my father, worked for me." He'd been a stubborn man who'd had to be dragged into the twenty-first century. "As long as I'm alive, there won't be any Wi-Fi up here at the ranch. Our guests come here for what they don't have at home," his father had said even as guest numbers had declined over the past few years.

"Times have changed, Dad," Will had argued. Not that it had done any good.

He shook away the memories. The day was cool but beautiful. The Montana sky was clear blue against the dark green of the pines. A light breeze stirred the boughs with that mountain spring smell Will loved. He would be making a lot of changes to the guest ranch over the next few months and couldn't wait to get started. Big Jack's retreat would pay for a lot of those improvements. It was another reason he'd agreed to it.

He could only hope that the weather cooperated. The retreat was only four days. But he'd heard about a storm coming out of Canada in a few days. The On the Fly crew should be gone by then, Will told himself. Not that weather wasn't unpredictable anytime in Montana—let alone in March. But this one was supposed to miss them and go east before it dropped much snow.

Will had made a point of mentioning the storm when Big Jack had called at the last minute about opening the guest ranch for four days right away.

Big Jack had laughed it off. "Not worried about a little weather."

Will had started to argue that the weatherman wasn't talking about a shower. This could turn into a late-winter storm. But the man cut him off.

"I'd consider this a huge favor. Like I said, I'm willing to pay extra. I have some big decisions to make about the future of the company and your ranch is the perfect place to do it. We'll need all the cabins you have available."

"Cabin nine is out of commission, but I can give you eight cabins, if that will work," Will had said, reminding himself again that his father and Jack had been good friends growing up. Big Jack had spent a lot of time at the ranch back when he was called Jackie.

"Great," Big Jack had said as if it was all settled. "I'll take cabin eight." He rattled off which cabin he wanted for each of his employees. Will had taken it all down, not surprised at how hands-on the man was being. "See you soon."

"I'll have a van pick you up at the airport as soon as you call me with your flight plan," Will had told him, since he could think of no more arguments that might dissuade the man. So they had opened the guest ranch early, with mixed emotions. If it worked out, this retreat would be a great start to the coming season.

Now Will watched the On the Fly crew headed for their cabins. Their names would be on the outside chalkboard at each cabin. He was sure Big Jack had already told them that since it was something his father had initiated years ago. What surprised him, though, was that none of the guests appeared that happy to be here. He told himself they were probably just tired from the long ride up from the airport. Once they got settled, they would get with the program and lighten up.

And yet all he could think was that he hoped he hadn't made a mistake agreeing to this, especially given his hesitation with hiring Poppy to cook and the possibility of a winter storm hitting too close to the ranch and dampening an already glum group.

He reminded himself that the weather was beautiful right now, that they had a cook coming and that Garrett said Poppy's food was good; at least Big Jack looked happy as he ushered his straggling few crew members toward the cabins as if they were ducklings. Given how much Big Jack reminded him of his own father, he wondered about Jack's relationship with his own sons. From the looks on both Lamar's and

Mick's faces when they'd arrived, Will would say the man might be as difficult to work with as Will's father had been.

As he opened the door to greet Big Jack—and he would never admit it to Dorothea—he couldn't shake the bad feeling that ran the length of his spine.

CHAPTER TWO

Will Sterling. As Poppy put down the phone, she saw that her hand was shaking. The realization made her laugh. She wasn't twelve anymore. And Will wasn't that impossibly good-looking fifteen-year-old cowboy who'd made her younger self swoon.

She wanted to pinch herself. He'd just offered her something she'd only dreamed of since the day her father drove her away from the Sterling ranch in tears. Will wanted her to cook at the ranch. True, it was only four days, but it still made her light-headed. Was this really happening?

"Good news?" her friend and only employee, Kara, asked from where she was finishing up a batch of iced cookies for one of their catering jobs.

Was it good news? For her, absolutely. But not so much for Will. "Interesting news." She thought about the phone call, telling herself it had been real. Will said he needed her. That he was desperate. That he owed her. All of the words she'd longed to hear in every retribution plot she'd ever dreamed as a girl.

How ironic was that? After all these years, Will needed her.

She grinned to herself. "That was Will Sterling. He needs a cook for four days up at his guest ranch in the mountains. He offered me my going rate without even asking what it was and a bonus at the end of the four days."

Kara's eyes widened. "You said yes, didn't you?"

Her catering business was just getting wheels under it so it wasn't as if she ever turned down anything reasonable. Right now, she couldn't give Kara more than an occasional part-time job and her friend needed more. If the business was going to grow, she would need the full-time help.

"Can you manage without me for that long?" Poppy asked her. "We have that birthday party and that upcoming luncheon to get ready for."

"Boss, it's a five-year-old's birthday party with six guests. Since we promised to keep it inexpensive, I think I can handle it. As for the luncheon, I have some ideas I wanted to run past you. I'll get them down on paper so you can see what I was thinking when you get back."

"Perfect." Kara was a godsend. She could depend on her and didn't want to lose her to a job with more hours. She'd been growing the business and hated leaving right now. But she couldn't pass up this opportunity on so many levels. Also it would be good money for a short period of time.

"So you told him yes?"

Poppy nodded. She could not help smiling even as she tried to contain her excitement at the prospect of four days at the guest ranch she had loved as a girl. Coming from the Midwest, she'd been enamored by the cluster of weathered old log cabins set back in the pines against the mountainside with their porches and willow rockers.

But it was the main lodge that had made her eyes pop that first time. She'd never seen such a huge rock fireplace in such an enormous room with its high log ceiling. She hadn't been able to resist walking around the entire room looking at all the mounted heads of deer, elk and moose. There were paintings of cowboys and Native Americans in headdresses, some signed by the artists themselves. And old spurs and lariats hung on the walls. It reminded her of the old Western movies she'd loved before moving to Montana.

She had touched the antler lamps and admired the massive ranch kitchen with all its counter space. Even at twelve and a tomboy, she had loved to cook. Back in the lounge, the well-worn leather furniture had looked so comfortable that she hadn't been able to help herself. She'd plopped down in one of the chairs and was running her hands along the warm smooth leather when Will Sterling had found her. She hadn't thought anyone was home and she'd been itching to see inside, so having never lacked courage, she'd dared enter without permission.

"What do you think you're doing?" he'd demanded.

Startled, she'd struggled to get out of the deep comfort of the chair. "I was just..." She had managed to get to her feet and turned. The cutest cowboy she'd ever seen stole any words she might have said. His longish brown hair under his Western hat was dusted with gold as if kissed by the sun. His brown eyes were the color of sweet molasses.

Dressed in a Western shirt, jeans, boots and a hat that looked a little too large for him, she'd fallen in love at that exact instant.

"I need to get moving," she told Kara. "I promised to get up there in a couple of hours and I have to pack. I also want to pick up some supplies."

"Supplies? I would think they would have those."

Poppy chuckled. "Buckshot Brewster is their usual camp cook. Apparently he broke his leg. To Buckshot, cuisine is a slab of beef and a side of beans."

Kara laughed. "Wait a minute. That cowboy you were telling me about who you met when you were twelve—"

"Will Sterling, the man who just hired me."

Her friend raised a brow in concern. "But I thought he broke your heart."

Poppy nodded. "Oh, he did."

"Wait, I know that look. What are you planning to do?"

She smiled, eyes narrowing. "If it's true that the way to a man's heart is his stomach... Well, then, I plan to give him a taste of his own medicine."

"You wouldn't."

Oh, but she would.

Lamar Hanson dropped his backpack in the bedroom that his brother, Mick, had been assigned at cabin one and went back outside hoping to see his father. He could see Big Jack talking to one of the Sterlings. He groaned inwardly as some of his father's boisterous words reached him since the cabin he was to share with his brother was the closest to the lodge. Big Jack was often too much of a blowhard. It was one reason Lamar had done his best to keep his father away from the business recently.

Now, he found himself wondering again whose idea this "retreat" really had been. He glanced from his father to the row of nine cabins, each set apart from the other with pine trees in between. His twenty-six-year-old brother, Mick, was helping Allison with her luggage in front of cabin four. That was Mick for you, he thought. Always chasing some skirt. Sometimes, Lamar questioned if he wasn't adopted since he and Mick were nothing alike.

At thirty-four, he looked the least like his father. His own hair was a reddish blond rather than the fire-engine red of his father's and his eyes were hazel rather than milky blue.

Mick was the blond in the family with piercing blue eyes and a slim build. He was the more handsome of the two brothers. But Lamar had gotten both height and intelligence. What his father and brother lacked in business acumen, Lamar made up for in spades. It was the reason he was doing his best to take over the small fly-fishing vest manufacturing company before his father sent them into bankruptcy.

But that wasn't his only problem, he thought as he watched Mick. Lamar had known that the twenty-eight-year-old Allison Landon, with her long dark hair, green eyes and baby-doll looks, would be too much of a temptation for Mick. Allison was in charge of invoicing and accounting. Mick was supposed to help by overseeing shipping and inventory, but did as little as possible.

As Allison's grating giggle trailed down to him, he considered the others his father had insisted on inviting on this four-day hideaway in the mountains of northwestern Montana. There was Kirk Austin from quality control and shipping, a big, good-looking blond former semi-pro snowboarder, who was watching Mick and Allison with obvious jealousy from cabin six's front porch.

Then there was the quiet wallflower, Lexi Raiser, head of the sewing department, trying to wrestle her luggage through the door of cabin five. Dean Donovan, a four-eyed nerd in his midtwenties with dark thinning hair who worked in the stockroom, had gone into the cabin right next door to Lamar, cabin two, seeming to want to distance himself from all of them as quickly as possible.

The newest hire, Ruby Alder, an attractive, fortysomething brunette graphic designer, who handled advertising, design and graphics, was sitting on the porch of cabin three with a book in her hand, pretending to read. He could tell that she was more interested in Big Jack than the book.

And last but not least, now ambling out of the van, Channing Palmer, the bored blonde from online ordering and distribution. Channing made no secret that she found all of this amusing. As she passed Lamar's cabin, she gave him a mocking glance as if he was the only one who didn't know what this retreat was all about. He didn't doubt it.

He groaned inwardly at the thought of this bunch together for four days. Big Jack swore that the employees had been picked at random. So why didn't Lamar believe that? And if his father really had been the mastermind behind this, what was Big Jack up to?

CHAPTER THREE

Dorothea had just finished checking the cabins and was working her way back when she heard the argument break out. She ducked between the cabins out of sight as a busty, brash blonde came flying out of her cabin to accost one of the other guests—a slightly built meek woman with lank brown hair.

Will had given her a list of the guests with descriptions so she could learn their names before they arrived. It didn't take much to put a name to Channing Palmer, the blonde.

"Leave me alone, Channing," the slighter woman said. Dorothea assumed this had to be Lexi Raiser. Lexi tried to step past the blonde, only to have the woman block her way.

"You really don't want to push me, Lexi," Channing said, glancing toward the lodge to make sure no one was watching.

Lexi tucked her stringy brown hair behind an ear and avoided Channing's gaze. "I told you, I don't want any trouble," she said in a small voice Dorothea could barely hear.

"It's a little late for that, wouldn't you say?" Channing demanded between gritted teeth.

"Is there a problem here?"

Both women turned as a third woman appeared. In her

forties, Ruby Alder was a good ten to fifteen years older than the other two, with dark hair pulled back into a ponytail. "Everything all right, Lexi?" the woman asked.

"Fine." Lexi dropped her head, staring at the ground.

"Butt out, Ruby, this doesn't have anything to do with you." But Channing took a step back, allowing Lexi to quickly escape.

Ruby hadn't moved. She stood glaring at the blonde until Channing swore and strode off toward her cabin—in the opposite direction Lexi had gone. After a moment, Ruby's gaze shifted to where Dorothea had been watching, as if the woman had known she'd been there the whole time.

Their gazes met and Dorothea had the distinct impression that Ruby Alder wasn't someone you wanted to mess with. But then neither was Channing Palmer.

As she hurried toward the lodge, she told herself that Will had no idea what he'd gotten himself into. A cook with a broken leg was just the beginning. Something was definitely amiss with these coworkers and she wondered if even a stay at the Sterling Montana Guest Ranch would tame this bunch.

When she arrived at the guest ranch, Poppy headed straight to the kitchen and went to work. She knew her way around the ranch from the hours she'd spent there as a girl. The kitchen had been one of her favorite places—that and the horse barn.

She wasn't surprised to see that the kitchen had been updated recently with high-end appliances. From what she could see, the rest of the ranch looked exactly the way she remembered it. From the row of cabins, the big barn, the corrals and the lodge with its log furniture in the dining room to the main lounge that she'd loved so as a girl, it was how she'd pictured it over the years.

Her nerves jangled but she was determined not to let it show. She could do this. Will had handed it to her on a platter. That cocky fifteen-year-old cowboy all grown up was due for a reckoning. She'd caught a glimpse of him down at one of the cabins talking to a guest when she'd arrived. He was tall and slim like he'd been at fifteen. But she didn't have time to think about how much he might have changed or what it would be like to come face-to-face with him after all these years.

She knew that the guests would be ready soon for an afternoon snack. Will hadn't told her about it, probably thinking he would throw out some cheese and crackers and call it good—much like Buckshot would have done if he wasn't laid up with a broken leg. Poppy had a little something more creative in mind.

As she moved to the edge of the dining room to look out the window down the row of cabins, she caught glimpses of the eight to ten guests—all adults, most in their twenties. She was surprised that Will had opened this early. It made her wonder what was special about this group.

She remembered his father saying years ago that they never opened the guest part of the ranch until May because the weather could be too unpredictable up here in the mountains. But she'd heard that Wyatt Sterling had passed away recently and now Will was running the guest ranch on the mountain, while his brothers worked the cattle ranch down in the valley.

Whatever Will's reason for opening early, it had certainly played right into her hands, she thought. This small group would be easy.

Turning to the job at hand, Poppy quickly set the oven at 350 degrees to preheat and put away the food she'd brought in the large walk-in refrigerator and freezer. Then she turned her attention to the afternoon welcoming snack. Since she'd been back, she'd heard about Buckshot's cooking at the ranch and now smiled to herself. Hers was going to be nothing like the chuckwagon cook's. Which meant Will was in for a surprise in more than one way.

As she worked, she tried not to think about that moment when she would have to face the grown-up Will Sterling. Would he see what she was up to? Or would he think she'd let bygones be bygones? If so, then he hadn't known her at all.

After twenty years, there was always the chance that he wouldn't even remember her. But she remembered him. Hard to forget your first love, especially since it had been unrequited. Just as it was hard to forget your first and last broken heart.

Since she'd returned to town about six months ago, she'd seen Will a few times—but only from a distance. What she'd heard was that the cute cowboy she'd fallen for as a girl had grown into a drop-dead-handsome cowboy. She'd heard stories about the women who'd tried to lasso him, but all of them had been forced to cut him loose. Will was a wild stallion who wasn't about to let anyone rein him in. At least, that's what she'd heard.

Poppy had never turned down a challenge, although this was going to be a tough one. She told herself not to get cocky. She was taking a risk just coming here. She had to use all her skill and then some if she hoped to accomplish her goal in such a short time.

She mixed up a few ingredients and popped her creations into the oven and set the timer. Then she looked around the kitchen. Fortunately, she was a fast cook. Also she'd had Kara lend a hand before she'd left town. She felt ready. At least cooking-wise. Heart-wise was another story.

When she heard the front door slam open and hurried boots thump across the old wood floor through the dining room toward the kitchen, she had to rein in her heart as it took off like a runaway horse.

Will came into the lodge on a breath of Montana mountain spring air. He'd been worried that Poppy would change her mind and not show up. It would serve the fifteen-year-old boy he'd been right. The memories he'd dredged up of Poppy since making that frantic call earlier had only left him more worried about having hired her. Maybe it would be the best thing that could happen if she didn't show up. He could try to find someone else. He and Dorothea could manage tonight without a cook, maybe, and tomorrow...

As he'd finished making sure his guests had all found their cabins, he'd seen a newer model SUV he didn't recognize parked next to the main lodge.

Poppy?

For a moment, he'd hesitated. Was he really that worried about seeing her again after all these years? After the way he'd left things twenty years ago? Why wouldn't he be?

He tried to convince himself that Garrett was right. Poppy probably didn't even remember. At least, he hoped not. He thought of her young tears and then quickly pushed the image away. It was just a silly little-girl crush. After she'd moved away from Montana, she'd probably fallen for a neighborhood boy and completely forgotten him within minutes of unpacking. She might even be married or have a fiancé or steady boyfriend. He tried to tell himself he was making too much out of a summer years ago.

Still, he couldn't shake the feeling that there had been something in her voice on the phone...

He braced himself as he headed for the kitchen. The past be damned, he had guests. That meant that they needed to be fed. In less than thirty minutes they would be coming up to the lodge for drinks and an afternoon snack—not to mention a dinner later this evening. Will had to make sure all of that was going to happen. He refused to think about what he would do if Poppy couldn't handle the job—or changed her mind when she saw him. Or hit him with a frying pan.

Will strode into the kitchen, ready to do whatever he had to. Even if he had to grovel to get a meal on the table tonight.

What he saw made him stop in his tracks. The slim, graceful-looking woman standing at the sink couldn't possibly be the girl he'd known. Maybe she'd sent one of her staff ahead— if she had staff. "Poppy?"

She turned. His jaw dropped. Gone were the pigtails and the braces. Her hair, now a deep mahogany brown, was still long and curly. She'd pulled it back in a low ponytail, which only accented her high cheekbones even more. And those eyes. He remembered them as being green. They were clear tropical seas with just enough gold in them to make him want to dig for treasure. She still had the freckles but now they only added to her beauty since she wore little makeup. She didn't need it. There was something so poised and confident about her. It was as if she'd walked into his kitchen and had made it her own.

"Hello, Will."

He told himself to close his mouth. He'd never been at a loss for words around women. It was from growing up around female guests his whole life. But his throat had gone dry and the floor under him suddenly seemed not nearly as stable as he remembered it. He swallowed, not sure what would come out when he spoke.

"Poppy, I didn't... I... You've changed."

Her laugh was musical. "So have you. Amazing what twenty years can do." Her smile lit up the already bright sunny kitchen.

He couldn't help being suspicious. Not that all cooks had to look like Buckshot, but... "And you *cook*?"

She looked amused. "Isn't that why you hired me?"

At that moment, he wouldn't have sworn to anything. He hadn't been expecting this. He'd been expecting that awkward kid he remembered only grown up into a woman who might have carried some old bad feelings against him.

He thought about what Dorothea had warned him about.

Normally, he would have scoffed, but… "Look, if there is any reason why you feel you can't or don't want to work for me—"

"What could there possibly be?"

He blinked. Had she just batted those big innocent green eyes at him? He swore silently. Dorothea was right. Poppy hadn't forgotten when they were kids. No way. If anything, she must have loved it when she got the call from him.

"Then I guess there's no problem," he said. He was in big trouble. "There was something else I was going to ask you." He opened his mouth, but she cut him off before he could make a bigger fool of himself.

"You were going to ask me if I was ready with an afternoon snack?" she suggested, a glint of laughter in those seaworthy eyes.

He nodded, used to feeling sure-footed around women. Usually, he was the one who made them uneasy. But this one… Was it because they had a history, one he'd hoped she'd forgotten? Or had he met his match in Poppy Carmichael?

"Yes, snack," he said. "Buckshot usually serves—"

"I've changed his menu a little. I hope you'll be pleased." She glanced at the sleek silver-banded watch on her slim wrist. "Twenty minutes in the main lodge?"

Will nodded, turning to leave, and promptly bumped into the island counter in a kitchen he knew like the back of his hand. "It seems you have everything under control," he said and cleared his voice. "Just keep doing whatever it is you're doing." This was going to be a disaster. He told himself it was only four days. How much harm could she do in four days?

Poppy watched him go. She relaxed her body and took a breath. Her pulse was pounding. Will Sterling. She'd thought she'd been ready for him. It had taken all of her composure. He was even more handsome close up. His brown hair still had those strands of gold interwoven through it—and it was still unruly when he removed his Stetson. His brown eyes edged by dark lashes were still warm molasses, with a hint of honey she hadn't noticed at twelve. His sensual mouth softened the strong jaw.

There was no doubt that he wasn't that fifteen-year-old anymore. Will was now all man. And all cowboy—just as she'd known he would grow into all those years ago. Still, he had taken her breath away.

First love, she thought with a curse as she put a hand over her patched-up heart. Did the ache never go away?

As her pulse began to slow, she told herself that taking this job could have been a mistake. How was she going to be able to bear seeing Will every day for four long days? What had she hoped to accomplish by agreeing to this?

But as she steadied herself on her feet, her courage and resolve returned. She could do this. She *would* do this. Will Sterling deserved it. At least, his fifteen-year-old self did. Anyway, it sounded like the cowboy playboy hadn't changed all that much since he'd already left a trail of broken hearts in town.

No, she would not weaken. She would have him eating out of her hand, she would steal his heart and then she would—

"Well, well," said a deep female voice from behind her, making her jump.

Poppy spun around to find Dorothea standing with hands on hips glaring at her. "Hello, Dorothea."

The woman laughed. "Just look at *you*." She shook her head. "Dear Lord, we are in for it, aren't we?"

"I beg your pardon?"

"Don't give me that innocent look. I see right through you."

"I can't imagine what you mean." She was surprised how little Dorothea had changed—including how outspoken she'd been. The only sign of the years that had passed was a streak of gray in the older woman's hair.

"First Buckshot breaks his leg and then you show up. Going to tell me that you had nothing to do with that?"

"With Buckshot breaking his leg?"

"You put the whammy on him, didn't you, you little minx?"

Poppy laughed. Dorothea, who'd been about thirty when Poppy had last seen her, was crazier than she remembered. She'd never taken the woman seriously, not when Dorothea was always threatening to put curses on guests she didn't like.

When Poppy, at twelve, had been skeptical of Dorothea's ability to actually put curses on people, the woman had said, "My mother was a witch and she taught me some of her spells. So you'd better watch it, young'un, or I'm turnin' you into a frog."

Poppy was no longer worried about being turned into a frog. "I didn't put a whammy on Buckshot. I'm only helping out for a few days."

"Sure you are," Dorothea said suspiciously. She narrowed her dark eyes threateningly. "I remember the crush you had on him. A girl doesn't get over that kind of starstruck young love easily. Just remember, I'll be watching you."

The timer went off on the oven. "Would you like to know what I'm making for the afternoon snack?" Poppy asked as she turned away to pull a tray of bite-size meatballs from the oven. When she turned back, Dorothea was gone.

Will made sure that Dorothea had the bar ready for their guests before he looked around for her. She'd been acting stranger than usual today. He was used to her sneaking around, checking everyone out, getting the lay of the land as she called it. Most people paid her no mind, but as he spotted her in front of the cabins, he saw Big Jack call to her. He seemed to be asking for directions. She pointed toward the large old barn down the mountainside. He nodded before turning away from her and started up the slope from the cabins toward the main lodge.

It was no wonder Will was feeling anxious, he told himself. He was still shaken after seeing Poppy all these years later. She was nothing like he'd expected and that worried him on a couple of levels. What if she couldn't cook? Garrett had said she owned her own catering company and the food at the party he'd attended was good. But what if she hadn't been the one to cook it?

On another level, he'd been taken aback by how attractive Poppy was—and his reaction to her. Hell, he'd been tongue-tied. He hadn't been tongue-tied around a girl since he was a boy. That thought did nothing to alleviate his concern.

He tried to relax. It was only for four days. He would be busy with the guests. He probably wouldn't even see much of Poppy. That made him feel a little better.

But still he realized that he wasn't normally this apprehensive about new guests. This was different, though, because it wasn't just any guest. It was Big Jack. Also these were his first guests since taking over the running of the guest ranch. He felt like a lot was riding on these four days. He wanted things to go smoothly, he thought as he stepped out front and rang the large dinner bell to call everyone up to the lodge.

Back inside, he watched the guests begin to make their way up the slope to the main lodge. He hoped Poppy had heard the bell and was getting the snacks ready. He couldn't help being antsy. It didn't help when Dorothea came in muttering about feeling as if there was a curse on the guest ranch.

"I forgot about the water leak in cabin nine," she said, nodding as if her prediction had come true. "First the water leak, then Buckshot tripping over himself and now that lady in the kitchen plotting revenge. Tell me bad luck doesn't come in threes."

"Don't have time for this, Dorothea." He stepped away

from her and saw Big Jack hanging back to talk to his oldest son as the others began to stream in. From their body language he could see the tension between the father and son. And what was that Dorothea had said about the lady in the kitchen plotting revenge?

He told himself this wasn't the time to start listening to Dorothea. He began to put names to the faces. Since his father took over the guest ranch, he'd insisted that the groups be small and that everyone who worked at the ranch knew the guests' first names and something about what they did. He wanted them to feel at home and believed in the personal touch. It helped having their names on the chalkboard on the front of their cabins.

Will thought about Big Jack wanting to pick the cabins for each of his employees. With number nine out of commission, the owner of On the Fly had taken the cabin farthest away from the others. The man should have the solitude he was looking for. Will could understand how he might want to be away from his younger, louder, more energetic staff.

"I need some space. Some rest. It's been a rough year, if you know what I mean," the man had said.

Will hadn't known what he meant, but he'd found most of his guests led busy, frantic lives and came to the ranch to relax, away from the stress. It was one reason his father had insisted that there was no internet in the cabins or the lodge. Nor was there any cell phone service. The last time Big Jack was at the ranch, there'd been no such thing as cell phones.

"I would imagine you've installed internet and cell phone service," Big Jack had said.

"I have plans to, but my father felt the only way to truly get away was to leave all of that behind."

Big Jack had laughed. "That does sound like your father. No television, either, as I recall."

"Nope. Not yet." Will wondered if the man would change

his mind. "We have the landline in the lodge for emergencies. That's really all we've needed. But by the next time you come up—"

"Sounds perfect," the man had said distractedly.

"You can have all the space and rest you need," Will had assured him. "I'm glad you thought of our ranch for your retreat."

"My father loved the place. I feel guilty that I never brought my sons up sooner. I don't know where the years have gone."

Big Jack had sounded sad—worse, regretful. Will had heard that the man had separated from his wife years ago, the separation ending in a nasty, costly divorce. That's when Big Jack had started On the Fly, making fly-fishing vests.

So maybe that was all this retreat was about. Sharing the Sterling guest ranch with his sons and employees. There was just one problem with that. While all of the cabins were some distance from each other with pine trees between to provide privacy, Big Jack had put his sons even farther away from him than his employees.

Will tried not to read anything into that, but he couldn't ignore the tension he'd felt from the group as they'd disembarked from the van. Big Jack had mentioned something about making some big decisions for his company. Is that what had them all on edge? His only hope was that Poppy's afternoon snack would soothe their angst.

As the guests now filed into the main lodge, Will introduced them to Poppy and Dorothea before he served everyone something to drink. Poppy excused herself, asking Dorothea for help in the kitchen.

His stomach roiled at the thought of what she'd cooked up. At least there wasn't smoke boiling out of the huge ranch kitchen. He supposed that was something. Instead, he thought he kept getting tantalizing scents. The guests were chatting among themselves, some sitting away from the others thumbing through the many Western magazines stacked on the large square coffee table in the center of the seating and others standing around the large fireplace where Will had a blaze going.

A few moments later, Dorothea brought in a tray filled with plates and forks followed by Poppy with an even larger tray filled with food that definitely smelled...interesting. He blinked as she put down the tray and began to remove lids one by one from the dishes she'd made.

"What I have for you this afternoon is a favorite of mine," she said as she took off the first lid from one of the serving dishes she set on the large square table. "Pork meatballs with crushed pineapple, rolled in toasted coconut, served with a chili mango sauce." She removed the lid of the mango sauce, then reached for another lid on another dish. "We also have chilled cucumber cups filled with my recipe for sweet potato hummus, and finally..." She lifted the last lid from a larger dish. "Black bean and goat cheese bruschetta."

Murmurs of excitement went up around the coffee table as everyone sat forward to see the beautiful dishes Poppy had made before they all grabbed plates and dug in. As they took bites of the afternoon snack, there were murmurs of enjoyment and surprise. None could have been more surprised than Will himself.

Poppy took a slight bow and said, "Please enjoy. Let me know if I can get you anything else." With that she turned and left.

He watched her leave. For the first time, he noticed that she was wearing jeans that fit her quite nicely, a T-shirt the same color as her eyes, sneakers and an apron that had tiny horseshoes on it. He was staring after her when Dorothea gave him a sharp nudge with her elbow.

"That woman is here to destroy you," she whispered. "So get that look off your face."

He wasn't sure what look was on his face, but he quickly changed it.

"Don't worry," Dorothea whispered. "I'm keeping my eye on her."

That was enough to make him worry. He waited until everyone had served themselves at least one helping before he made himself a plate. He listened to the oohs and aahs around the table as he tried the meatballs first. *Oh, my word,* he thought. The meatballs were divine.

"This is all so delicious," Ruby, an attractive fortysomething brunette, said. "My compliments."

Lamar agreed and looked to his younger brother, Mick. But Mick seemed more engrossed by what was going on across the coffee table from him. Kirk, the blond former semi-pro snowboarder, was talking quietly with Allison, the cute dark-haired young woman.

"Let's not forget our manners," Lamar said pointedly.

Channing rolled her eyes at him. "Who made you the manners police?" the bored-looking blonde mocked. "Good food, Poppy," she called into the kitchen before mugging a face at him.

Lamar ignored her and looked at Dean, who pushed his thick black-framed glasses up his nose and nodded in agreement. Lexi lifted her head from her plate, which looked so clean Will doubted she'd tried any of the food. "It's real good." Then she put her head down again, her lanky brown hair hiding her face.

"I'm going to put on ten pounds before we leave here if all of her cooking is like this," Allison said with a laugh and playfully hit Kirk when he told her she'd still be perfect.

Will tried to ignore the intrigue around him as he helped himself to the rest of the dishes Poppy had laid out. Every bite blew him away. It was all amazing. He hadn't expected this. Hell, he hadn't expected the Poppy Carmichael now in his kitchen. But could she keep this up?

He glanced over at Dorothea, who had made herself a plate and was sitting away from everyone by the window. She was devouring the meatballs and looking as if she hated herself for it. But she was also studying their guests.

No doubt waiting for the other shoe to drop.

Lamar ate very little even though it tasted wonderful. He was upset about what his father had said to him on the way in. All he could think about was getting Big Jack alone so he could find out what was going on.

Now as he looked around the table and listened to the chatter and laughter, he saw that the employees seemed to be enjoying themselves. They no longer appeared concerned as to why Big Jack had suddenly wanted to do a retreat in the mountains, isolated and so far from anything.

The only one who wasn't eating at all was Lexi Raiser. The shy introvert seemed uncomfortable. As if feeling his gaze on her, she looked up, met his eyes and quickly looked back down again at her plate in her lap. He'd been warned by his brother that Lexi had a crush on him.

"I swear to you," Mick had said with a laugh. "I catch her staring at you all the time. She's got it bad."

He'd scoffed since his brother wasn't the most reliable source when it came to women. "As usual, you don't know what you're talking about," Lamar had said since Lexi seemed interested in everything going on at the company. She was one of those people who was like the wallpaper. No one noticed her, but she could see all of them.

But Lamar did think that something was bothering Lexi. A couple of times over the past few weeks, she'd come into his office as if she needed to talk to him and then seemed to have changed her mind and told him something about the sewing department that he really didn't need to know.

Maybe he should have tried to draw it out of her. But he hadn't had the time or energy since he found himself running the place on his own with little help from his father or brother. He knew he hadn't been doing his best because of it.

He swore softly under his breath as he stood and moved to the fireplace. The warm blaze crackled and popped. He touched the rough rock absently and told himself Lexi's problem could be anything. He didn't need any more complications at the office. Lexi might have to go if she posed a problem and he hated that because she was good at her job in the sewing department.

"Going on the horseback ride?" Mick asked as he joined him in front of the fire. His brother kept looking back at the large leather couch where Allison was laughing at something Kirk had said.

"What are we doing here?" he asked his brother quietly.

"What?" Mick said, looking confused. "We're going horseback riding. At least I am if the girls are going."

"They're young women *and* employees, and no, I don't mean— Why did Dad set up this stupid retreat?"

"He told me he wanted to reward some of the workers and show you and me where he used to spend a lot of time with his father when he was young," Mick said.

"And you believed him?" Lamar shook his head. "If that were true, then why does it feel so…wrong?"

"I have no idea what you're talking about. I'm having fun. Maybe you should try it sometime." With that his brother returned to the couch to say something to Allison, who quickly rose, and the two left, apparently to change for their horseback ride.

He glanced at his father to see if he was finished eating so maybe they could talk, but Big Jack was busy sipping his drink and looking in a completely different direction. He had sat apart from them during the afternoon snack, saying nothing. Lamar suspected he hadn't eaten anything. Often his father preferred to drink his meals.

Now he followed his father's gaze—straight to Ruby Alder, their fortysomething graphic designer. Ruby was chewing absently on a piece of crust from the bruschetta, her gaze locked with his father's.

As the guests got ready for the horseback ride, Will helped Dorothea take the plates and what little food was left to the kitchen. Poppy was busy chopping something, no doubt for their supper.

"Your…snacks…were a huge hit," he said as he put down the nearly empty dishes he'd brought in. "Everything was delicious."

"I'm glad you liked it." She turned to face him, a large butcher knife in her hand. The blade caught the light, blinding him for a moment. She chuckled as she put the knife down and wiped her hands on a dishtowel. "I made the meatballs with you in mind."

Again he felt a little tongue-tied. What was it about this woman? "With me in mind?"

She smiled. "I remembered how you used to love meatballs. I helped your mother make them when I was here that summer."

That summer. Was it his imagination or did she keep reminding him of that summer in their past? Or maybe it was his own guilt reminding him. He didn't know what to say.

She raised an eyebrow as if seeing his discomfort. "Did you want to talk about dinner? I found Buckshot's menu plans for the four days your guests will be here. But as I said, I hope you don't mind if I deviate a little from it."

What could he say after what she'd just served? "Of course not."

Poppy gave him another smile. "Then I guess we're all set."

He smelled something baking in the oven and realized he shouldn't be all that surprised that she'd started cooking for later. He took a step closer and caught a whiff of something buttery and rich that rocketed him back to his childhood. "What is that?"

"It's actually your mother's recipe for her butter cookies."

Will felt his eyes widen. "Where did you find that?"

Poppy looked away for a moment. "I borrowed the recipe before I moved away," she said guiltily. "Every time I made them, they reminded me of this ranch and your family…and you, of course."

He swallowed the lump in his throat. He'd been right about Poppy not forgetting the last time they saw each other all those years ago. *So she stole the recipe to get back at him?*

"Your mother knew it by heart. I'm sorry I borrowed it. If I'd known that your mother was going to…"

"She died too young."

Poppy nodded. "Well, now I've brought the recipe back so Buckshot can make the cookies for you." She smiled broadly again. The timer went off. "Would you like a cookie?"

He did and didn't. The scent of them baking had brought back so much of his youth, including visions of his mother in this kitchen—and Poppy perched on the counter. The two of them with their heads together as his mother had Poppy stirring something. The two of them laughing as Poppy licked the spoon while his mother put the cookies into the oven to bake.

How had he forgotten how close Poppy had been to his mother? He could still see her sitting on the counter smiling at him. Her knees scabbed, her cowboy boots scuffed, her green eyes bright as her smile.

Poppy held out one of the cookies she'd scooped up with

a spatula. "I know how much you like them when they're still warm."

"No," he said, taking a step back. "I'll wait." With that he turned and left, feeling assailed by so many memories, good and bad. That Poppy. That long, hot summer. And this Poppy.

It's only for four days, he told himself. Then Poppy would be gone, along with the guilt she made him feel. And all the other feelings she evoked in him. Feelings he didn't even want to put a name to. Four days.

Poppy heard Will announce to the guests that Dorothea would be leaving fresh cookies in their cabins for when they returned from their horseback ride. As she began to box up the cookies for each cabin, she thought about Will's shocked expression when he'd smelled the familiar cookies baking.

She was sorry that she'd taken his favorite cookie recipe. At the time, she'd wanted something of Kate and the ranch to bring with her. And, like Will, she adored the cookies. She'd known that his mother hadn't needed it because she made the cookies by rote. But then Kate had died that next spring, which meant she'd taken the recipe with her to her grave. She hadn't meant to hurt him or the rest of his family since she figured his mother wouldn't miss it.

Looking at the neatly printed recipe card written in Kate's hand, Poppy felt a wave of grief. She'd loved the woman. Having lost her own mother at three, she'd been instantly drawn to Will's. Some of her fondest memories at the ranch were of sitting on the kitchen counter while Kate cooked and taught her culinary skills.

It was there that she'd decided she had to learn to cook, especially since much of what her father made was out of a can. Not that she could fault him. He was busy with his forest service job and raising a headstrong daughter all alone.

She took the last batch of cookies from the oven, breathing in the buttery scent. She could almost see Kate standing here next to her, explaining how to cream the butter with the sugar gradually to make the cookies light and airy.

Setting down the pan, she carefully lifted each one off the cookie sheet and set them aside to cool. She had eight boxes of cookies ready for Dorothea to take and some extras that would be available in the lodge. Her guests wouldn't be going hungry. She took a breath, pleased. Her guilt for taking the recipe aside, she thought her plan seemed to be working so far. She'd caught Will off guard. He seemed a little unsure of his footing and what was going to happen next.

If he'd forgotten that shy twelve-year-old whose heart he'd broken, well, she'd be happy to remind him.

CHAPTER FOUR

Lamar had no interest in a horseback ride. But when he'd tried to corner his father after they'd left the lodge, Big Jack had said they could talk on the ride and walked off.

As several wranglers arrived by pickup to help get the horses ready for the ride, it became clear to Lamar that the guest ranch was operating short-staffed. Picking up one of the ranch's brochures by the front door, he'd realized that the guest ranch didn't even open for guests until May and certainly not this early in the spring. There was still deep snow in the high peaks behind the ranch. While today was pleasant, it wasn't exactly warm. Why here? Why now? Why so last-minute?

He had so many questions and no answers. He couldn't shake the feeling that his father was up to something. Whatever it was, Lamar planned to find out—if he could get his father to talk to him.

At least they wouldn't be staying long. He told himself he could put up with this so-called retreat for four days. But he couldn't help worrying. Something was going on with his father. He was used to the intrigue between the employees. It ebbed and flowed in waves, often due to his brother, Mick, flirting with certain members of the staff and then moving on to others.

The company had a no-dating rule that also applied to his brother, not that Mick paid it any mind. After the way he'd seen his father looking at Ruby Alder, Lamar knew he'd have to remind his father that the rule applied to him, as well.

Looking out his cabin window, he spotted his brother in deep conversation with Kirk Austin, the twenty-seven-year-old former semi-pro snowboarder. He had no doubt that they were arguing over Allison. He noticed that his brother was doing most of the talking.

Just when he considered breaking up whatever was going on, he saw Dean Donovan standing in the nearby pines. As he watched Dean push his glasses back up his long nose, he realized that the stockroom worker was eavesdropping on Mick and Kirk's conversation.

With his boots on, he headed out of the cabin. Dean spotted him and pretended to be looking for something in the pines. Mick and Kirk separated at the sight of Lamar, but neither looked happy.

Shaking his head, Lamar headed down to the barn, the others following at an uninterested saunter. Horses whinnied from the corral as the wranglers saddled up mounts and helped the guests into the saddles. There was both tension and excitement in the air as he climbed onto his horse. He'd ridden some with friends when he was younger, but he was far from comfortable in the saddle.

Will swung up onto his horse, clearly at home there. He took the lead with one of the wranglers as they began to walk their horses toward a path that led past the cabins and along a trail beside the creek.

Lamar tried to relax, but he saw that his father had purposely ridden up beside Will at the front of the line and was now way ahead of him. So much for talking on the horse-back ride.

As the line began to string out, with some of the riders going much slower than others on the narrow trail, he was even farther from his father and that discussion Big Jack had promised. He swore under his breath and tried to enjoy the country. It really was beautiful—just as his father had always told them. He breathed in the sweet scent of the pines. Closer, the creek ran clear over colorful rocks. From a tree limb, a squirrel chattered above him as he passed.

His calm was broken as, ahead, he overheard raised voices. Kirk and Mick were arguing about something again. He caught just enough of the heated discussion to guess it was about Allison. He was going to have to talk to his brother about this. Again.

Kirk reined in and rode back a few horses to get away from Mick. Lamar shook his head. Never a dull moment with these two.

The wrangler at the rear of the group was urging Dean to go a little faster when, in front of Lamar, Lexi suddenly brought her horse up short.

Back at the ranch, Dorothea was glad to see that all of the guests had left on the trail ride. Earlier, she'd been watching them surreptitiously as she'd always done with the various groups that came to the ranch. She prided herself on being able to tell almost at once which ones were going to be trouble.

With this group, she'd seen something that she was sure Will and the others had missed. The quiet, plain one, Lexi? She'd stolen a shaker of salt from one of the dining room tables as she'd left earlier. The young woman did it with such finesse that Dorothea would guess it hadn't been her first brush with kleptomania. One moment Lexi was passing the table. The next moment the saltshaker from the dining table was tucked into her shoulder bag. The woman didn't even break her stride.

In the kitchen, Dorothea didn't see Poppy anywhere around, but she found the boxed-up cookies ready to be taken to the cabins. She carefully packed them into a basket and headed out into the beautiful day.

She made stops at each cabin, dropping off the boxes of cookies. When she reached Lexi Raiser's cabin, she paused for a moment, unable to ignore the strange feeling that washed over her.

From the get-go, she'd sensed that something was wrong with this group. She'd known it the moment they climbed out of the van. She just couldn't put her finger on what it was exactly. At least, not yet.

She took just a moment in the young woman's cabin. Some guests came in, dumped the contents of their suitcases on the spare bed in the second bedroom. Others neatly hung their clothes on the provided hangers in the closet or folded them just as neatly in the large antique bureau drawers. And then there were those who left everything in their suitcases on the luggage rack and never unpacked, as if they weren't planning to stay long.

Lexi, it appeared, was one of those. Her room was so neat it looked as if the room wasn't even being used.

Dorothea put the cookies on the small table and turned to leave, wondering what Lexi had done with the saltshaker, when she glanced toward the door and saw what she'd missed on the way in.

Salt. It gleamed in the dull light. A thin trail of it had been spread along the edge of the floor and threshold.

Dorothea hugged herself as a chill shuddered through her. She recognized the spell. It was one to keep negative energy away—and one her mother had taught her. But who was it that Lexi believed she had to fear? Channing Palmer? Or someone else at this retreat?

★ ★ ★

Will had been reminiscing with Big Jack about the days when he and his father were regulars at the ranch when he heard the commotion followed by the screams and brought his horse up short.

Reining his horse around, he rode back on the wide trail to see what was going on. The first thing he saw as he came around the bend was Lexi clinging to her horse as it bucked and jumped. She was hanging on as if her life depended on it.

His wrangler was trying to get hold of Lexi's horse's reins.

Will jumped off his horse and hurried toward them when suddenly Dean's horse began to buck and jump, as well. Unlike Lexi, Dean wasn't hanging on. He flew through the air, landing hard on the ground in the middle of the trail with a grunt and a whimper as his glasses flew off, but fortunately didn't break.

The other horses whinnied and stomped. Will got Lexi's horse settled down and handed the reins to his wrangler, who had grabbed Dean's horse's reins. As he hurried over to where Dean lay crumpled on the ground moaning, he wondered what the devil was going on. All horses could get spooked for whatever reason and act up occasionally, but these were seasoned guest horses that were as docile as sleepy old dogs.

Poppy was prepping for dinner service when Dorothea came in the front door. She glanced toward the main lodge area around the fireplace and then turned into the dining room and headed toward the large open kitchen.

But as she walked past one of the dining room tables, she stopped abruptly and picked up an empty saltshaker to stare at it for a long moment. The woman had always been peculiar, Poppy thought, but at the same time rather endearing. Kind of like an addled aunt.

"If you bring that shaker into the kitchen, I'd be happy to refill it," Poppy offered.

Dorothea came out of whatever trance she'd been in. She entered the kitchen and handed the empty shaker to her. As she watched Poppy refill it, the older woman said, "I can see what you're doing."

She finished filling the shaker and looked at Dorothea. "Filling the saltshaker?"

The woman let out a grunt. "You took this job to settle a score with Will."

Maybe not as addled as Poppy thought.

"I don't know exactly what you have planned," Dorothea continued, narrowing her eyes as she openly studied her. "But I can't let you hurt him."

"I'm just here to cook," Poppy said.

"Cook." Dorothea chuckled. "Cooking up trouble, that's what you're up to. As for the rest of the guests…" She shook her head. "Just remember—"

"You're watching me. Got it. Would you like a cookie?" She offered the full plate to her.

Dorothea's gaze narrowed as she studied the cookies for a moment before she picked up one. She took a bite, clearly savoring the taste for a few moments before her eyes flew wide open and she cried, "The boys' mother used to make cookies like these."

"Kate taught me how when I was a girl. It's my favorite recipe. Would you like another one?"

The woman looked longingly at the plate of cookies, but declined. "You are diabolical. But it isn't going to work, you know."

Poppy gave her an innocent look.

"It will take more than his mother's cookie recipe to get him to fall for you."

But it was a start, she thought as they both turned to see that Will and his guests had returned—early. One of the guests was limping and holding his arm.

CHAPTER FIVE

Will wasn't surprised when Dorothea was the first one to come rushing out of the lodge toward them. The woman had an insatiable curiosity, but she also was always there to help with whatever needed to be done. It was the worry on her face that concerned him. Had something else happened while he was gone?

"Why is one of the guests holding his arm?" she asked as Will drew up his horse to let the others proceed on to the barn and corral.

"A couple of the horses started bucking," he said. "Dean was thrown off."

"Not Lexi?" she asked, her gaze going to where Lexi alone was leading their horses toward the corral. Past them, the wranglers were unsaddling and taking care of the horses.

Will frowned. "Why would you ask about Lexi?" He shook his head. "Never mind. Yes, Lexi's horse was the other one. Dean got bucked off. He's limping and his arm seems to be sprained, but not broken, thank goodness. Lexi's horse tried to buck her off, but she stayed on."

Dorothea nodded. "I knew it. Didn't I tell you?"

Will groaned. "Don't start, okay?" He didn't need this. He was worried about Lexi and Dean. He was also worried about the horses and still puzzled over what had caused the problems. "I need to check the two horses. Can you see to Dean? Ice, bandage on his wrist, rest, you know the drill." He rode off, leaving her standing outside the barn.

"I'm the one who taught you the drill," she said to his retreating back.

Dismounting, he walked his horse the rest of the way. As he passed Lexi, he noticed that she was pale as fresh snow. Clearly she was still shaken. He hated that her first ride had gone so badly. Dean was limping toward the lodge. Dorothea had joined him. She'd had nursing training in college, which had certainly come in handy here on the ranch. Will could see that she was questioning Dean about what had happened. The woman loved knowing what was going on, he thought with a shake of his head as he went to join the wranglers to help with the horses.

Will especially wanted to check the horse Lexi had been on. It was a gentle mare that he'd never had any trouble with before. He was checking the saddle to see if it had been correctly cinched. He also checked for burrs or anything that could have set off the mare.

"I don't think that was the problem," Huck, the oldest wrangler, said as he joined him. Huck had worked for the ranch for years. He motioned to the tack room. Will followed him inside and closed the door.

"Did you see something?" he asked the wrangler.

"I stayed behind and checked the area after the rest of you headed back. I knew something had to have spooked those horses." Huck reached into his pocket and pulled out a snake.

Will's first reaction was to jerk back until he realized that the snake was made of rubber. But it was real enough that it

had fooled him. Coiled on the ground, it would have definitely spooked the horses.

He swore. "Where did that come from?"

Huck shrugged. "It isn't weathered so I'd say it got dropped
on the trail today."

"One of the guests purposely dropped the snake to spook
the horses bringing up the rear?" Will shook his head. "To
be funny?"

"Maybe. These are greenhorns."

Or trying to seriously hurt someone?

"Who was riding in front of Lexi and Dean?" he asked
the wrangler.

Huck thought for a moment. "There was you and Big Jack,
his youngest son…"

"Mick." Will remembered that Kirk had been riding up
there near Mick, but when they got in an argument, he'd ridden back a few horses.

"Behind Mick would have been the dark-haired flirty one
and the older brunette."

"Allison and Ruby."

"Then the blonde, Channing."

Will grinned at the wrangler. "You remember her name,
but none of the others?"

Huck ignored that. "The moody blond snowboarder."

"Kirk."

"Then Lexi, Lamar and Dean. The way I figure it, someone ahead of Lexi dropped it. Her horse saw it, might even
have kicked it out of the way. Once her horse started bucking, Dean's horse either then saw the snake or was reacting
to Lexi's mare."

"So Lamar's horse didn't react?"

"He'd reined in when Lexi stopped and Dean started to pass
him and Lexi," Huck said as he tried to reconstruct the scene.

"So Dean tried to pass Lexi's horse on the trail," Will said, trying to understand what had happened. "He could have dropped the snake but you said her horse had already stopped for some reason."

"I didn't see anyone drop anything, but I wasn't watching the whole time, either."

Will realized it would be hard to nail down who might have dropped the snake. "Not all the horses might have seen the snake. Or the ones in front could have kicked it up. Lexi's horse reacted first, though, right?"

The wrangler nodded. "I was busy trying to calm Lexi's horse so I didn't notice the snake until I stayed behind to search the area. That's when I found it on the edge of the trail in the bushes. When I first saw the snake, I thought for a second it was real, too. Wrong time of year, though. Too cold for rattlesnakes even if we had them at this elevation."

"Let's keep this to ourselves for now. Hopefully this is the last of the pranks." If that was what it had been.

He pushed open the tack room door and stepped out. As he glanced toward the main lodge, he saw Big Jack and his oldest son in what was clearly a heated argument. Past them, he could see Lexi. She'd stopped on the front porch of the lodge and was looking toward the cabins.

Will followed her gaze. Mick was standing outside of cabin four talking to Allison. Kirk was on the porch of cabin six. He had appeared to be watching Mick and Allison with interest before he looked past them to Lexi.

When Will returned his gaze to Lexi, he saw her hurry inside the lodge as if suddenly cold—or scared. But he had that bad feeling again that he was going to regret opening the guest ranch early for Big Jack and his employees.

With first aid kit in hand, Dorothea joined Dean in cabin two. He'd been sitting on the bed in the first bedroom with the door open, his head down, his hurt wrist cradled on his lap. She'd knocked, but he hadn't seemed to have heard. She'd tried the front door to find it not even closed all the way.

As she pushed it open and stepped in, she realized that he hadn't seen or heard her enter so she studied him for a long moment. Was he in pain because of his wrist? Or was there more going on with him?

As usual, Will had prepped her on who was coming so she'd known all of their names, their jobs at On the Fly and a description of each guest. Wyatt Sterling had prided himself on the personal touch, which meant everyone who worked closely with the guests had to be able to call them by name. Dorothea had seen staff get sent packing for breaking one of his rules.

Dorothea was a quick study and had had a pretty good feel for each of the guests even before she'd laid eyes on them. Dean's description had been so nondescript that she wasn't surprised how average he was from his height to his appearance.

In his midtwenties, his hair had begun to thin. He wore thick glasses with black plastic frames that he continually was pushing up his nose. But he also acted as if something was bothering him besides his wrist, she thought.

He must have sensed her because he looked up.

She quickly said, "I knocked. You didn't hear me. I brought something for your wrist."

Dean pushed up the glasses and got to his feet as she stepped into the cabin. She noticed three shirts hanging in the open closet and several pairs of slacks. He'd also brought dress shoes, along with what were obviously new cowboy boots on his feet.

"Let's do this in the living room, maybe at the desk," Dorothea suggested, seeing how uncomfortable he was to have her in his bedroom.

"I don't think any of that is necessary. I'm sure my wrist is fine," he said.

"It will heal faster if you put some ice on it for twenty minutes at a time over the next few days until you can have a doctor take a look at it. For now I can wrap it. The main thing is to let your wrist rest."

He looked as if he wanted to argue, but then seemed resigned. "Why did my horse do what it did?" Dean asked as she bandaged the wrist and then had him hold the ice pack on it.

"They're horses." She shrugged. "They're skittish and can get spooked. Usually don't, though. That's why it's always good to be hanging on. Sounds like your peaceful trail ride turned into a rodeo. It will go better next time."

"There won't be a next time."

"Haven't you heard that old saw about how important it is to get back on the horse?" she joked as she stood to leave. "You can bring the ice pack to the lodge when you come up for dinner and I'll replace it."

"I'll pass on dinner." He sounded sullen and angry, caught apparently in a why-me loop.

"Suit yourself." Dorothea thought about giving him a pep talk, but decided against it. Let him pout. He might be better off in his cabin alone since she didn't think being bucked off his horse was his only problem with being here. He seemed alienated from the rest of the crew. Which could also be a blessing.

"Call on the phone if you need anything," she said.

He glanced at the phone as if seeing it for the first time.

"It isn't connected to anything but the lodge," she told him in case he was hoping to call someone to get him out of here.

He grunted and she left him to mope, worried that his accident was the beginning of another set of bad luck.

As Will walked into the lodge later after helping with the horses, he caught a strong whiff of sage and groaned. He wasn't surprised to find Dorothea had a green candle on the large square coffee table in front of the fireplace and she was now waving a sage branch around. He'd been here before with the woman and since the guests usually didn't mind the smell—and didn't know what was going on—he ignored her home-remedy attempts to protect them all from evil.

Actually, he hoped it worked, because it appeared one of the guests had purposely tried to hurt one of the others with that rubber snake, and they may need all the positive energy they could get.

Big Jack had come in and gone straight to the bar to pour himself a drink. With the ride being cut short, they had more downtime than normal before dinner was served. Will thought he could use a drink himself so he joined the man, who looked as if he had a lot on his mind.

"Dorothea tended to Dean's sprained wrist," he told the owner of the company. He merely nodded as if that was the least of his concerns.

"I hate to see anyone get hurt the first day."

"It's Dean's luck," Big Jack said. "If anyone was going to get hurt, it would be him."

Will could see that the man wasn't interested in visiting. "I think I'll check on dinner," he said and, taking his drink, headed for the kitchen.

Big Jack didn't seem to notice, dropping into one of the deep leather chairs and staring into his glass as if he thought he might see the answer to his problems in the ice bobbing around in the amber liquid.

In the kitchen, Will found Poppy hard at work. She was singing softly to herself, a song he didn't recognize. At the sound of his step behind her, she abruptly stopped singing and turned. Her cheeks flushed as she said, "I didn't realize I had company."

"Pretty song," he said.

"It was one my father used to sing to me at night when

we lived in the cabin near here," she said, turning back to her work. She was chopping green onions with obvious skill. Next to her, she had butter melting in a large skillet. He watched her stop to stir the butter slowly. The woman could make melting butter feel like an aphrodisiac, he thought with a groan.

"Was there something you needed?" she asked as she put down her spoon and scraped the chopped onions into the pan.

His stomach growled as she added finely minced garlic. "No, I was just checking to see how you were doing."

She turned to smile at him. "I'm glad you're here. I need you to tell me what you think of this." She dipped a spoon from the drawer into something she had cooking in a pan on a back burner and offered him a bite.

It happened so fast that he didn't have a chance to decline. At least, that's what he told himself. He took the spoon in his mouth, aware of how intimate it felt as she stepped close and slipped the mouthful between his lips.

The moment the sauce touched his tongue, his senses sky-rocketed. He'd never tasted anything like it. It was sweet and savory with a depth of flavor that made it hard to discern all the ingredients.

He closed his lips over the spoon so as not to waste a drop of the wonderful potion. Poppy smiled and slowly withdrew the flatware from between his lips.

"What do you think?" she asked, her gaze locking with his as she waited for his verdict.

"Oh, my word." He licked his lips. He couldn't help himself. "That is…amazing."

Her smile broadened. "I'm glad you like it. It's my top-secret recipe."

He was still savoring the sauce with all his senses on alert when she reached over with her finger to catch a dab at the corner of his mouth. He watched her finger, still wet with the dab of sauce, go from his lips to her own mouth. He felt a flutter low in his belly as her gaze met his as she sucked the savory sauce from her finger.

Will's body reacted even as he told himself there was no denying it. This woman had come up here to take him down— just as Dorothea had warned him.

"That *is* good," Poppy said with a laugh. "What was I going to tell you? Oh, yes, I'm serving that sauce tonight with the honey-glazed roast beef now in the oven, along with whipped garlic potatoes, asparagus hollandaise and roasted root vegetables in a maple reduction with a side of smoked duck salad in a light citrus vinaigrette. For dessert—"

"Stop," he said, raising a hand. "You're killing me." He wondered if that was her plan. But that wasn't all she was doing and she knew it. "Surprise me."

She smiled, her gaze locking with his. "There is nothing I would love more. Than to surprise you."

Will took a breath. Now that he knew the score, he told himself Poppy couldn't get to him. Not with her amazing food or her secret sauces. And yet, he couldn't forget the way she'd taken the dab of sauce from the corner of his mouth and put it in her mouth, her lips closing over her finger... He cleared his voice. He had to put an end to this.

"I love your cooking," he said, "but I hate to see you toiling over a hot stove the whole time you're here."

"It's a labor of love for me and it's what you hired me to do."

Not exactly. Buckshot's menu tonight was barbecued beef, beans and baked potatoes with ice cream sundaes for dessert. Buckshot spent as little time in the kitchen as was absolutely necessary.

"I was thinking that while you're here we should get you out on a horse. I remember how much you loved riding. I'd hate to think of you in this kitchen working nonstop."

She smiled as if she thought it was his guilt talking. "You don't have to worry about me."

But he feared he did. Now that he was onto her, though, he thought maybe he could turn the tables. She wanted to play games? This cowboy was more than ready. He just needed to get on even footing, which meant getting on the back of a horse.

Poppy had been touched by Will's offer to take her horseback riding in spite of herself. It had seemed to come from his heart. She quickly reminded herself that it was probably just guilt for the way he'd treated her when they were young. She really doubted he was concerned about her wearing herself out cooking since that's what he'd hired her to do.

She had so few days to pull this off she couldn't help but worry that it wouldn't be enough time. Today was Sunday. The retreat was over Wednesday after a late breakfast and she would have no reason to stay any longer. It would be back to Whitefish with possibly no other chance to ever get this close to Will.

"Patience," she told herself. She tried to relax as she recalled the look on his face when she'd given him a taste of her secret sauce. He was definitely enraptured with her cooking.

Which was a start.

But she'd decided to pull out all the stops when she'd taken that drop of sauce from the corner of his mouth to her own. She'd gotten to him, she was sure of it. It had been cheesy and childish and yet she couldn't help taking pleasure in that moment. She told herself that Will deserved it and so much more.

"Poppy?"

She was so lost in her thoughts that she hadn't heard him come back into the kitchen. She spun around, feeling her face heat with embarrassment as if afraid he could read her mind.

"Sorry, didn't mean to startle you," he said. "I was just

thinking as I was leaving. The guests have free time tomorrow morning to do things on their own. So if you'd like to go for a ride… I have something I want to show you."

He looked so glad to be able to do something for her. She told herself it was just his guilt motivating this, but at the same time, she wished he wouldn't be so nice and thoughtful. He was making this so much harder.

"I'll plan on that," she said, excited about the prospect of a horseback ride with him. Maybe too excited about it.

As she watched him go, she warned herself not to fall for the cowboy again. "Not a chance," she said under her breath, even as she couldn't help noticing how handsome he was as he left—not to mention the wonderful way his jeans fit his perfect backside.

She shook her head, reminding herself to keep her eye on the prize. Will Sterling's reckoning. So deep in her plotting, she didn't hear Dorothea come up behind her.

"Now I get what you're doing," the woman said. "You're a kitchen witch."

Poppy shook her head and tried to laugh it off. "That's ridiculous," she said, turning back to what she had cooking on the stove.

"You are seducing that cowboy with your culinary skills. I saw the look on his face when he tasted whatever concoction that was you gave him. He was besotted—just like you were with him when you were twelve."

Poppy hoped Dorothea hadn't witnessed *everything*. "Isn't it possible that I merely enjoy cooking?"

"Cooking up trouble for our Will with your cookies and your secret sauces. You've got him literally eating out of your hand."

She wished. "You're making too much out of one small bite of tonight's sauce for the roast beef," Poppy said, turning to the woman. "Let me get a spoon so you can have a taste—"

"Oh, no, you don't," Dorothea said, stepping back. "You can't work your powers on me with your conjuring sauces."

"Don't be silly," she said, turning back to the stove. "As if with one spoonful I could put you or Will under my spell." She laughed. "You'll be sorry, though, if you don't try this sauce at dinner. It is really good."

"I saw how good it is." Dorothea left, muttering to herself.

Poppy wished the woman wasn't onto her. But as long as Will didn't suspect what she was up to…

Lamar went straight to his cabin after his run-in with his father. Big Jack could be impossible—especially when it came to running a business. He was too impulsive, priding himself on making decisions without giving them any thought.

And when he'd called his father on it, Big Jack had come back with, "That's why I named the business On the Fly. That's how I live my life."

"Like the way you sprang this retreat on me?" Lamar had demanded. "Do you even care what this is costing the company? And what was the purpose?"

"I don't have to explain my decisions to you. But I will tell you this. I have an announcement I'll be making at the end of the retreat."

"An announcement? And you aren't going to tell me until the end of the retreat?" When his father had said nothing, Lamar snapped, "Actually, you do need to explain your decisions to me. You put me in charge of On the Fly and since you are running the business into the ground with your… decisions, I'm sorry, but it's time for you to step down, Dad."

Big Jack had looked as if he was going to bust a major blood vessel. "I knew that's what you'd been up to, trying to kick me out of my own business."

"You turned it over for me to run when you got bored with it," Lamar had pointed out. "You can't suddenly decide to jump back in and take over again, especially when your motives are questionable."

"What is that supposed to mean?"

"Ruby. You think I didn't notice the way the two of you were looking at each other?" he had demanded. "You should be aware of the no-dating policy since you were the one who implemented it after Mick got us in hot water with one of the female employees."

"This is none of your business."

"None of my business? Are you serious? You want to start running things and dating one of the employees."

"We're not dating."

"Whatever you want to call it," Lamar had snapped. "It has to stop. I have power of attorney. I don't want to fight you, Dad, but I will to save the company and our employees' jobs."

"Don't you mean the nice little setup you have going?" Big Jack had spat and lowered his voice threateningly. "You think I don't know what's going on?"

"What are you talking about?"

"The money going out the back door of On the Fly. Is that why you want me out?"

Lamar had been so shocked he couldn't speak. Nor had he gotten the chance before his father had stormed off toward the lodge.

He'd stared after his father, wanting to go after him and yet knowing he wouldn't get a straight answer out of him right now. Maybe after they both calmed down, he'd thought on his way to his cabin.

With every step, he played back their discussion. Big Jack could not think for a minute that Lamar was stealing from the company. But was someone? No, that wasn't possible. Their bookkeeper would have caught the discrepancy. Unless it wasn't a discrepancy. Unless the thief was stealing product out the back door before it had been inventoried. Was that what his father meant?

Lamar had been so busy trying to keep Big Jack from bankrupting the company with his bad decisions and his excessive spending that he hadn't been paying close attention to what might have been going on at On the Fly. If one of their employees had been stealing...

Now he glanced out the window of his cabin. He could see horses in the nearby pasture running in the afternoon breeze, their manes aloft as they kicked up their heels. Behind them pines towered over the bunkhouses, the scene so picturesque he knew he'd seen it on the Sterling Montana Guest Ranch brochure.

A terrible thought struck him. Was this why his father had insisted on an impromptu retreat in Montana? Were these four days about cornering the thief?

CHAPTER SIX

Will could have cut the tension in the room with a chainsaw as he joined his guests before dinner was to be served later that evening. The only ones who didn't seem to notice the mood of the group were Mick and Allison. They had managed to sit next to each other in one of the large deep leather love seats, while everyone else was scattered around the massive lodge.

Dean had come up from his cabin even though Dorothea had said he'd planned to skip the evening meal. Will thought he was looking for sympathy the way he held his injured wrist, but he got none from this bunch. If anything, all he managed to do was look pathetic, making several of the guests snicker.

Channing had said something no doubt rude and, laughing, now hid her face behind the open magazine she'd been thumbing through.

"Lexi, that was amazing the way you stayed on your horse today," Kirk said and grinned. "I thought it was your first time on horseback. That was an eight-second ride, wasn't it? Ever thought about joining the rodeo?"

"Or the circus," Channing said.

Lexi said nothing, as if she could tell Kirk was only saying

these things to rub it in that Dean had fallen off. Will saw
Dean push his glasses up and glare at Kirk, who only laughed
when Lamar told him to knock it off.

Lamar and his father sat on opposite ends of the room,
neither apparently speaking. Ruby and Channing were both
thumbing through magazines, appearing to tune Kirk out as
he began talking about one of his rad snowboarding half-pipe
tricks he used to do.

"Used to do," Dean mumbled loud enough for everyone
to hear.

Kirk scowled at him and turned back to Ruby, continuing
with his story about when he was a semi-pro snowboarder.

Lexi sat alone, pretending to read an article in one of the
magazines. Will saw that she had it open to a how-to on horse
grooming, something he doubted was of interest to her. She
still looked pale and scared and he doubted they would be
able to get her back on a horse. A trail ride was scheduled for
the day after tomorrow. Will wasn't looking forward to it.

He was relieved when Dorothea announced it was time for
them all to go into the dining room for dinner. Ruby threw
down her magazine and left in the middle of one of Kirk's
stories. The others followed, taking chairs either with or away
from the people they'd been avoiding in the lounge. No one
looked happy. Not even Mick and Allison. She seemed to flirt
with him one moment and then push him away the next. Will
could tell that he wanted more than she was willing to give.

Glancing toward the kitchen, he couldn't help but wonder about Poppy. He felt more sure-footed now. He wasn't
sure exactly what it was that she had in mind when it came
to him. But at least now he knew what was at stake, which
he told himself was more than she knew.

Will reminded himself that Poppy was only a small concern given this group of guests. Big Jack had consumed several drinks. His face was flushed and his eyes rheumy as he

took a chair at the far end of the table. Will took his place at the head and was glad when Poppy came out with her cheerful countenance. He hoped the food was half as good as the afternoon snack—and that bite of sauce she'd given him. Just the memory stirred more than his appetite. That had been the point, he reminded himself. But now that he was onto her...

"Tonight, what I have for you," Poppy said as she and Dorothea brought out the serving dishes, "is a honey-glazed beef with my top-secret sauce recipe." Her gaze lit on Will for a moment, their eyes meeting across the long table. "It will be served with whipped garlic potatoes, asparagus hollandaise and roasted root vegetables in a maple reduction, along with a side of smoked duck salad in a light citrus vinaigrette." Poppy's offerings were met with one compliment after another and more excitement than he'd ever heard from any of Buckshot's meals. "Please enjoy and let me know if there is anything else I can get you."

Will had to admit, Poppy was definitely lightening up the table of guests with her rich, mouthwatering dishes. Truly, she had outdone herself. He had to hand it to her. The woman could cook. And to think he'd actually questioned whether she could handle this.

He'd definitely underestimated her talents, he thought. But quickly reminded himself how much trouble he was in. Of course she wanted payback for the way he'd hurt her all those years ago. He'd thought she might get her retribution by being a horrible cook. Or that she might even poison him.

Now he knew different. Her plan was much more insidious. He'd seen it in her smile. She was using her amazing cooking skills to wrap him around her finger. But then what?

It came to him in a flash. She'd left the ranch brokenhearted twenty years ago. Now she'd come back to lure him in with her cooking and then break his heart when she left.

Not that he didn't deserve it. But she was wasting her time. He couldn't let this go on. What would she do when she failed? Maybe that was when she poisoned him. He had to show her that he wasn't that cocky fifteen-year-old cowboy. Once she saw the real him…

"Poppy," he said impulsively. "Won't you join us for dinner?" She looked surprised and hesitant. "Please pull up a chair. We'd love to have you enjoy the meal with us."

Several of the guests chimed in. "Do, sit with us."

She smiled and reluctantly took an open chair near Dorothea, who shot him an alarmed look. Hadn't she heard the old saying about keeping your friends close and your adversaries even closer?

As the plates and utensils were passed around, the guests helped themselves, filling their plates.

"You are an amazing cook," Allison gushed. "How did you learn to do this?"

Poppy shrugged. "I learned from great cooks," she said and met Will's gaze. "And I experimented, honing my craft." She looked embarrassed. Her cheeks were flushed. But she also looked flattered.

He smiled down at her. He would make sure she joined them for every meal during this retreat. And not just so he could keep an eye on her. She was a ray of sunshine and this group definitely needed the light. He noticed, though, that she took only a small portion of each dish. Had he been as suspicious as Dorothea, he might have thought she'd done something to his meal. But he thought she was more worried about there not being enough. She shouldn't have. There was plenty even with everyone taking seconds and, some, thirds.

Will had to admit as he ate the incredible meal that, his and Poppy's past aside, hiring her was the best thing he could have done. He could well imagine this meal with Buckshot in the kitchen. This group was morose enough without that. While a decent cook, Buckshot had no social charms in the least. Don't like his food? Don't eat it, that was his motto. He was fine with letting the guests starve if they wanted to be picky.

They all ate in a pleasant contented atmosphere. Poppy's doing, he thought as he stole glances at her. She looked so sweet and innocent that for a moment he thought he'd only imagined all that innuendo earlier with the spoonful of sauce. But as he saw her take a bite of her meat dripping with that very secret sauce and lick her lips, her gaze came up to meet his.

Oh, yeah, there it was. That come-hither look and that luscious mouth of hers. He reminded himself it was only four days. He prided himself on his willpower. This woman was not going to get to this cowboy. He would kill her with kindness, so to speak. He would derail her plan starting with their horseback ride.

When everyone said they couldn't eat another bite, Poppy rose to help Dorothea clear the table and announce dessert.

"I have fresh raspberry cake drizzled with dark chocolate shavings resting in a cloud of sweet clotted cream," she said as she brought her masterpiece to the table.

Even though he was stuffed himself, he wasn't about to let her think he was afraid to taste her cake. "I'll take a small piece," he told her. He watched her carefully slice it, the flesh of the cake a pale pink against the white of the sweet clotted cream reminding him of her skin.

He knew she was watching him as he took a bite. He'd told himself that he was ready for whatever magical potion she'd put in the cake. But he hadn't been ready for the rush of flavors. He closed his eyes for a moment, unable not to moan in delight. If he thought he could resist her food, he was kidding himself.

Will opened his eyes and met her gaze. She wanted to play

dirty? "Okay," he said. "You've got me. I'm in love with this cake."

Poppy smiled, that gleam in her eyes, and everyone laughed. Everyone but Dorothea.

Lamar wanted nothing more after dinner than to go to his cabin. He had brought some paperwork and was anxious to get on it, especially after what his father had said. If someone was stealing from the company, he needed to find out who, how and how much, and put an end to it quickly.

"Will, I believe you mentioned line dancing," Big Jack said as they all left the dining room.

Lamar saw that he wasn't the only one who wanted to escape, but his father wasn't having any of it.

"Sorry, but some of the events on this retreat are compulsory," he said in his booming voice. "Line dancing is one of them."

Everyone was steered into the dance hall behind the main lodge living room for Western line dancing. The wranglers, Slim and Huck, who'd helped saddle the horses earlier came in to get the music and dancing started. Lamar watched Allison light up when Slim, a handsome young wrangler, pulled her out on the floor to kick things off. Mick followed, making sure he was next to Allison.

Lamar could see that his father had had just enough to drink that he wasn't going to let anyone out of this. He groaned under his breath as Huck dragged Lexi out on the floor. Big Jack pretended to lasso Ruby and pull her onto the dance floor. She came out laughing to fall in between Huck and Big Jack.

Lamar motioned for Kirk and Dean to get their behinds out there. Dean pointed at his wrist and shook his head. He took a chair near the old stereo and watched, looking miserable.

When Poppy appeared in the doorway, peering in as if enjoying watching, Will went to her and drew her out on the dance floor. She looked flushed, but both pleased and surprised. Lamar saw her darting glances at Will. Was it as obvious to everyone else what was going on there?

He felt his father glaring at him. Going to the back of the dance group so no one could see how bad he was at this, he tried to keep up with what everyone else was doing. He didn't know his left foot from his right, and on every turn, he came out facing the wrong way.

But Big Jack seemed to be enjoying himself. Some of the others, not so much. Lexi was worse at this than even Lamar. But Ruby, Allison and Channing were naturals. As he watched and tried to keep up, he noticed the way his father and Ruby would look at each other and swore.

Completely on the wrong foot, he bumped into Kirk, who cussed at him and glared at Allison's back as if he would have liked to kill her. Allison was flirting with Mick—and the wrangler next to her—and having a grand old time as the song ended and another began. Slim was surprisingly good at this, no doubt having had a lot of practice here on the guest ranch.

After stumbling through the last dance, Lamar saw an opportunity to duck out the back door. His father be damned. He'd deal with his wrath when Big Jack realized he'd gone. But right now, Lamar needed to find out if it was true that someone was stealing from their company—not bumbling around like a fool on the dance floor.

As he started toward his cabin, he saw a dark figure come out the back of the lodge. It was too dark to tell who, but whoever it was wore the navy On the Fly coat. Apparently someone else had ducked out, as well. He wondered who was brave enough to incur his father's wrath. The figure disappeared around the other side of the lodge.

It wasn't until he'd gone into his own cabin, turned on a light and pulled out the paperwork he'd brought and had begun to go through it that he saw something move in front of his window. He quickly got up to look out as Ruby rushed past, headed back in the direction of the lodge. He realized that must have been her that he saw earlier as she left and was now sneaking back into the dance.

He wondered what she might have been up to, but quickly put it out of his mind as he turned his attention to more important things.

Will had never been impulsive. Far from it. His brothers kidded him about being as solid as the old pine tree next to the lodge and just as exciting.

"You both should thank your lucky stars that I'm so solid," he'd told them. "You want to run the guest ranch? I didn't think so. Then be glad I'm content to spend my off-season kicking up my heels and the rest of the time right here being solid as an old pine tree running the guest ranch."

That's why it was so out of character when he saw Poppy standing in the doorway; he'd rushed to her and drawn her out on the dance floor. She'd balked for a moment, stopped to take off her apron and, taking his hand, had let him tempt her. In her T-shirt, jeans and boots, she couldn't have looked more sexy and cute.

And she'd turned out to be a great line dancer.

While getting her out on the dance floor had been impulsive, he'd told himself it was about keeping her close so there wouldn't be any surprises. But as they danced, he realized it had more to do with a painful pinch of his conscience. When he saw her standing there, he'd remembered her as a girl watching the ranch's guests from the sidelines. He hated the memory of the yearning on her young face. She'd wanted to join them so badly, but Will's father had said not to encourage her.

"She has a crush on you, son," Wyatt had told him. Apparently everyone was aware of it. "I won't have you leading her on."

He'd argued that he wasn't.

"Let her down easy. Your job is to make sure the guests have fun."

He'd felt so torn. When guests weren't around, he spent time with Poppy. She was enough of a tomboy that it felt like they were buddies. But when guests were around, especially the cute girls closer to his age or older with their families, he'd done his job. Not that he'd minded it. But Poppy had rightfully been confused by him running hot and cold. Worse, he'd been embarrassed when there were guests around to have a twelve-year-old kid following him around like a puppy dog. It was worse when she'd look at him with those big green eyes...

Now, as he danced next to her, he looked into those beautiful green eyes and felt something entirely different. Attraction. He told himself it was a normal male reaction. She was beautiful, especially with her cheeks flushed, her eyes bright. She was smiling, clearly enjoying herself, and he thought this was how she would look after making love.

That thought made him misstep and crash into her. She caught him, laughing, and at that moment he couldn't help himself. He looked at that luscious mouth of hers and it had taken all of his common sense not to kiss her. But he knew she'd seen the need in his expression. He'd never felt more vulnerable. She was determined to seduce him with her cooking, when he was already feeling hopelessly smitten with more than her cuisine. But he wasn't about to do what he'd done to her twenty years ago. He couldn't leave her on the sidelines, not ever again. Nor could he hurt her again.

Which meant he had to keep her at arm's length while defusing this situation between them. Smitten or not, he wasn't the marrying kind. Women didn't believe that. They thought they could rope him, hog-tie him and change his mind. None ever had. Poppy would be no different.

When the song ended and another began, he said, "I need to see to something in the barn. Stay and dance. Enjoy yourself."

Poppy looked surprised and disappointed, but she hid it quickly. She followed him out of the dance floor to the quiet of the lodge. "Thank you, but I have an early morning. Thanks for the dance." Her gaze locked with his.

He was the first to pull away. Just standing this close to her was torture. "I'm going to turn in early." Dorothea had put her in a room next to hers—on the opposite end of the hallway from his apartment.

"You're doing an amazing job," Will said, reminding himself and her that she was here to cook.

"I'm glad you think so. It's nice to be back here. Even for a short while. I'm glad you called me."

He thought he saw a flicker of something in her eyes, a reminder of how he'd treated her back then, but it was gone so quickly he thought his conscience had only imagined it.

Poppy couldn't believe Will had pulled her out on the ranch dance hall floor tonight. Just like earlier when he'd asked her to have dinner with him and the guests. He'd caught her off guard. He was being so nice to her... Was it possible he suspected what she was up to?

As she got ready for bed, she couldn't help smiling at the memory of finally being out on the guest ranch dance floor. It had been her twelve-year-old girl's heart's desire. From the sidelines, she'd watched the other kids dancing and having fun. Not that she'd known how to dance at that age. Back then it had been square dancing, but she'd dreamed of dancing with Will and having him look at her the way he did the older girls.

Now after all these years, her dream had come true. Somewhat, she reminded herself. She at least had his attention. She thought about the way he'd smiled at her as they were dancing. He looked as if he was having fun. And when he'd stumbled and bumped into her? He'd almost kissed her. She was sure of it. The way his gaze had settled on her mouth with a longing that she knew only too well. So why did she feel guilty?

Because her motives for coming here were less than honorable. She hadn't broken Buckshot's leg, but she'd wished something would happen so she could return to the ranch one last time and make Will Sterling hurt the way she had all those years ago. It was a silly, spiteful wish. A girl's fantasy that had made her feel better on those lonely nights years ago when she couldn't sleep after moving away from him.

Not that she could discount those hurt feelings at twelve or now. She just wanted Will to know how it felt. The feelings had been so real that she'd never been able to forget him. When she'd gotten the opportunity to move back to Whitefish, and be near the Sterling ranch, she'd jumped at it.

Just as she'd jumped at taking this temporary cooking job. She had only three more days to get him to fall in love with her and break his heart. The whole plan seemed foolish now, a child's dream of reckoning. She had been wishing that she could let go of that old hurt earlier when she'd looked in on the dance and Will had reached for her—instead of pushing her away as he'd done all those years ago.

Now she was where she had longed to be. Will was finally seeing her, Poppy Carmichael, all grown up and a woman to be reckoned with. Poppy smiled and told herself everything was going as planned…so why did it feel so bittersweet?

CHAPTER SEVEN

Poppy cooked breakfast early Monday morning in a daze. She'd had a terrible time getting to sleep last night. The dancing had been fun and she'd realized that she hadn't had fun in a very long time. She'd been so focused on starting her catering business, on succeeding and on somehow getting back at Will Sterling that fun had been out of the question.

This morning, she'd run into Will on the way to the kitchen. She hadn't thought anyone else was up since it wasn't even light out.

"Good morning," he said, seeming as surprised to see her as she was him.

"I was just going to slip a note under your door." He wadded up the paper in his hand and tossed it in the wastebasket by the desk in the lounge. "Big Jack said a continental-type breakfast would be fine. He wants his team to have some free time until noon. So I see no reason we can't go for that horseback ride this morning like we talked about. Unless you don't want—"

"I do," she said quickly.

"Great. Meet you at 8:00 a.m.?" he asked, all business.

"Perfect. I'll be ready." She watched him leave, and when she was sure he wasn't looking, she retrieved his note from the trash. Smoothing it out, she saw that it said pretty much what he'd told her. It was signed only Will.

She felt foolish for retrieving it, but still she put it in her pocket and headed for the kitchen. Even with Will being all business this morning, she couldn't help feeling pleased and guilty and excited and maybe too happy about getting on horseback again. The last thing she needed to do was lose focus. And there were times last night dancing next to Will that she had lost more than focus.

Maybe it was from being close to him on the dance floor, having him be so nice and caring about getting her back on a horse, but she'd had to remind herself that the plan was to pay Will back, not fall for the handsome cowboy all over again. She'd assured herself that that wasn't what was happening.

In the kitchen, she ignored Buckshot's menu of store-bought sweet rolls, cereal and fruit, and made two large Dutch baby soufflé pancakes with brandied apples and a dozen miniature Brie and chive omelets, along with a fresh fruit salad.

Then she changed and headed for the corrals where she found Will saddling up their horses. The morning was bright and crisp, the needles on the towering pines glistening in the sunlight. She breathed in the day, remembering the smell and the feeling of being completely in love with all of it—including Will Sterling.

The Will she found at the corrals was much more relaxed than the one she'd run into this morning in the lodge. She knew it had something to do with the horses and his love for them. He was a man at home in the saddle.

He looked happy to see her as she walked up. "You remember how to ride?" he asked and grinned over at her.

"It's been a while, but isn't it like falling off a bike?"

He laughed. He had a nice laugh and a great smile and

both made her heart flutter more than they should have. She reminded herself of the day she'd decided to show Will what an amazing girl she was. When she rode Lightning, the wild horse his father had brought to the ranch to break.

"I'm afraid I don't have a wild stallion for you to ride today," Will said as if also remembering that calamitous day. "Hope you don't mind."

She had to laugh. Her plan had gone awry that day. If she'd proved anything to Will it was that she didn't have a lick of good sense. She wondered about her current plan as he handed her the reins to her horse and she swung up into the saddle.

They rode out on a different trail than the one he'd taken the guests on yesterday, avoiding the cabins and riding west through the mountains. She was surprised how comfortable she felt in the saddle, always had. Another reason she'd thought that she and Will had been perfect for each other, if the foolish boy would have just realized it. That summer, she'd believed that she'd end up on this guest ranch with the cowboy she loved—if she could only find a way into his fifteen-year-old heart.

"I'm glad you agreed to this," Will said after they'd ridden for a few minutes without speaking. He brought his horse alongside hers and looked over at her. "It's been good to see you. I'm glad we could reconnect. But more than that I've had a chance to think about…my behavior… And I—aw, hell…" he stammered. "I want to apologize for the way I acted toward you all those years ago. I was rude and disrespectful and a stupid, cocky kid." He met her gaze. "I hated the way we left things that day when you moved away. I hope you don't hold it against me."

She tried to swallow around the lump in her throat. She hadn't expected this. Instead, she'd always told herself that he probably hadn't even understood how heartbroken she'd been that day. She was leaving Montana, leaving the ranch, leaving the boy who she loved to distraction.

Poppy had always figured that if he'd understood, he hadn't cared. She'd thought he didn't even remember that day that had been so painful to her. Now she realized that she'd wanted to believe he was callous and unfeeling, she'd wanted to believe the worst, because it made her feel better about her revenge plot. Just as she'd needed to believe he hadn't changed, that he was that same arrogant, cocky cowboy who broke hearts willy-nilly without even a pang of remorse.

"I don't know what to say." She really didn't. He was messing up her plan by not being the cowboy she wanted to believe he still was. He kept doing kind things and now he was apologizing? She felt her eyes burn with tears.

"You don't have to say *anything*. I just wanted you to know that I'm sorry. I didn't mean to hurt you. I was a jerk and I deeply regret it." With that he gave her a sad smile. "I hope I haven't spoiled your ride. That certainly wasn't my intention. Maybe with luck, we can be friends." With that he gave his horse a nudge and headed up the trail.

Friends? With luck? She rode after him, still choked up and hastily wiping at her foolish tears over his apology and the hurt of his last words. Friends. He couldn't have made it any clearer. Her attempts at seduction now felt laughable. He'd seen right through her and was trying to let her down easy.

She groaned to herself. Scratch that plan. She'd failed miserably. What had made her think she could be a seductress to begin with? A cowboy with Will's experience with women? Of course he'd seen what she was up to.

Poppy told herself to just be happy that he'd apologized. In truth, it had touched her deeply—before he'd said maybe with luck they could be friends. She wasn't even sure he wanted that!

Ahead he had reined in his horse and was waiting for her.

As she rode over the rise and brought her horse to a stop beside him, she saw the cabin where she and her father had lived for that life-changing summer. He'd brought her here? To remind her of the past?

"This is what I wanted to show you," he said. "I heard it's going up for sale. I've made an offer on it."

"What?"

"I'm thinking about restoring it." He shrugged, looking embarrassed. "I thought it would be a nice extra cabin for guests who wanted their privacy or that I might even live here one day." He ducked his head shyly. "You probably think it's silly, but I was feeling nostalgic when I made the offer. There was talk that the cabin might be torn down." He looked over at her. Their gazes locked. "I didn't want to see that happen. Remember the good times we had there? I never forgot you, Poppy." He laughed. "How could I? I'd never met anyone like you. Still haven't."

She was too shocked to speak. This man was killing her. She'd spent all these years plotting her revenge, determined to pay him back for hurting her while he'd...

He saw her discomfort and suggested they ride a little farther up the trail before they had to turn back.

"You remember the waterfalls?" he said over his shoulder. "I thought you might want to see them again."

Will felt like a heel. He'd made it clear that he and Poppy could never be anything but friends—just as he had when she was twelve. She'd taken it better twenty years later. But still he was mentally kicking himself. In his attempt not to hurt her again, he feared he'd done just that.

She'd seemed surprised by his apology for the past. But even more surprised by the part about them possibly being friends someday. He thought that she'd like that he was trying to save the house she'd lived in that summer. Instead, she'd seemed even more upset.

He told himself still it was better to stop this foolishness now before either of them got in any deeper. She hadn't said two words on the way back to the ranch.

To fill the quiet he was tempted to remind her that it was her own fault, her and her plan to extract her revenge—if that's what it was. While he loved her food, he was determined not to hurt her. Which meant he couldn't let her keep trying to seduce him. It wasn't going to happen, so better to nip it in the bud quickly.

He had wanted her to see that he wasn't that cocky kid he'd been. She had cried that day twenty years ago and she had looked like she could do it again today as they reached the guest ranch. He hoped she would now let go of her revenge scheme because he had a challenging group of guests for the next two days that he needed to deal with. Besides, she was wasting her time trying to corral him. He thought of the other women who had tried and failed. Then again, none of them had been Poppy.

He shook his head at the thought. No, not even Poppy could lasso him. Did she really think he would fall for her teaspoons of love potion? No matter how enticing, he wasn't that easy.

When they reached the corral, he said he would take care of the horses. She gave him a quick "Thank you for the ride," and hurried up to the kitchen, saying she needed to make preparations for lunch.

As he unsaddled their horses, his mood worsened. He told himself that he'd rather cut off his right arm than hurt Poppy. The woman had him where he didn't know which end was up. He'd handled it all badly and wished they could start over. But there was too much water under the bridge. Anything he did now to try to fix things between them would only make it worse.

He thought about last night at the dance. Had he been trying to make up for the past? Or had he just wanted to see her smile? Either way, it had been a mistake. Maybe his best bet was just to stay clear of her as much as he could. Distance, he reminded himself, since they only had two more days here at the ranch.

It wouldn't be easy. When he was around her, he felt a pull toward her stronger than gravity. His memory of their past had pockets of sweet, endearing moments that he'd forgotten until he'd seen her again. He could see her sitting on the counter in the kitchen cooking with his mother, a smudge of flour on her cheek, and looking so serious that it had made him want to laugh.

Or that day he'd run to her after she'd been thrown off Lightning and was almost trampled to death, to find her covered with mud from head to toe. He could still see those green eyes shining out of that dirty face. She'd been trying so hard to be tough and not cry. He couldn't help recalling his awe and relief that Poppy was all right. The girl had tried to ride a wild horse, proving she had more guts than he did.

There were other memories of her, ones he'd thought he'd forgotten. He wished they could be friends again so he could share them with her. He wondered if she had good memories from that summer catching frogs with him in between guests or eating ice cream on the front porch together on a hot summer day at her cabin while her dad fly-fished the creek out front.

When his brother Garrett called as he was putting the tack away, he was glad of it. He needed to get his mind off Poppy. "How are things going?" Garrett wanted to know.

"I don't know." He glanced toward the main lodge where Poppy had just disappeared inside and said, "Strange."

"Strange how?" His brother sounded worried. "Poppy's working out, right?"

"She's amazing." His brother chuckled. "Her meals are—"

"Amazing," Garrett interjected. "Sounds like she's won *you* over. I guess she didn't agree to work for you to get back at you for breaking her young heart."

He didn't want to share his suspicions with his brother, who he knew would think he was just being paranoid. "I wouldn't blame her if she did." He stared at the lodge for a moment. "Wait, you thought that was why she'd taken the job?"

"I was joking."

"So was I," he said.

"Why?" Garrett asked. "Has she done something that makes you think she really is plotting against you?"

Oh, has she. He thought of the spoonful of sauce she'd had him try and felt an ache of desire. If her plan was to seduce him with her food as Dorothea thought, then the woman had succeeded. But he wasn't like some wild horse that was going to be broke to ride by giving him a cube of sugar.

"You sound odd," Garrett said. "You sure everything is all right?"

"The guests are a little strange," he said, moving the subject as far away from Poppy as possible. "We've already had one accident. Nothing serious. One of them brought a rubber rattlesnake and dropped it on the trail ride. Got two of the horses bucking. One of the riders stayed seated, but the other went off, sprained his wrist."

"Another day at the office, huh," Garrett said, since he knew from growing up at the guest ranch for the summer months that it often involved some kind of drama. "Bet Dorothea is fit to be tied. Her and her proclamations of bad things coming in threes. So if Poppy hasn't poisoned you, then I guess you're okay. Unless she's cast some kind of spell on you." He laughed. "You can always have Dorothea break it for you."

But Will wasn't laughing. He was looking toward the lodge and thinking about Poppy. He was already under her spell and had been longer than he'd realized. He reminded himself that it would be over in two more days.

Lamar questioned why his father had scheduled free time until noon today. He'd seen Lexi sitting on her cabin porch pretending to read a book. Most of the time, she was looking around as if expecting something to happen.

Mick and Allison were playing horseshoes at the pits on the other side of the main lodge with Kirk and Channing. He'd heard horseshoes ringing off metal since after breakfast.

The person he hadn't seen was his father. He'd gone down to his cabin, knocked on the door, but gotten no answer. He'd tried the door, only to find it locked. Restless, he'd stopped by Dean's cabin to check on him, only to find him looking bored and ready to go home. He knew the feeling.

He'd gone through the paperwork he'd brought until late in the night but hadn't found anything suspicious, let alone felonious. This morning after breakfast he'd taken his fly rod and, wearing his On the Fly vest, had gone for a walk along the trail they had taken yesterday on horseback until he came to a stream.

After catching a half dozen nice trout, which he'd released, he was headed back when he saw his father come out of the pines behind the cabins and headed for his. A few minutes later Ruby emerged, as well. She was brushing dried pine needles out of her hair as she headed for her own cabin.

Lamar swore and headed for his father's cabin. This time, he didn't knock but burst right in.

Big Jack turned in surprise. For a moment Lamar was at a loss for words. His father had been looking at his phone, a strange smile on his face. Since there was no cell phone service up here, Lamar assumed he must be looking at a photograph on his phone. Or an old message?

"Ruby?" he finally managed to say.

His father stood his ground as he put away his phone and said, "What about Ruby?"

"She works for the company you own."

"Not for much longer. Not sure there will be a company for long the way things are going, anyway. But I'm washing my hands of the business. You want it, it's yours. I'm going to retire."

"Just like that?"

Big Jack nodded. "Just like that. Also Ruby won't be staying, either."

Lamar wasn't going to ask about that relationship. "Who is stealing from the company?"

His father raised a brow.

"You can't believe it's me."

Big Jack shrugged.

"I need to know what you've uncovered."

"Haven't uncovered anything. I just know."

He stared at his father. "You just know?" Was Big Jack getting senile? *"You just know."*

"That's what I said. Now if that's all, I need to get ready for lunch. There is a hayride afterward and a hike. I don't want to miss seeing the waterfalls. Haven't seen them in years."

What was this? A trip down memory lane for his father?

"By the way, the hayride and hike are mandatory," Big Jack said.

Lamar started to argue, but saved his breath. If this was his father's last hurrah, so be it. He would play along. It was only a couple more days.

Poppy had the radio on in the kitchen while she and Dorothea cleaned up after a lunch of thinly sliced roast beef with

huckleberry-barbecue sauce on homemade buns, sweet potato fries and chipotle molasses baked beans.

Again Will had asked her to sit with all of them, but this
time she excused herself, saying she had to take care of what
she had baking in the oven. No one had put up a fight. They
all just wanted to know what it was.

She enjoyed their excitement when she'd brought out warm
oatmeal cake with a rich, buttery brown sugar sauce. She'd
stood for a moment, waiting for Will to take a bite; when he
did, he groaned with pleasure and looked at her and gave her
a thumbs-up.

Poppy was delighted that the guests were enjoying her
meals. True, she was pulling out all the stops since she had
only two more days left to hook Will Sterling and reel him
in. Earlier, she'd been discouraged after their horseback ride.
But she wasn't a woman to give up easily, although it was
clear that Will had been warning her to do so.

She smiled when, at lunch, she saw him take a bite of his
sandwich, close his eyes and lick his lips. But he still wasn't
where she needed him to be yet. She kept thinking of last
night on the dance floor when he'd come so close to kissing
her. He had tried to warn her earlier that there was no hope
of them being more than friends, but now she questioned if
he was warning himself off more than her.

From down the table, he'd met her eyes and there had been
more than his usual warmth in those brown eyes before he'd
quickly looked away.

No wonder she felt confused and off balance. Will had
surprised her. That thought almost made her laugh. He'd
shocked her. First by apologizing and then by telling her that
he'd made an offer on the house she'd lived in that summer,
the summer that had changed her life. It wasn't just falling
in love with her first cowboy, Will. It was also the time she
spent at the ranch, helping make beds in the cabins, cooking

with Will's mother, Kate, feeling like part of a family, not to mention being able to ride a horse whenever she wanted.

She'd fallen in love with all of it. Montana, the guest ranch, Will and his family. She'd been thinking about that and questioning her motives for being here, so she hadn't heard what the radio announcer said until Dorothea nudged her.

"You hear that?" the older woman demanded.

Clearly Poppy hadn't. "Sorry, my mind was elsewhere."

"Yes, I can imagine where," Dorothea said as she turned up the radio. "Big winter storm coming."

"This late in the season?" Poppy listened with concern. Apparently weather forecasters had thought the late-winter storm coming down out of Canada was going to miss the western part of the state. Now, though, they were saying it was a much larger, more dangerous storm than they'd first predicted and it would be hitting the mountains and the Whitefish, Montana, area by midmorning tomorrow.

"Will needs to shut this down and get everyone out of here," Dorothea said with conviction.

Poppy realized she wasn't ready to leave. She needed more time. "Surely it won't be that bad."

Dorothea gave her an impatient look. "A winter storm? Buckshot broke his leg, you showed up with your charmed concoctions, a guest was bucked off his horse...now a winter storm? If that isn't a sign, I don't know what is." Poppy had no idea what the woman was talking about. It must have shown on her face because Dorothea added, "There's a curse on this retreat. I knew it. Once bad luck starts... I told Will..." Dorothea waved a hand through the air. "But does anyone listen to me?"

As much as Poppy hated to admit it, maybe the woman was right and Will should cut the retreat short. She'd heard that snowstorms this time of year could dump several feet of heavy snow or more, knock out power, close roads. "You should probably mention the storm to Will in case he hasn't heard yet."

Dorothea looked surprised. "It would mean you leaving tomorrow before you got what you came here for."

"I'm more concerned about the guests getting out before the storm."

"Right. Has nothing to do with Will. You're only worried about the guests, that's why you look so disappointed," the woman pointed out snidely.

"This retreat was important to him. I hate to see it spoiled."

"Yep, that's the reason," Dorothea said with a huff. "Has nothing to do with the plan you cooked up, huh. Don't even bother to deny it."

Poppy wasn't going to. She'd thought she could seduce Will with her cooking. While he did seem to love her food, that's as far as she'd gotten. Apparently it wasn't true about the way to a man's heart being his stomach. He'd seemed to have enjoyed all of the meals she'd cooked and been impressed by her expertise. But he hadn't succumbed to anything more than her culinary seduction and now she was running out of time.

They both turned as Will came into the kitchen. Dorothea rushed to tell him about the latest storm warning, but he said he'd already heard.

"The storm's not expected to last more than a day or two," he said. "I already mentioned it to Big Jack. He wants to stay so we'll weather it as best we can. I was just coming to tell Poppy that the retreat will continue."

She looked up to meet his eyes. "Are you sure?" She realized that some of Dorothea's superstitious fears might have merit. There was already tension among the guests. A storm would only put everyone more on edge.

"I was thinking that maybe you should leave early," Will said to her. "We can make do, if you want to get out before the storm hits. I'll still pay you the bonus. Actually, I'd feel better knowing you got out of the mountains safely tonight rather than wait until tomorrow."

He was trying to get rid of her? She didn't know what to say for a moment. She'd thought she was growing on him. Well, at least her cooking was. Then she glimpsed something in his expression.

He wanted her to leave. Because her plan was working! Well, he wasn't getting off that easy. "The storm isn't supposed to hit until after breakfast. I'd just as soon stay. I'll leave after the guests do."

A smiling Dorothea shot her a knowing conspiratorial look.

Will didn't say anything for a moment. "If you're sure. I just wanted to give you the option." He met her gaze and started to say more, but stopped. Looking uncomfortable to realize that Dorothea was watching them both closely, he turned and left.

"You have him where he doesn't know which end is up," Dorothea muttered.

Did she? It sure didn't feel like it most of the time. But him wanting her to leave told her that Dorothea might be right. Going back to cleaning the kitchen, she told herself that maybe she really was getting to Will. His worrying about her staying might have nothing to do with the storm. Could he be worried that she might steal his heart before this was over?

She told herself that she was dreaming if she thought that could happen. Also she felt a little guilty. She liked this grown-up Will Sterling. From everything she'd seen, he was a nice, considerate man—no longer that cocky fifteen-year-old cowboy who'd broken her heart without a second thought. Broke it, smashed it, walked on it.

This Will…well, he was sensitive and caring and—

She realized the trail her thoughts had taken and mentally slapped herself. The plan had been to come here, steal his heart, break it and get her retribution. Will had hurt her.

That hurt was still alive in her, though it felt weaker every day being here with him. She'd thought for sure being reminded of where the offense had taken place would make it even stronger.

Still, she told herself this was her chance and she might never get another one. Yes, she needed retribution, but she also needed closure. She'd get what she came for and then put Will and this guest ranch behind her forever so she could finally move on.

But even as she thought it, she wondered if she was losing her taste for revenge.

Lamar had never been on a hayride in his life. Nor did he see the thrill in piling onto a flatbed wagon covered with hay bales to be dragged around the mountainside by a team of horses.

To make matters worse, Allison and Channing both were flirting with the wranglers. So Mick and Kirk were sulking. Lexi had taken a seat with her back to the rest of them while Dean chewed on a piece of straw. Ruby leaned against a bale of hay, her eyes closed, appearing to be asleep, Big Jack perched nearby.

"So tell me what it's like to get on a wild bull and try to ride it," Allison was saying to Slim, who apparently had been a rodeo bull rider in his younger days.

"It's scary and thrilling. The idea is to match your wits against the bull's. All the bull wants to do is throw you off and stomp on you."

Everyone laughed but Mick, who seemed to be tearing his hay bale apart piece by piece and sending it flying into the air behind them. Maybe he was leaving crumbs so they could find their way back, Lamar thought moodily.

His father was pretending not to notice Ruby. Out of the blue, Channing suggested they sing something and the wranglers were ready with a half dozen Western songs, starting with the classic "Home on the Range."

By the time most of them were singing badly along to "You Are My Sunshine," they had reached the path to the waterfalls. As they climbed down, Lamar saw his father buttonhole Ruby. The two started up the trail to the falls together with his father whispering something to her that made her laugh.

Kirk helped Allison off the hay wagon. She stood waiting for Mick, but he jumped off the other side and headed up the mountain without her. Channing trailed after him.

"Trouble in paradise," Dean said as he passed Lamar and pushed his dust-covered glasses up his nose.

Groaning under his breath, he planned to bring up the rear, but Lexi kept stopping to pick spring flowers until he couldn't take it anymore and passed her. He caught a glimpse of Kirk walking alone. So had Mick and Allison met up on the trail? The last he'd seen Channing was ahead of Kirk.

He couldn't see the others on the trail ahead and quickened his pace, just wanting to get this over with. He still couldn't understand the purpose of this so-called retreat. If it was to make them all bond, then good luck with that. If it was a trip down memory lane for his father, then it was a costly one.

As he came around a bend, he saw Mick and Allison. They'd stepped off the trail and were arguing.

Lamar, having had enough, walked up to them. "Maybe you aren't familiar with our no-dating policy at On the Fly, but let me remind you of it now. Knock it the hell off."

"We aren't *dating*," Allison said and stormed off.

Mick chewed at his cheek as he looked after her, his expression one of angry funk.

"Do I even have to ask what is going on between the two of you?" he demanded.

"It isn't what you think, big brother, so don't worry about it," Mick said and stormed off up the trail, as well.

Shaking his head, he followed. A few more curves in the path and he saw the others gathered at the falls. His father had his cell phone out and was taking a photo of Ruby with the falls in the background. Allison was flirting with the wrangler who'd apparently decided to make the hike. Lamar realized that Huck must have passed him when he was talking to his brother. Mick was sulking off to the side. Channing had taken off her shoes and was wading in the water at the edge of the creek. She was calling everyone else a wuss for not coming in even though the icy water had to be making her feet ache.

Kirk showed up and decided to climb up the rocks along the edge of the falls and was only halfway up when Mick scrambled up, as well.

"Bad idea," Lamar said under his breath, wondering what their insurance covered on an employee retreat.

"King of the world!" Mick announced when he reached the top, having found a faster way than Kirk.

Lamar groaned. Those two would be the death of him. Or each other. It was always a competition. He tried to remember ever being that young or that foolish. He motioned for his brother to come back down. Mick ignored him until Big Jack said it was time to go. They scuttled down, slipping and sliding and starting a small rockslide.

"Boys will be boys," his father said beside him.

Lamar shook his head. Mick would always be a boy, he thought. Just like their father. But that was why his brother and father got along so well. Two peas in a pod.

After everyone had taken turns snapping photos, they were ready to make the hike back to the hay wagon. Lamar realized with a start that Lexi had never joined them.

"Has anyone seen Lexi?" he asked. There were shrugs and head shakes and a general disinterest. Apparently no one had. She should have reached the falls a long time ago. Unless she was still picking flowers.

"I'm sure she probably turned back," said Dean, who'd been sitting on a rock drawing circles in the dirt with a stick. "Probably waiting for us with the other wrangler who stayed with the horses. Probably flirting with him."

Lamar couldn't imagine that. Fortunately, the hike down went much faster. Mick and Kirk of course had to race each other, busting through the trees, hooting and hollering. Ruby and his father held back, the line stringing out so when Lamar reached the hay wagon Mick and Kirk were lounging on bales of hay, laughing like old friends.

"Where's Lexi?"

The two looked around, clearly having forgotten her. "Wasn't she with you?" Mick asked, confirming his lack of interest earlier when Lamar had questioned everyone to see if anyone had seen her.

Lamar turned to Slim. "Slim, it seems we've lost one of the group. Have you seen Lexi?" He started to describe her but the wrangler seemed to remember her.

"Last I saw her, she was headed up the trail with you," Slim said.

He looked back up the trail as Allison and Huck came out of the pines followed by Dean and finally his father and Ruby. "Did any of you see Lexi on your way down?" No one had. "We have to find her."

"Let's give her a few minutes," Big Jack said as he helped Ruby up into the wagon. "I'm sure she couldn't have gone far."

Huck said he would run back up and see if they'd missed her on the way down. He took off up the mountain.

Twenty minutes later, he returned and got on his two-way radio to the lodge. "We have a missing guest."

CHAPTER EIGHT

Poppy had just come out of the kitchen when the call came in. Dorothea had been straightening the magazines on the coffee table in the living room. She went to the radio as the alert came in full of static.

"I'll let Will know." The older woman turned to her and she put the headset back. "Seems they lost one of the guests."

"Who?"

"Lexi. I knew something bad was going to happen. Even Lexi knew this was going to happen."

"She knew she was going to get lost?" Poppy asked, confused.

"Never mind."

"You think she got lost on purpose?"

Dorothea sighed. "I think she's scared of someone on this retreat with her." At Poppy's still-perplexed expression, she said, "I'd seen her pinch a saltshaker from one of the dining room tables yesterday not long after they'd gotten here. When I dropped off the cookies in her cabin, I realized that Lexi had taken the salt to try to protect herself." Poppy knew she looked even more confused. "She'd poured it along the threshold of the cabin's front door to keep evil out. And now she's missing."

Poppy wasn't about to ask what salt had to do with anything. Instead, she said, "What do we do now?"

"We find Will and tell him." The older woman turned on her heel and started for the door. Poppy hurriedly took off her apron and went after her, catching up as Dorothea reached the barn. Will was just coming out when he saw them.

"What's happened?" he asked, looking from Poppy to Dorothea.

"Lexi got lost on the hike up to the falls," Dorothea said. "They can't find her."

He swore. "I knew I should have gone along but Big Jack had insisted. I figured they'd be fine since that's a good trail to the waterfalls. The only way you can get lost is to—"

"Step off the trail?" Dorothea suggested.

He nodded at her sarcasm with a sigh before running up to the house and returned wearing a sidearm.

As he started for his pickup, Poppy asked, "Could you use some help?"

He turned, seeming surprised by her offer. "Sure, come on."

Dorothea started to say something, but Will cut her off. "Hopefully we'll find her long before Poppy has to worry about dinner."

They climbed into his pickup, buckled up and went roaring down the road.

"Maybe they have already found her," she said, seeing how upset and worried he was.

"Let's hope so. There is always that one guest you have to worry about, but with this bunch…" He shook his head and glanced over at her for a moment. "You are the best thing about this. I really don't know what I would have done without you. Your cooking has calmed the beasts. It's amazing, truly. But your cheerfulness… We've really needed that." He reached over, touched her hand and then seemed to think better of it, and quickly drew his fingers back. He stared straight ahead as if regretting both his words and his actions.

Poppy was surprised not just by his words, but his touch. The warmth of his fingers had her hand still tingling. Chemistry? She smiled and murmured, "Thank you," all the while feeling giddy with pleasure. He'd felt it, too, she was sure of it.

She watched the pines flash past in a blur of green, her smile broadening. She could still feel the warmth where he'd touched her hand. Just friends? She didn't think so. Will could say what he wanted, but there was a spark between them. He'd felt it and she could still feel it working its way to the tips of her toes. She breathed in the unique male scent of him mingling with the great outdoors, wanting to remember it.

With a start, she realized she was acting like that enamored twelve-year-old. She couldn't let a touch of his hand or the scent of him make her light-headed. That she'd felt anything was enough to make her want to scream. This was not her plan. Not to mention Will had made it clear. Friends. Maybe.

She wiped the smile off her face.

And yet, she couldn't help feeling pleased as they bumped along the road in the close confines of his warm pickup.

Will hadn't meant to say the things he had to Poppy. They'd just come out because they were all true. He told himself that he shouldn't have brought her along. He especially should make a point of not touching her. He'd taken her hand on impulse and quickly let go as if he'd grabbed a frayed electrical cord.

He couldn't tell if she'd felt it as well or noticed his reaction. It was getting harder and harder to hide how he felt around her. He couldn't help being thankful she was here. He couldn't imagine these four days without her. Buckshot's cooking and his gruff disposition would have only added to the doom hanging over this retreat.

Glancing over at her, he felt that pull so sharply that it almost took his breath away. He felt a sliver of fear and rightly so. If he was right, this woman was determined to seduce him. He'd been so cocky at first, saying *bring it on*. But the more he was around her, the more he thought she just might be able to do it. She'd already seduced him with her cooking. It wouldn't take much more and he'd be falling for her only to have her break his heart.

He suddenly realized that the cab of the pickup had seemed a whole lot too intimate. He felt overheated, closed in. He rolled down his window to let in the warm afternoon air. Out of the corner of his eye, he saw Poppy staring out her side window. The sunlight fired her hair. Every time he looked into those sea-green eyes, he felt as if being invited to dive in. But once he did, he knew he would drown in them.

He swore under his breath. He'd prided himself on being strong and determined. But he'd never known a woman as strong and determined as Poppy. He felt defenseless against her, which he knew was ridiculous. But keeping her at arm's length was getting harder and harder with each day, with each hour.

With each dish she served, he felt himself falling more deeply under her spell.

That thought brought him up short. It was one thing to fall in love with her food—they'd all done that in the past two days. But falling for her? Not that she wasn't attractive to distraction. But it was more than that and he knew it. He *liked* her. He *admired* her. He thought way too much about kissing those amazing lips.

He swore silently, realizing the path his thoughts had taken and how much trouble he was in. Ahead he could see the horses and wagon. He pushed Poppy and the thought of kissing her out of his mind as he looked around for Lexi, hoping she'd already turned up. Unfortunately, he didn't see the young woman. What he saw instead were a lot of worried faces waiting for him to solve the problem.

Poppy listened as Will questioned everyone and talked about getting a small search party together. She could tell he didn't like the idea of turning the guests loose in the woods. What were the chances that he would lose more of them?

"Okay, who saw her last?" he asked the group.

"I did," Lamar said and looked guilty. "She was stopping to pick flowers and I got impatient and passed her. That's the last I saw her."

"All right, can you take me to that spot? The rest of you stay here. No one leaves." He motioned to one of the wranglers to go with him. She noticed that, like Will, Huck was wearing a sidearm.

"Mind if I come along?" Poppy asked. "I know the area."

He studied her for just an instant. "Sure." And they headed up the trail with Lamar leading.

Poppy could feel the air cooling around them as they walked through the shadows of the towering pines. The sun had warmed the day but was now about to disappear behind the mountain. She knew how quickly the temperature could drop—especially this time of year—in the mountains. She could feel Will's anxiety. They had to find her. It wouldn't be that long before it got dark. If they didn't find her soon, he would have to call in search and rescue from down in the valley.

"This is the spot I last saw her," Lamar said. Of the bunch, he seemed the most grounded, she thought. Unlike his brother, Mick.

"Lexi!" Will called. "Lexi!"

Poppy heard nothing but the echo of his voice. She couldn't help thinking about what Dorothea had told her. The salt aside, it would seem that the young woman was afraid of something. Or someone. One of the other employees on the retreat?

"Okay," Will said. "Let's divide up and take each side of the trail and see if we can find her." He glanced at his watch. "We meet in twenty minutes back here. Lamar go with Huck. Poppy, you come with me. Stay where you can see each other. I don't want to lose anyone else. If you find her, fire one shot," he said to Huck. "The other group will fire an answering shot. Three shots if you're in trouble."

With that Lamar and Huck dropped off the trail to the right. Poppy let Will lead as they headed to the left. They hadn't gone far when she saw that Will had topped a small hill off to her right. Poppy remembered a spot on the creek where the water made a beautiful little pool. She thought about calling to him, but before she could he motioned to her where he was going and dropped over a rise. She knew he wasn't worried about her getting lost so she angled toward the spot on the creek.

The terrain was fairly easy walking as it slanted downhill at an slight incline. But she knew it didn't stay that way. Soon the hillside would drop straight down to the creek. If a person wasn't ready for it...

She could hear the babble of the water and noticed all the flowers that had come up from the lush ground after the winter snow had melted. No wonder Lexi had been enticed off the trail.

Her hope was that once Lexi got turned around and realized she didn't know her way back, she would follow her own tracks back up to the trail. At worst, that she would follow the creek down the mountain rather than strike out farther into the trees where she would only become more lost. The creek would eventually hit a road. But would Lexi realize that?

As she neared the ledge over the clear pool below it that

she'd visited so many times as a girl, Poppy heard a sound that chilled her heart. Crying.

"Lexi?" she called.

She heard a whimper, then nothing. Ahead all she could see were pine trees. She remembered as a girl finding bear paw tracks in the wet mud near the pool. This time of year the bear were no longer hibernating, but out, hungry and searching for food. If Lexi stumbled across one...

Moving cautiously toward the whimpering sound, Poppy could hear the sound of the creek growing louder. A twig snapped off to her right. She held her breath for a moment. "Lexi?" she called. She could hear her crying quietly; why wasn't Lexi answering? She was almost to the vertical drop of the creek. "Lexi? It's Poppy. Where are you?"

"Poppy?" She began to sob loudly. "Down here."

She stepped to the precipice of the steep bank that fell to the creek and looked down to where Lexi was lying on the ground near the edge of the water. The young woman tried to get up, but let out a gasp and began crying harder. Clearly she was scared—and injured.

"Stay there," Poppy ordered. "I'm coming down to you."

As she looked for a way off the steep ledge, she saw where the ground had given way and realized that Lexi had fallen down the slope to the creek. Frowning, she looked back up the mountain toward the trail. There were skid marks in the leaves and soft earth as if... Why would Lexi have been running?

Thinking again of the bear prints she'd seen by the creek that time, Poppy made her way carefully around the cliff to where the young woman had landed.

"What happened?" she asked as she looked around to make sure they were alone. She hadn't seen bear tracks on her way down. Nor did she see any large dark shapes up or down the creek.

"I fell and twisted my ankle. I think it might be broken."

She knelt down beside the young woman and thought about the tracks she'd seen on the hillside above them. "Were you running when you fell?"

Lexi looked away. "Why would I have been running?" she demanded through her tears.

"I thought I saw… Never mind." Clearly the woman was lying. Poppy wanted to chide Lexi for getting off the trail to begin with and making everyone worry about her, especially Will, but just then she heard another twig break and looked up to see him coming through the trees.

Her heart did that familiar loop-de-do she remembered only too well, making her ache inside. She couldn't help herself. The cowboy was something to see coming through the pines wearing his Stetson over his curly sun-tipped brown hair and wearing a gun on his slim hips.

"I thought I might find you here," he said to Poppy. "This was always one of your favorite spots."

She looked up at him in surprise. How had he known that? Let alone remembered? She felt that ache grow more intense. That Will knew about this spot and how she always came here all those years ago… Her heart seemed to beat harder in her chest. She'd thought that he had never really seen her when she was twelve. He'd pushed her away because all he saw was a silly little kid. But now she remembered that there had been times when he hadn't pushed her away. Sometimes it felt as if they were…friends back then.

She groaned. Friends. That's all he'd ever wanted to be. She was the one with all the fantasies about something more. She listened to him talking softly to Lexi, asking if this hurt, if that hurt. He was good with guests, she thought. He made a good friend.

"What happened, Lexi?" Will asked.

"I fell." She began to sob again. "Is my ankle broken?"

"It's not broken. Probably just sprained," he said.

Poppy stepped over by the crystal-clear pool and tried to breathe. She was such a fool. Did she really think that her cooking and her cute tricks were going to get Will Sterling to fall to his knees in love with her?

Behind her, Will was saying, "You're going to be just fine." Lexi sniffled but quit crying. "Have you tried to stand?"

"I couldn't."

Poppy turned back then, telling herself she should be more worried about Lexi than about herself and Will. Clearly there was more to the woman's story.

Will looked to her. "Okay, I'm going to fire a shot to let them know that we found her. Do you think between the two of us we can help her to her feet?"

Poppy nodded, wondering what Lexi was hiding. What would have possessed her to run down a mountainside? And why had she lied about it? She'd rather they think she just walked off that ledge?

As Will moved a few yards away, she thought about what Dorothea had told her about the salt Lexi had put at the door of her cabin. She crouched down beside her and whispered, "If you saw something that scared you, that made you run, you can tell me."

Lexi wagged her head and covered her ears as Will pulled the pistol from his holster and fired it into the air. The sound reverberated through the pines. A moment later there was an answering shot from Huck in the distance.

Poppy gave it another try. "Lexi, if you're in some kind of trouble—"

"I'm not. I just fell." She started crying again, her gaze going to the ledge above them where she'd been running before falling.

"Okay, let's get you moving," Will said as he joined them again. "Poppy here has to get back to the ranch if we're going to have anything to eat tonight," he said and winked at her. "Poppy, tell us what you're thinking about making for dessert."

"Field berry pie," she said.

Lexi seemed to perk up at the sound of dessert. She wiped her eyes and let them help her to her feet. She even took a tentative step.

"Okay," Will said. "I'm going to have to ask—what is field berry pie?"

Poppy laughed, playing along. "I guess it's going to be a surprise. But I can give you a hint."

They kept up the distracting chatter as they made their way slowly up the hillside—crossing Lexi's running tracks as they did. Poppy was glad when Huck and Lamar hurried down the hillside to help them. But she didn't miss Lexi's reaction when the two men had first appeared. She'd felt Lexi stiffen for a moment before she recognized them.

"Here come the recruits," Will said, glancing over Lexi at her. He looked worried and Poppy wondered if he'd seen the same tracks she had.

CHAPTER NINE

Monday evening, Will knew that Poppy had outdone herself even before he saw what she'd cooked. He'd smelled it the moment he'd come into the lodge. Now as she and Dorothea approached the dining room with tonight's dishes, there were murmurs of excited expectation. Will felt his stomach growl. He had to admit, he was filled with a lot more anticipation than he'd ever been with Buckshot's cooking.

He reminded himself that they would be going back to simple fare after this retreat. That didn't bother him as much as the thought of Poppy no longer bringing her cheerful bright smile to the table. She loved cooking. It was written all over her face every time she brought out one of her creations. He envied her for having that kind of love for her job. He'd been born into running the guest ranch, and while there were days he enjoyed it, there were a lot he didn't, especially when he'd been working for his father.

But if he had learned anything the past few days, it was how easy his father had made running the guest ranch look. Things had definitely not been going as smoothly as he'd thought they would once he was in charge. The thought made him smile at his own arrogance. His father used to say that he had a lot to learn. Apparently so.

"Tonight, what I have for you is a mustard-maple pork tenderloin served with roasted squash and a mushroom risotto," she said. "Along with a sweet beet and goat cheese salad."

Will looked around the table. He hadn't missed the change that came over the guests at mealtime. After the hayride, it had appeared that the group was arguing among themselves. They'd all trudged into the lodge after freshening up, saying little. Was it possible that each day the tension was getting worse between them?

But once Poppy brought out the first dishes, the mood shifted radically. It was like magic. Like he'd said earlier, she calmed the beasts and he was more thankful for that than he could ever express to her. She filled this room with something close to love, he thought as he watched the guests dig in.

Poppy hesitated a moment as if not sure she should sit with them again, but Lamar got up to pull out her chair for her. Her cheeks were flushed and her eyes bright as she looked down the table smiling. When that smile lit on him, he felt his heart flutter. What was wrong with him? Hell, who was he kidding? The best part of his day was seeing her. The last thing he'd wanted to do today was push her away.

Friends. What had he been thinking? He couldn't be friends with this woman. *Are you crazy?* With that body, with that mouth that he fantasized about kissing the moment he closed his eyes at night? So what was he going to do about it? Throw caution to the wind?

He didn't know. He'd hoped to talk to her after they'd found Lexi, but there hadn't been an opportunity, since Poppy had opted to let Lexi ride back in the pickup cab while she climbed onto the hay wagon with the guests.

Once they were back, Dorothea bandaged Lexi's ankle in

the lodge and Poppy had headed for the kitchen to get the night meal on.

Will had started to follow her, anxious to talk to her. Did he really think that by laying all his cards on the table he could make some sense of this? At least he could warn her that where she was headed was dangerous. How far did she want to take this? What if they ended up in bed together? It wasn't like the thought hadn't crossed his mind. It was getting harder and harder not to think about the two of them naked upstairs in his bed.

That's why she had to quit this. Otherwise, he couldn't be responsible, he told himself. Which was why he had to talk to her. If she really was determined to seduce him—

He'd wanted desperately to say these things to her, but had been stopped by one guest after another with a problem he needed to see to. With each passing hour, he had more respect for his father, who wasn't easy to work for, but had made running this guest ranch seem easy.

Now as the food was passed around in the dining room, followed by the clatter of knives and forks as everyone enjoyed the meal, Will watched in surprise, noting that not even the Lexi scare earlier had dampened their appetites.

He looked down the table and realized that Poppy seemed to be waiting for him to take a bite of the pork. The mustard-maple sauce was both sweet and savory and a wonderful mahogany color that reminded him of her hair. He breathed in the scent, realizing how much she put of herself into each dish and how much he was enjoying both her and her cuisine. If this was what making love with her was like...

"Do I detect a note of sage?" asked Dean, making Mick and Kirk snicker.

Poppy grinned. "You do indeed. Nice palate."

Dean beamed. His wrist was better. He was threatening to get back on a horse again. There was some kidding and jok-

ing, but even the usually dour Dean seemed to be enjoying himself and the meal.

Everything had been going fine until Ruby knocked over the saltshaker in front of her.

"Quick, throw the spilled salt over your shoulder," Dorothea ordered in a stricken voice from down the table.

Ruby laughed. "That's an old wives' tale. No one believes that."

Will saw Dorothea bristle. "That's how those women lived long enough to become old wives," she snapped.

Next to Ruby, Big Jack scooped up a little of the spilled salt and tossed it over his left shoulder. "Happy?" he asked Dorothea and laughed. "I think Ruby is safe now from evil."

"I wouldn't bet on that," Dorothea mumbled under her breath, loud enough that everyone at the table had to have heard.

The room went too quiet, but leave it to Poppy to save the day as usual. "I hope you're all leaving room for dessert," she said into the death-like doom that had descended on the table moments before. "We're having pie. Field berry pie, for those of you who haven't had it, is a fusion of blackberries, raspberries, blueberries, strawberries and apples. It's kind of an everything-but-the-kitchen-sink kind of pie. Who wants ice cream with theirs?"

Hands went up all around the table and everyone went back to eating, the tense moment over at least for now. This was an odd bunch of guests, Will thought. He glanced at Dorothea, who looked up to give him one of her I-told-you-so looks. He had to admit that there had been more accidents in two days than ever before. Just his luck?

As dishes were cleared away and Poppy got up to get the pies, he rose to help scoop the ice cream. She was cutting the pies next to him when he whispered over to her, "Can we talk later?"

She glanced at him, maybe a little surprised, but nodded, then returned to the table and began passing around pie and ice cream for their eagerly waiting guests.

Poppy thought she already knew what Will wanted to talk about. All during kitchen cleanup and putting the food away—what little there was left to put away—Dorothea had been more quiet than usual. When she did speak it was to tell Poppy that she feared things were going to get much worse.

"Can't you feel it in the air?" the older woman had demanded.

She hadn't shared her own concerns with Dorothea or anyone else for that matter. "It's only two more days. I'm more worried about the storm that's coming. Imagine if they're all confined to their cabins because of the snow. Or worse, the lodge?"

"I heard Will earlier trying to talk Big Jack into cutting the retreat short but the man wasn't having any of it." Dorothea shook her head. "Retreat," she said with disdain. "Doesn't look like it's bringing any of them closer together, if that was the plan. In fact, it's just the opposite."

Poppy couldn't argue her point. She wondered how they'd all gotten along before this. Maybe they'd never had to spend this much time together. So why was Big Jack determined that they were going to no matter what?

Dorothea finished her work and left, taking a box of salt with her. "You'd be smart to put some down by your door, as well," she said as she left.

The woman hadn't been gone long when Poppy looked up to see Will come into the kitchen. He smelled of campfire. Past him, she could see the blaze going outside at the fire pit. The guests were huddled around it, their faces lit by firelight. She was surprised to see that even Lexi was there. She'd limped out after supper.

"Your food was amazing as always," Will said as he leaned against the kitchen counter with a nonchalance that didn't quite ring true. He seemed...nervous. "I'm sorry I don't have more staff to help you. How are you and Dorothea getting on?"

She smiled. "Just fine. I think we're bonding."

He laughed at that. "She told me to watch out for you. That you're plotting against me and to be careful if you offer me anything to eat that you haven't taken a bite of yourself."

Poppy had to laugh, as well. Why was he telling her this now? She'd already suspected that he was onto her. But she played along to see where he was headed rather than call him on it. "She thinks I'm trying to seduce you with food."

"Well, if that's the case," he said, meeting her gaze, "it's definitely working."

They stood looking at each other for a long moment before Will cleared his voice and changed the subject so quickly it almost gave her whiplash.

"I need to ask you something about earlier today," he said, dropping the unlikely nonchalance and going back to all business. "I saw tracks where it appeared—"

"Lexi had been running when she went off that ledge and fell?"

He nodded and let out a long sigh. "Did she say why she was running through the woods like that?"

"She denied it. But it was clear she was lying. She was definitely scared. I thought maybe she'd seen a bear or something else that had frightened her."

"Or someone." He looked away for a moment before he turned back to her. "I hate to even mention this but Dorothea—"

"Told you about the salt Lexi borrowed for her cabin."

He nodded, smiling. "I'm sure you find all this hocus-pocus

stuff as silly as I do, but it does sound like the young woman is afraid of someone."

"Are you going to mention it to Big Jack?"

Will chewed at his cheek for a moment. "I'm afraid he'd laugh it off. Not that I blame him. Or worse, that it might affect her job."

"Do you think he'd fire her?"

He shrugged. "Maybe that's what this retreat is about. Finding out which employees he wants to keep. He said he had some decisions to make while here. Lexi's behavior would make any employer worry."

"I'm sure Dorothea broached this subject with you," Poppy began.

"The storm," he said with another sigh, realizing they were finishing each other's sentences—something they'd done twenty years ago when they were just kids. "She wants me to talk to Big Jack again about them leaving tomorrow right after breakfast. The storm isn't supposed to hit until noon. You haven't changed your mind about staying, have you?"

She shook her head. "I'm here for you until the end."

He nodded and looked as if he wanted to say more, but changed his mind as he started to leave. She got the impression he'd come in here to talk about more than guest ranch business. "You're welcome to come out by the campfire. Dorothea brought out the marshmallows, crackers and chocolate for s'mores."

Poppy was still wondering at all the things Will hadn't said. "I think I'll pass and make it an early night, but thank you." A lot had happened today and she'd realized that she needed time alone—away from Will. Earlier, being with him in the truck, seeing him in his element up in the woods, and later witnessing how tender and caring he'd been with Lexi, it had left her shaken to her core.

Not that she'd forgotten the sparks he'd ignited with just

the touch of his hand or his apology. Will Sterling was way too likable even when he was warning her that they could never be anything but friends.

Isn't that why he'd brought up Dorothea's suspicions? He wanted her to know that he was onto her. Well, she'd gotten the message. So why hadn't he just come out and told her that he knew what she was up to and it wasn't working?

Unless… She felt her heart do a little bump in her chest. Because it was working? It was just the food she cooked for him. Is that why he'd seemed…off tonight? She was getting to him. Why else try to warn her off? If she really had no chance of seducing him, then why would he mention it?

She felt way too much hope suddenly and didn't like the way her pulse began to pound. Easy, she warned herself. The last person she was going to let ruin her plan for a Will reckoning was herself. She had two days left. That's if Big Jack and his crew stayed until Wednesday afternoon.

Looking out at the campfire and the people standing around it, she was reminded of what she'd seen in the woods today and the state she'd found Lexi in. As she headed up to bed, she walked through the dining room and was tempted to take a saltshaker. She would lock her door tight tonight, though.

Something about this group of guests was enough to make anyone feel a little spooked.

Lamar studied his employees standing around the campfire. The scare earlier with Lexi getting lost and hurt seemed to have restrained even his brother, Mick. Or maybe it was just because Allison appeared to have lost interest in him and was now chummy with wrangler Huck. At least his father and Ruby were keeping their distance.

But it was Lexi he was more concerned about. She'd been acting stranger than usual. Now she was huddled by herself at the edge of the group. Will had dragged up a log for her to sit on so she wasn't on her ankle. Why she'd insisted on coming to the campfire, Lamar couldn't imagine. Maybe she didn't want to be alone. She seemed to be watching them all with suspicion.

"Having fun?"

He turned in surprise to see Allison next to him. She wasn't looking at him, but studying the people around the fire as she warmed her hands over the flames.

"I need to talk to you," she said, lowering her voice, still not looking at him. "Alone."

"Okay." He started to move away from the fire, but she stopped him.

"Not now. Meet me in the barn. Midnight. Don't tell anyone."

He stared over at her. Was she serious or just joking around? He wondered how much she'd had to drink. But when she looked up at him, he saw that she wasn't joking. She actually looked scared.

"I need another beer," she announced loudly. "Anyone else?" As she moved away from him to head for the cooler filled with ice and beverages, he saw that both Kirk and Mick had been watching him and Allison with interest. Lexi, too, he saw as he looked around the campfire. She met his gaze for a moment and quickly looked away.

But none of that bothered him as much as seeing his father studying him with a mixture of anger and concern.

Will managed to get Big Jack aside as the campfire burned down. "I really think you should consider cutting the retreat short and leaving tomorrow before the storm hits. I know you don't want—"

"We'll leave right after breakfast."

He'd expected the man to put up an argument. He couldn't help being surprised. Big Jack was the kind of man who stuck to his guns even as the life raft was sinking. Will hadn't thought he'd be able to change his mind, even though he'd been determined to give it another try.

"So you changed your mind already? Can I ask why?"

The man glanced back at the dying campfire. Most of his employees looked as if they were staying until the last embers blinked out. "Lexi getting lost and hurt today... Dean getting bucked off his horse—"

"I should tell you. My wrangler found a rubber snake that someone must have brought along as a joke. They'd dropped it on the trail and when the horses saw it..."

"I was afraid it might be something like that," Big Jack said, shaking his head. He looked tired and much older in the faint dying firelight where they stood.

"I'm sure whoever did it thought it would be funny," Will said, not wanting to get anyone in trouble. It had been a stupid thing to do, but then again, these were greenhorns. What did they know about horses?

Big Jack looked skeptical. "Maybe," he said. "Or maybe one of them has an ax to grind against me."

"I doubt that's the case."

Big Jack smiled. "Nice of you to say but a man makes enemies, even within his own family."

Will said nothing, since he'd seen the man arguing with both of his sons at one point or another. He suspected this wasn't what Big Jack had hoped would come out of this trip.

"I'll let everyone know what time we'll be leaving," the man said, sounding defeated. "But, Will, I wanted to thank you for opening up early for us. Even with the...drama, I've enjoyed being here. I need to make some changes in my life and this retreat has helped me make my decision. I spent a lot of wonderful hours here on this ranch as a boy. It was nice to come back one last time."

His words startled Will. "I hope it won't be your last," he said, suddenly afraid the man was terminally ill.

Big Jack laughed. "So do I, but we never know, do we?" With that he walked over to the group still around the campfire to announce that they would be leaving after breakfast. No one seemed upset by that news as he walked away.

Will looked toward the main lodge. He could see that Poppy's light was on in her room upstairs at the lodge. He caught movement behind the curtains and quickly looked away as he struggled with his feelings. Earlier, his plan in the kitchen was to tell her he knew what she was up to and that it wouldn't work. That he didn't want things to be awkward between them. That he hated that she'd come up here looking for retribution—if Dorothea was right about that.

But he couldn't get the words out. Dorothea was convinced that Poppy had put a love curse on the food she'd served him. As crazy as that sounded, it seemed that she had.

He smiled and shook his head as he said good-night to the guests still around the campfire and headed toward the lodge. While Poppy's culinary skills were nothing short of amazing, it wasn't just her food. The woman had gotten to him—just as Dorothea had warned would happen.

So what was he going to do about it?

Nothing. He reminded himself of the girl Poppy had been and how he'd hurt her all those years ago. He couldn't do that to her again. As tempted as he was, if they ended up in that big bed of his upstairs he feared they would both regret it. He'd have to stay clear of her. Keep it all business. He'd get her to leave in the morning with the guests. It was the only way.

As he headed to his office, though, all he could think about was her standing in the ranch kitchen, the sun coming through the window and lighting up her hair. And then her turning and him thinking about kissing her and carrying her upstairs.

Closing his office door, he resolved not to let that happen. He thought of the other women he'd been attracted to and how quickly he'd moved on for one reason or another. Even as he argued that Poppy Carmichael wasn't like any woman he'd ever known, he couldn't bear the thought of her being just another woman he'd loved—for a while.

He dove into the paperwork waiting for him on his desk.

CHAPTER TEN

Lamar reached the barn a little before midnight. On his walk there, he didn't see anyone. But he noticed that the temperature had dropped and a chilling wind had come up. Clouds scudded across a dark sky, a sliver of moon playing peekaboo as he made his way toward the barn. The wind kicked up dust, whirling it around him. He was glad for the heavy coat and stocking cap. As he bent his head against the wind and cold, he felt foolish for agreeing to this rendezvous and, at the same time, a little on edge.

The guest ranch was so quiet that when an owl screeched from high on the barn, he jumped a foot. "Calm down," he told himself impatiently. "You have nothing to worry about." But he *was* worried. He'd been worried ever since he'd spoken with his father. Maybe there was even more trouble at the company than he thought.

He couldn't imagine what Allison had to tell him—in the middle of the night—instead of merely pulling him aside and saying whatever it was. She wasn't hitting on him, was she?

That thought made him chuckle under his breath. Could he really not tell the difference? He needed to get out more and not spend every waking hour taking care of On the Fly. As his father had pointed out, the business wasn't even his. He was merely the owner's oldest son and the guy who got left with all the work and worry, he thought, grumbling under his breath.

When he reached the hulking structure of the barn, he hesitated. He couldn't see anything in the darkness inside. He stood for a moment out in the wind and finally, chilled, stepped in. Once inside, he realized that there was a faint light in the far back, but still it took a moment for his eyes to adjust. If possible, he felt colder in the barn than he had outside. He wished he was in his warm bed. Better yet, off this mountain and back in sunny California. This clandestine meeting had him not just chilled but jumpy.

At a sound behind him, he spun around. Allison rushed in and motioned for him to follow her to a dark corner out of the light. Seriously? He groaned inwardly, but followed her, wanting to get this over with as quickly as possible.

She seemed even more nervous than he was. She kept looking at the barn doorway and past it to the cabins as if expecting that she'd been followed.

"Allison, I have no idea why you—"

She shook her head, interrupting him to say, "There's something I thought you should know, okay?" Then she hesitated.

Oh, for the love of God. He moved restlessly, trying to keep his feet warm. "What is it, Allison? It's freezing in here and what's with all the secrecy?"

"There might be something going on at On the Fly."

He stopped moving, stopped trying to stay warm. "Like what?"

She looked away. "I don't know exactly. It's just—"

He groaned, reminded of his father saying he just knew that something was wrong at the company. "Allison, it's too cold for this. Spit it out."

"Okay," she snapped, looking as if she wished she hadn't started this. "I saw someone the other day at the plant. He pulled into the back after-hours. I could tell he was there to meet with someone."

Lamar shook his head, losing patience. "Someone to meet someone. Get to the point, please."

"The man I saw was a drug dealer."

He stared at her. "A drug dealer?"

"I know what you're thinking."

"I doubt that. Is he *your* drug dealer? Is that how you know him?"

"No. That is, I know who he is, all right? It was a long time ago. Another life."

"Look, if you used to buy pot from some guy—"

"He isn't that kind of drug dealer. He wasn't at On the Fly to sell someone a dime bag," she snapped impatiently. "He's big-time."

Lamar felt himself go still and even colder. "Who was he there to see?"

"That's just it. When he saw me, he recognized me and turned around and left. Clearly he hadn't expected me to be there. I wouldn't have been, but I was running late and got this call…" She sighed. "I'm sorry, but the fact that he was coming in the back way as if he'd been there before…"

His head was spinning. "What is it you're saying, Allison?"

She looked away and bit at her lower lip for a moment. "Just that it got me thinking. He was there. He had his business face on. So…" She finally blurted it out. "Someone could be using On the Fly to send out more than fly-fishing vests." She pulled her coat around her as if suddenly as chilled as he was.

He didn't know what to say. His first instinct was to laugh it off. Just because she saw some drug dealer at the back of the plant…

"Look," she said, grabbing his arm tightly. "You can't tell

anyone that you heard it from me," she pleaded. "It's bad enough that he saw me, you know?"

He didn't. He knew nothing about the drug world. He didn't want to know. "Thank you for telling me."

She smiled as tears filled her eyes. "I have to leave."

He nodded, thinking she meant go back to her cabin.

"I can't stay at On the Fly. Not now. If you start asking questions…" She swallowed and looked terrified. "He'll know it was me. I have an aunt who lives down south. I might go there."

That seemed unnecessary, to uproot herself and run away, but she knew more about that world than he did. She'd known the man. She would know what she had to fear. Though he couldn't imagine it being that serious.

"Have you told anyone else?"

She shook her head.

"Not Mick?" Another head shake. "Not my father?" She shook her head but added a shrug. Was it possible Big Jack knew? Or suspected? Is this why he was so upset about the business?

"I have to go. Please promise you won't tell anyone it was me."

He promised and watched her go, feeling numb and scared at the same time. He thought about hiking down to Big Jack's cabin and demanding answers. But it was the middle of the night. And surely if his father thought someone was running drugs through the company he would have…

With a snort of derisiveness, Lamar realized he wasn't sure what his father would have done. Maybe something as crazy as an impromptu retreat at an isolated guest ranch high in the mountains of Montana, where he invited all the suspects.

Poppy couldn't sleep. She'd tried reading but after a few minutes realized that she didn't know what she'd just read.

She put the book aside and walked to the window, surprised.
The wind had come up. She'd heard it howling along the edge
of the eaves. One of the wranglers had doused the campfire
earlier. Now the wind hurled ash into the air. The pine trees
swayed, reminding her of other nights up on this mountain
when she was young and couldn't wait to wake up. Each day
back then had been filled with so much hope and promise.

She realized that she'd felt the same way her first night here.
Being back on the ranch, seeing Will… Poppy pushed that
thought away as she let the curtain fall back into place. The
howling wind outside made her worry about the approaching
storm. Had Will talked Big Jack into leaving early? She hoped
so. And yet, the thought made her sad. She didn't want to
leave. She told herself it was because she hadn't accomplished
what she'd come up here to do.

But even as she thought it, she was no longer sure. Had
she really wanted Will to hurt as much as she had when he'd
broken her heart at twelve? Or had she wanted him to finally
see her? See that she wasn't a kid anymore. She was a woman.
Is that what she really wanted? She no longer knew.

Worse, she felt as if her plan was backfiring. Her feelings
for Will had grown stronger as she'd gotten to see the man
he'd become and he saw the woman she'd become. No longer was it a young girl's crush on an older boy who treated
her like a kid sister. What she felt when she was around him
was a powerful chemistry. It seemed to electrify the air. One
little spark and boom!

The game she was playing had become dangerous. Over the
past two days, she'd realized that Will had grown into a man
she could love. Not for a retribution fling, but for long-term.

Angry with herself, she headed back toward bed when
there was a knock at her door. "Who is it?" she asked as she
grabbed her robe and snugged it around her as she moved toward the door.

"Will."

Her pulse quickened. She glanced toward the mirror on the wall. Earlier, she'd showered and now her hair was a mass of damp curls that hung around her shoulders. Her face, without even a little makeup, looked like a field of freckles on snow.

"Poppy?"

Her throat had gone dry. She opened the door and couldn't help herself. She smiled. Every time she saw him, it made her smile, but especially to see him standing at her door with his Stetson in his hand looking almost bashful.

"I'm sorry. I know it's late. I got busy downstairs in the office and didn't realize the time." His gaze met hers. "I hope I didn't wake you."

"You didn't," she assured him.

"This will only take a moment," he said. "I talked to Big Jack. They'll be leaving right after breakfast."

Her heart sank because she knew what was coming next.

"I thought you might want to leave then, as well." He didn't sound as if it was what he wanted.

"Are you and Dorothea and the wranglers leaving tomorrow morning?" she asked.

"We'll leave as soon as we get everything closed up here. This storm sounds like a big one. We'll move down to the main ranch to help with calving until the guest ranch opens for the season." He closed his mouth as if he realized he was talking too much. Him being a little nervous made him all the more irresistible.

"I'm sure you could use help getting things closed up in the kitchen," Poppy said lamely.

He shook his head. "I think it would be best if you went when the guests leave. That way I don't have to worry about you, too."

She nodded. He couldn't make himself any clearer. "If that's what you want."

He let out a curse and shook his head. "That's just it. It's not what I want." He raked his free hand through his hair. "When Dorothea told me that you'd only taken the job to put some kind of curse on me, I laughed it off. Then I saw you, tasted your food and realized, hell, bring that love potion on. Other women have tried to rope me in so I wasn't worried. But, Poppy, I swear, you throw a mean lasso." His gaze tenderly grazed her face. "I don't want you to leave. But that's the best thing you can do. If you stay…"

She swallowed the lump in her throat. "If I stay?"

He let out a chuckle as he looked down at his boots for a moment, then back up at her. His eyes locked with hers. "Then all bets are off." Her heart swelled to near bursting as he reached for her, cupping the back of her head as he buried his hands in her hair and pulled her into a no-nonsense kiss.

Her lips parted. She breathed in the night air and the scent of the campfire on his clothing as she leaned into his strong, masculine body and opened herself for his kiss. His mouth took hers possessively, the tip of his tongue brushing teasingly over hers before it got serious.

Lost in the kiss, neither of them heard Dorothea's door open until it slammed loudly. They both jumped, pulling apart and looking embarrassed as if they'd been caught by their parents making out on the couch.

"I shouldn't have done that," Will said as their gazes met again. "I promised myself that I would keep my distance. That if there was any chance that I could hurt you again…" He stared at her. "Do you see now how dangerous this could get? We're playing with fire here, Poppy. I don't want to see either of us get burned."

She opened her mouth to say something, but she had no idea what. She didn't get the chance before he said, "But damned if I haven't wanted to kiss you since seeing you standing in my kitchen that first day. Good night, Poppy."

She could only nod mutely as he walked down the hall to his apartment. Dorothea opened her door and peered out before slamming it shut again. Poppy stepped inside her room and closed the door. She locked it, leaned against it and smiled as she tried to catch her breath. This time when she curled up in bed, sleep welcomed her as the wind roared outside the lodge, making the old building creak and groan.

CHAPTER ELEVEN

When Poppy woke again, it was dead quiet. Until she heard the bloodcurdling screams.

For a moment, she thought she'd only imagined them. Then she heard the thunder of Will's boots on the hardwood floor in the hallway outside her room and Dorothea's frightened voice asking what was happening.

Getting up, she hurriedly dressed and rushed downstairs. She stopped abruptly at the bottom of the stairs. Through the front windows, she could see nothing but white for a moment. Snow was falling so thick that she caught only an occasional glimpse of the barn in the distance.

As she stared in horror, realizing that the storm had blown in much sooner than predicted, the front door flew open. Ruby stumbled in wrapped in a down comforter from her cabin and a pair of flannel pajamas with moose on them. She was followed by Dean, who looked as if he'd dressed in a hurry, and Kirk, who was wearing sweats and his On the Fly winter coat. All three of them had snowflakes melting in their hair and on their clothing as they closed the door behind them.

"What's happened?" Poppy cried as she started toward them. "I heard screams." Ruby looked as if she was about to say something when the door blew open again. Lexi limped in, looking terrified. She'd gotten dressed, including her coat and boots. Snow had soaked her shoulders and made her hair hang limp. Clearly she'd been out in the storm longer than the others. She stepped to the fireplace even though there were only black embers remaining from the day before.

Everyone looked at Lexi, including Poppy. "What..." she started to ask when Lexi burst into tears. Through the woman's sobs, she was able to make out enough of her words to understand that someone was dead and apparently Lexi had been the one to find the body.

"Who?" Poppy cried.

Lexi looked up at her and choked out two words, "Big Jack," before she began to wail again. Ruby moved to her, to put her arm around her, but Lexi shrugged it off.

Poppy was debating what to do when Dorothea came bursting in from outside. She took one look at Poppy and ordered, "Build a fire." Then she went to the old black landline phone and picked up the receiver as if to call the sheriff, but Poppy saw at once that the line must be dead because she put the receiver back down with a curse.

"Has anyone been able to make a call?" she asked.

There were head shakes. Lexi didn't seem to hear or care. "No cell service," Kirk said. "Remember? It's in your damned brochure. So now the landline isn't working, either? Don't you have, like, a two-way radio?"

"Don't worry," Dorothea said not very convincingly. "It's all going to be fine."

But Poppy could see that something was wrong as Dorothea stepped over to the two-way radio they had used the day before to communicate when Lexi was lost.

Trying not to worry, she quickly went to the fireplace and

started a fire, then headed into the kitchen to put the coffee on before she began breakfast. She had no idea what would happen next. But when she was upset, she cooked. People said they weren't hungry in a crisis, but she'd found they would often change their minds when food was put before them.

She wanted to go outside and find Will. But she knew she wouldn't be of any help out there. In the kitchen, she felt stronger, more capable and always useful. When she looked at the clock, she was surprised at how early it was. She'd had no idea what time it was. Outside there was nothing but falling and whirling snow as gusts sent the huge heavy flakes whipping past the windows.

In the main room, she could hear the pop of the blaze in the fireplace. She turned on the radio only to get the grim news. The winter storm was paralyzing not just the mountains but the valley, as well. No one had planned on the storm to come in so early or with such force. With the wind and the amount of precipitation, roads were closing. Everyone was warned to stay home unless it was an emergency.

With a tray of coffee, mugs, cream and sugar, Poppy went back into the main lounge. Apparently everyone had heard the weather report. They'd taken a seat in front of the fire, but no one was talking as she put down the tray.

"Coffee," she said. "It will help you warm up." When no one reached for a mug, she went back into the kitchen. Dorothea followed her and pulled her aside.

"Do you have any other powers besides cooking like you do?" the woman asked.

Poppy wanted to laugh, but she was too worried. Dorothea still thought she was a sorceress? "I'm afraid not."

"That's too bad because we could really use them right now," the woman said in all seriousness. "I've done what I could, but it's not enough. The landline is down and..." She dropped her voice even lower. "The two-way radio has been disabled."

Poppy frowned at her, uncomprehending. "Are you saying—"

"Someone wanted to make sure we couldn't get a call out to the sheriff."

She couldn't believe this. She glanced toward the lounge. "Who would—"

"Your guess is as good as mine."

"Big Jack is really dead?" Dorothea nodded. "What happened?"

The woman hesitated for a moment. She pulled Poppy even farther back into the kitchen so they couldn't be heard. "He was murdered. In the barn. Lexi found him. Who knows what she was doing up in the wee hours of the morning. She says she was awakened by something, looked out and saw him and thought he looked strange, like he was sleepwalking. She was worried and followed him to the barn, but didn't go inside because she got scared. She said that she looked down and saw that his tracks and hers weren't the only ones in the snow. Someone was waiting in the barn for him.

"She was debating what to do when someone rushed out, knocking her down. She didn't see the person's face and could give no description. When she got up, she went into the barn, saw Big Jack and started screaming."

"You think Big Jack had gone to the barn to meet someone?"

Dorothea shrugged. "Or had followed someone."

"Does everyone know that he's dead?" Poppy said, motioning toward the other room.

"That's all they know. When they all came running up to the barn to see what was going on, Will sent them in here. He told Lexi not to repeat her story until she tells the sheriff. But I have no idea when that is going to be since the lines are down, and now with the two-way radio out… I suppose Will plans to drive her down when he goes to notify the sheriff. I don't know. He won't want to leave us here with a murderer."

She felt her eyes widen. She hadn't thought of that. "I just heard on the local station that a lot of the roads are already closed because of the amount of snow that's fallen and still coming down. Because of poor visibility, it's emergency traffic only," Poppy told her.

"Well, I'd say this constitutes an emergency. I just wish they had all left yesterday."

"The storm wasn't supposed to hit until noon," she reminded her. "Will told me that Big Jack had agreed to leave right after breakfast."

"Is that why Will stopped by your room last night?"

Poppy didn't answer even though she could hear the challenge in the woman's voice. They had more to worry about now than a kiss and how dangerous it could be to take it any further. But it had been an amazing kiss, one that promised of things to come—if they didn't stay away from each other.

"I'm going to make breakfast," she said as she heard the front door open. They both moved to where they could see who'd entered. Allison was dressed and so was Mick. They both came in covered with snow. Behind them was Lamar and Will. Trailing even farther behind was Channing.

As the others made their way toward the roaring fire, Will came through the dining room to the kitchen. He immediately lowered his voice. "You've heard," he said to Poppy. She nodded. His grim gaze shifted to Dorothea. "I tried the phone in the barn. The landline is down in here, too?"

The woman nodded. "But I have worse news. The two-way radio. Someone disabled it."

Will swore. "Whoever killed Big Jack doesn't want us getting help." He shook his head and glanced toward the other room, looking as worried as Poppy was feeling.

"Are you going to try to get through the storm for help?" Dorothea asked.

He shook his head. "I need to be here to make sure all of you are safe. I sent Huck to notify the sheriff, but I'm not sure he can get through. With the storm like it is..."

"A lot of roads are closed. They're saying emergency travel only," Poppy told him.

"Let's hope Huck gets through. He knows these roads and the best way to get down off this mountain. But if the valley is bad, too... Our only other option is to wait out the storm. Once the phone lines are up again we can call for help. In the meantime..."

"We're trapped here with a killer," Dorothea said, her voice breaking.

They all turned at the sound of someone coming into the kitchen behind them.

"Did you reach the sheriff?" Lamar asked, his voice rough with emotion.

Will stepped toward him, seeing how upset he was. "The landline is down because of the storm and as you know cell phones don't work here even under the best weather. Apparently the two-way radio isn't working, either."

"We have to get help," Lamar pleaded.

There was no help for Big Jack. All Will could do was hope that Huck got through to the sheriff. That didn't mean, though, that the sheriff could get up to the ranch any time soon. He shook his head. "I've sent Huck for the sheriff. That's all we can do at this point. Even if the roads weren't closed because of the storm—"

"Don't tell me we can't get out of here," Lamar said, sounding panicked.

"Please keep your voice down. I don't want to scare the others."

"They're already scared," he shot back.

Will hesitated, reminding himself that the man had just lost his father. "I sent Huck for help, but quite frankly, even if he can get through, I'm not sure the sheriff can reach us until the storm lets up. So I think we all need to settle in and make the best of it until the roads are open again. I'm sorry. In the meantime, we've locked up the barn. Your father's body will be secure until the storm lets up and the sheriff can get here."

Lamar raked a hand through his blond hair. "I can't believe this is happening."

"Neither can we," Will said, glancing back at Poppy before he turned again to Lamar. He wished he hadn't gotten her into this and yet he didn't know what he would have done without her the past few days. "Do you know anyone who might have wanted to harm your father?"

The young man laughed and glanced toward the living room. "Just about anyone in that other room might have had reason to want him dead. I don't know. He told me when we arrived that he thought someone was stealing from the company. It might be the reason he planned this retreat. It certainly wasn't my idea."

"Stealing from On the Fly. You don't know who he meant?"

He shook his head. "But whoever killed him might have thought my father was onto them and wanted to keep him from having them arrested."

That seemed a long shot. He also suspected that Lamar wasn't telling him everything. It was one thing to be a thief. It was another to resort to murder to cover up the theft. He said as much to Lamar.

"Unless that person was desperate. I don't know. This was all news to me. I wasn't aware of any problems at the company."

Will said, "Last night your father mentioned to me that he'd made enemies."

Lamar laughed again. "True enough, but I have no idea who he was talking about. You know how he was—self-centered, impulsive and often clueless about other people's feelings. He never met a rule he didn't want to break. Or a woman he didn't want to bed." As if realizing he was talking about the dead and his father, he turned away with a curse.

When he spoke again, his voice was filled with emotion. "I loved my father, but he was a difficult man. We'd been butting heads over the company. I wish I knew what he hoped to accomplish with this out-of-the-blue retreat." He met Will's gaze. "Knowing him, he probably thought he'd draw out the thief. That would be just like him." Lamar's voice broke. "Apparently he succeeded."

Will recalled that Big Jack had said he thought this would be his last visit to the guest ranch. "Is there any chance your father was ill?"

The question seemed to take the man's son by surprise. "Ill?"

He told him what Big Jack had said.

Lamar shook his head. "I have no idea. That's another thing about my father. He could have been dying and he wouldn't think to share that kind of news with his sons." Will saw his expression change. "Unless he told Mick. But even if Dad was dying, that doesn't explain why anyone would want to kill him. In fact, why not wait until whatever disease he might have had did the job? Why risk murder?"

Good question, Will thought, and again suspected Lamar knew more than he was telling him.

Poppy had overheard the conversation before Lamar went back into the other room to join the others. Like Lamar, she couldn't believe this was happening. Will had gone with him only to return looking even more worried.

"I don't know how much you overheard," he said, keeping his voice down. "Lamar thought there might have been a thief in the company and that Big Jack had hoped to expose the thief at this retreat. I suppose that could be a motive for murder if the person felt backed into a corner. Dorothea, what in heaven's name are you doing?" Will barked the last, his nerves obviously frayed.

"I'm filling this bottle with herbs and spices to make a protection potion," she said belligerently. "What do you think I'm doing? I need to go to my cabin for a white candle and my amethyst stone."

Will rolled his eyes. Poppy could tell he didn't really need this right now. "I was just about to say that we need to keep everything as close to normal as we can," he said.

"I suspect this *is* normal for Dorothea," Poppy whispered. The woman ignored them both. Poppy smiled at Will and met his gaze for a moment, reminded of their kiss. It was all she'd thought about last night lying in bed before she'd gone to sleep. "I'm going to make us a special breakfast."

"Thank you," he said, impulsively taking her hand and bringing it to his lips.

She felt a shiver of desire as his lips touched her skin. "You're welcome." Their gazes held for a long moment. She couldn't help but think again of their kiss last night and that promise of things to come if they didn't stop. She felt her insides go molten. Having a killer among them only seemed to heighten her senses. If there was a chance that the two of them wouldn't make it out of this...

"I'm so sorry I got you into this," Will said quietly. "As much as I've loved having you here."

An argument broke out in the living room. Will groaned and let go of her hand to leave. "I need to take care of things. Will you be all right?"

"I'll be fine. Don't worry about me," she said and smiled, while at the same time remembering her earlier thought.

Funny how when there is a chance of dying, a person forgot all about retribution. Nothing mattered but being with the people you cared about.

Dorothea was shaking her. "The two of you can't really be thinking about… Not at a time like this."

Poppy had to laugh. "Is there a better time?"

The woman waved a hand through the air as if to extinguish all thought of that. "Well, he can't be serious about acting like nothing is wrong. Besides, you aren't really going to cook for those people?"

She'd always cooked when she was upset. Right now she was scared for all of them, maybe especially Will. But she was determined to do as Will asked and try to keep things as normal as possible even though her hands were shaking.

"Will's right. We need to stay calm." In the other room, whatever had been going on, Will seemed to have taken care of it. "And we all need to eat."

Dorothea stared at her in disbelief. "We're supposed to feed a killer?"

"Tell me which one is the killer and I won't give him or her anything," Poppy said.

"This isn't funny." Dorothea sounded close to tears. "You heard Will talking to Lamar. He's trying to find out who might have wanted Big Jack dead. He's putting himself in danger, as if we aren't all in enough danger as it is."

Poppy knew exactly what Will was doing. He wanted to narrow down the suspects, hopefully find the killer before anyone else could be hurt. She thought it was the only thing he could do. Actually, she'd been thinking she might talk to Lexi. There was obviously more to her story yesterday. After everything that had happened, maybe Lexi would open up to her.

But she wasn't about to mention that to Dorothea. If anything, she hoped to keep the woman as unperturbed as possible.

"I knew something bad was going to happen," Dorothea was saying. "I tried to warn Will, but he wouldn't listen. No one ever listens to me."

"Dorothea, we can't panic. Just think about it," Poppy said, trying to reason with her. "If you were the killer, you'd be nervous, right? As it is, I'm sure they're all in there looking at each other wondering who did it. So the best thing we can do is let the person believe he or she got away with it."

The woman huffed. "Well, you're a better actor than I am. I'm not turning my back on any of them. I'm going to be watching them all closely. Like you said, the killer will be nervous. I'm betting he or she will make a mistake and when that happens..." She drew a sharp knife from the block on the counter and wrapped it in a dishcloth and stuck it into the deep pocket of her apron. "I'm going to be ready."

Great. "Isn't it enough that you have your potion to protect you?" she asked, knowing that pointing out that the knife was a really bad idea wouldn't get her far.

"A spell potion can only do so much." She narrowed her eyes. "I put a spell on you to keep you from captivating Will with your cooking and look how well that's worked. Some forces are too powerful."

Poppy shook her head. "Why don't you get me out some butter and eggs. I'm thinking I'll make sourdough pancakes with wild huckleberry syrup, along with a slab of honey-grilled ham, fried potatoes with onions, and Brie and herb omelets with roasted tomatoes."

"You can't be serious."

"Just look at it this way," she whispered. "While the killer is eating, he or she won't be murdering anyone else."

Dorothea, of course, took her seriously. "You don't think the killer is going to stop with Big Jack, either, do you?"

CHAPTER TWELVE

Will had no idea how he was going to contain this as he looked around the lodge at his guests. Mick and Kirk had been going at each other when he'd walked in. He'd broken up their argument, overhearing just enough to suspect it had to do with Allison rather than Big Jack's death. How the two could argue over a woman at a time like this, he did not know.

But tensions were high. Mick was emotional, which was understandable. He'd just lost his father. Worse, one of the people in this room had bludgeoned Big Jack to death in the barn.

So now what was Will going to do? His hope was that Huck got through the storm and returned with the sheriff. But he wasn't counting on that. He suspected they would have to wait out the storm. He couldn't imagine anything worse. The animosity in this room felt like a powder keg ready to blow.

Meanwhile, he couldn't keep the guests locked up in the lodge until the storm let up and the sheriff arrived. There weren't enough bedrooms upstairs for that even if he had some way to lock them in. They would have to stay in their cabins. Which meant he had no way of actually making them do that.

"Poppy is making breakfast," he announced. "I see she made you coffee and it is nice and warm in here. So everyone is fine. We can weather this."

"When can we leave?" Dean asked without looking at the others. He was rubbing his wrist as if it still hurt from being bucked off the horse.

"I've sent Huck down to bring the sheriff back if possible," he said. "Unfortunately, the storm has closed a lot of the roads already, according to the latest weather update on the radio. I'm afraid we won't be able to get out until the storm lets up and the plows get the roads open again."

"Why don't you just call the sheriff?" Dean demanded.

"The landline is down," Will said. "It happens in storms like this."

"That's insane," Allison said, her voice breaking.

"Insane?" Channing echoed. "We're in the mountains in the middle of a storm. I'd say it was pretty typical."

"Channing's right," Will said. "It isn't all that unusual for this time of the year in Montana to have these problems. All we can do is wait it out." He'd warned Big Jack of this, but the man had been determined to have his retreat in March in Montana at the ranch.

"We can't stay here now, not with…" Allison began to cry.

"There must be a way to leave," Dean said. "You have four-wheel-drive SUVs parked out there."

"He's right," Kirk agreed, even surprising Dean. "I saw a couple of trucks with plows on the front. You can open the road."

"In the first place, the plow trucks couldn't get through the drifts at this point even if we could see the road. In this type of storm with so much snow coming down, and add the wind, visibility is the problem," Will explained patiently. "With roads in the valley closed as well as in the mountains, no one is going to be getting anywhere until the storm lets up."

"What I want to know is if you're going to try to keep us all here in the lodge," Channing said with a flip of her blond hair. "Because staying here with a killer, not to mention hysterical people, would drive me, for one, insane." She shot a glance at Allison to make her point.

He shook his head. "I don't see how I can do that. There isn't room for all of you, and even though I'm sure the sheriff would detain you if he were here, I don't have the authority. But I would like you all to do me a favor." He went into his office off the back of the lounge and came back with pens and Sterling ranch notepaper.

Turning to the group, he said, "Please write down where you were when you heard the screams and what you did after that. If you saw anything suspicious. Anything that might help the sheriff find out who did this, and sign your names." He began to pass out the paper and pens.

"You really don't expect the killer to confess," Ruby said with a laugh.

"I don't think we'll get that lucky," Will agreed. "But this is something that might help the sheriff when he gets here." As he handed out the Sterling Montana Guest Ranch notepads, he said, "It's important to get it down now when your memory is the freshest. Also if you heard anything, saw anything suspicious. Be sure to put your name on the paper, the date and time." He could see that no one wanted to do this, but a few began, hiding what they were writing from the person next to them.

He grabbed a large Native American basket from one of the tables that had been part of the lodge's decor from as far back as he could remember, and set it in the middle of the large square coffee table. "Just drop them in here."

Ruby still looked amused but complied, as did the others. Will stepped back. He could feel the suspicion in the room. They didn't trust each other. He didn't blame them because since no one had come to the ranch last night without him knowing it, one of the people in this room had to be the killer.

Kirk scribbled something on his paper, folded it and tossed it into the basket. "So you can't keep us here, right? Like you said, you don't have the authority to do that."

"No, I can't," Will hated to admit. Short of tying them all up, he did not. And he couldn't keep them locked in their cabins for what could be a couple of days. Nor could he keep an eye on them all the time.

"So we can leave," Kirk said, getting to his feet.

"You can go to your cabins. Slim will be watching the barn. You all need to stay away from there—"

"I mean, we can get off this mountain if we want to," Kirk interrupted.

"If you're thinking about walking out—"

"I saw a pair of old skis."

Will shook his head. "I certainly wouldn't advise that. There is more than a good chance that you would get lost in the storm, if not injured, and die of hypothermia. It is nice and warm here. We have plenty of food. There's no reason to leave the ranch until the storm breaks and the sheriff arrives."

"As you said, you can't keep us here," Kirk said and started for the door, but his way was quickly blocked.

"Why in such a hurry to get out of here?" Lamar demanded as he stepped in front of him to keep him from leaving.

"Are you kidding? There's a killer on the loose," Kirk said as he turned to look back at the others. "I'm not staying here with a murderer."

"Or maybe you don't want to wait for the sheriff for another reason," Lamar said. "Where were you last night?"

Will knew he had to step in. If everyone started accusing each other… "Lamar—"

"You can't keep me here," Kirk said and took a threatening step closer to Lamar. The men were about the same size and weight, but Will could tell that Kirk had fear on his side.

Will stepped between them. "This is exactly what we can't have. Kirk, you want to leave, I'm not going to stop you, but it's a suicide mission if you try to get off this mountain in this storm. It's miles to the nearest main road, which will be closed to traffic. You'd be lucky to make it to a farmhouse in the valley in this kind of weather because unlike Huck, who I sent off this mountain, you don't know your way. It is easy to get turned around in a storm like this. You could end up going in circles and not even realize it."

"Let him go," Channing spoke up.

"If he's worried about waiting for the sheriff," Dean said, "then he's probably the killer, so I agree with Channing— let him go."

Kirk turned back to the group to glare at Dean. Will thought he might have to break up a fight before this was over, but Kirk spun around and gave Lamar a shove. "All of you had better watch who you accuse of murder. I had nothing to do with Big Jack's death. I was in my cabin all night. If you don't believe me, ask Allison."

A hush fell over the large room. Lexi looked up as if just now taking an interest in the conversation. Everyone stared at Allison, who had looked down, shaking her head but not denying it. Her mascara was smeared from crying. She'd been writing on her notepad and, now finished, folded her paper and tossed it and the pen into the basket. She didn't look up at anyone as she got to her feet and moved to stand with her back to the room in front of the fire.

"So we can go back to our rooms?" Dean asked, cutting through the tension that felt thick as dense fog. He pushed up his glasses and rose to leave.

"I'll ring the bell when breakfast is ready," Will said. "I'd ask that you all come back then so I know everyone is all right. Also I recommend staying close to the row of cabins when you leave here. I don't want anyone getting lost in the storm. I guess I don't have to tell you to lock your doors."

Those not already standing began to push to their feet and head for the door.

As Mick started to leave, his brother intercepted him. "We need to talk," Will heard him say as the two stepped out into the whirling snow.

"You're just going to let them go?" asked a small female voice.

He turned to see Lexi hadn't moved from where she'd been sitting on one end of the long rock hearth—the farthest from the people who'd been in the room. He hadn't even realized she hadn't risen to leave with the others.

"I can't keep them here," Will said as he moved to her. She'd already told him how she'd found Big Jack, but he suspected there was a lot more to the story.

He saw that she hadn't touched her paper or pen. "I was hoping to ask you a few more questions." But as he neared her, she leaped to her feet.

"I think I'm going to throw up," she said and rushed to the front door and out into the blizzard.

Lamar was still in shock as he and his brother walked the short distance to the cabin they shared. As he made his way through the falling snow, head ducked down inside the collar of his coat, he realized that Will was right. Trying to go anywhere in this weather was suicide. He could barely make out the cabin next to his and Mick's.

There were tracks in the snow where some of the others had broken a trail as they headed for their cabins, but the tracks were filling in fast, their existence to be quickly erased.

He pushed open the door of their cabin and his brother followed reluctantly. Mick had been in a sour mood off and on since their father had announced this retreat. Mick had argued that he would stay behind and make sure everything was fine at the company.

But their father had thanked him and said no. Mick, like the others Big Jack had chosen, were going. No exceptions. No argument.

Mick's mood had seemed to pick up a little when he'd heard that Allison would be going. The two had either been flirting or arguing the whole trip. Now that they'd heard the news about Allison spending the night with Kirk…and the death of their father… Lamar couldn't imagine a worse time to confront his brother.

When he turned to look at Mick, he saw that he looked close to tears. His brother plopped down on the end of his bed and raked a hand through his hair. "Can you believe he's gone?" His voice was muffled with his head down.

"No. I'm still in shock, too. I don't think it's really set in yet." He sat down next to his brother.

Mick lifted his head, tears in his eyes. "Who do you think did it?"

Lamar shook his head.

"You didn't see anyone last night?" his brother asked, giving him a start.

"Why would I have seen—"

Mick shook his head. "I thought I heard you go out last night."

He saw the way his brother didn't quite meet his gaze. Had Mick heard him sneak out last night before midnight to meet Allison? What if Mick had followed him? Overheard the conversation? Or worse, just saw them together and thought there was something going on between them?

He wanted to tell his brother what Allison had told him, but couldn't break his promise. With Big Jack murdered, Lamar feared he might be jeopardizing her life, as well. He had a feeling she'd spent the night with Kirk to cover her sneaking out at midnight to meet in the barn. She'd given herself an alibi.

But what if last night she hadn't gone back to her cabin, but doubled back to meet Big Jack?

"I couldn't sleep. I went for a walk. I wasn't gone long. This place was dead quiet. I didn't see Dad. I didn't see anyone on my walk." That at least was true. "What about you?" Lamar asked. "You have any idea who might have done it?"

Mick shook his head. "I know you two had an argument over the company."

Lamar jerked back in surprise. "You can't think that I—"

"Dad said you were trying to take On the Fly away from him."

He swore and got to his feet to look down at his brother. "I don't want to get into this with you, but you know how he kept taking money out of the company. He was putting us in a position where we could lose everything."

"That sounds like a motive for murder," Mick said, finally looking up to glare at him.

Lamar tried to be patient. He could see how upset his brother was. But at the same time, he couldn't believe he was being accused of murdering their father. "Dad and I had our problems, but he knew that I was only trying to save the company. Come on, Mick, you knew how he was. Even Dad would admit how he was. It was why he was going to step aside and let me take control. He said he was leaving the company and taking Ruby with him."

"*Ruby?*" Mick repeated like a curse.

"Yeah, Ruby."

Mick stared at his feet for a few moments. "Don't you wonder where Ruby was last night? What if Dad went down to the barn because he was looking for her?"

"Why would she be in the barn?" Lamar had to ask.

His brother shrugged. "I saw her headed in that direction. After I heard you go out, I left my bedroom, went into the living room to look out our cabin window. It hadn't started snowing yet. I saw Ruby walk in front of our cabin and head toward the barn."

Lamar felt his heart lodge in his throat. "What time was this?"

Mick shrugged again. "I don't know. It was dark out and I was half-asleep."

He stared at him. "You're sure it was Ruby?" With them all wearing the same coats and hats and the women all being about the same size and height... Mick could have seen Allison.

"It was her because a few moments later I saw Dad slip into the barn like he was spying on her." Lamar felt sick. Wasn't it more likely that Mick had seen Allison when Lamar had been in the barn waiting for her? If Mick had seen their father enter the barn *after* Allison... Then Big Jack was in the barn last night while Lamar was talking to Allison. He might have heard every word.

He tried to remain calm. "Did you write this down on the notepad Will gave you?" He saw at once that Mick hadn't. "Why not?"

His brother shot to his feet. "Because I don't have to tell Will Sterling anything."

"You can't keep this from the sheriff when he gets here. Mick—"

"Don't lecture me. I know what I need to do."

Lamar shook his head, telling himself that he'd been so sure that when he'd sneaked out, his brother had been asleep in the second bedroom. So it was possible that what Mick had seen was Allison. Because why would Ruby go to the barn? Why would his father unless he'd followed not just Allison but his own son?

Lamar groaned inwardly. His father had made it clear that he'd suspected him of whatever was going on at On the Fly. He tried to remember everything that was said between Allison and him, wondering what his father's last thoughts were before he died. But who caught him alone in the barn after that?

From what he could gather, no one knew what time Big Jack had been killed. Definitely after midnight. After Lamar and Allison had left the barn. Was his father inside there all that time? But Lexi said she'd seen him go by her window before daylight. If she was telling the truth...

His head ached. He was regretting more and more meeting Allison in the barn last night. He didn't want to keep secrets from anyone, especially his brother. Maybe Mick was right and it had been Ruby looking for Big Jack. She could have been in the barn when Lexi said she saw Big Jack go down there. The two might have planned a lovers' tryst—but in a cold barn?

None of it made any sense. All he knew was that his father was dead and something had been going on at On the Fly that he'd missed. Now one of his employees was a murderer and they were all trapped here with the killer.

"Maybe the sheriff can sort it all out," Lamar said, feeling shaken. Would they ever know the truth? Will was right. By the time the sheriff got there, invaluable evidence could be lost. The killer would have covered his tracks. Or her tracks, he thought. In that case, whoever had murdered their father might never be caught.

Lamar had little faith that anyone had told the truth on the notes they'd written and put into the basket. He certainly hadn't and neither had Mick.

"Are you going to be all right?" he asked his brother.

Mick nodded. "I can't help feeling guilty, though, you

know? He could be such a bastard. There were times I hated him. And now that he's dead..."

He put a hand on his brother's shoulder. "I do know. He was our dad and now he's gone. And we have no idea who he pissed off enough to kill him."

CHAPTER THIRTEEN

Poppy finished making breakfast and sent Dorothea to tell Will that it was ready. A few minutes later, she heard him ringing the dinner bell. Glancing outside, she saw that the storm hadn't let up. On the contrary, it looked worse than it had earlier. She hugged herself, growing more concerned.

She knew Will was hoping that Huck made it to town and reached the sheriff. But she couldn't imagine how. Even if he did, would the sheriff be able to make it up here or Huck be able to return? She tried not to worry about it as she heard the guests begin to file in. Dorothea returned looking wary. She patted her apron pocket and gave Poppy a knowing look.

"I just hope you don't accidentally stab yourself," she said to the woman as she shoved a plate filled with individual omelets at her. "I'll take the rest." She followed Dorothea out to the dining room where only a few guests had come in out of the cold and were now seated around the fireplace. Their coats hung by the door, the snow melting onto the floor. They all looked as if they wanted to be anywhere but here. Will had been out shoveling to keep a path from the cabins to the lodge.

Poppy couldn't blame them. She thought they all felt that

way right now. She put a smile on and said, "This morning we have sourdough pancakes with wild huckleberry syrup, along with a slab of honey-grilled ham, fried potatoes with onions, and individual Brie and herb omelets with roasted tomatoes." She put down the platters of food, but she could tell there was little interest. "I also made a nice fruit salad."

"Everyone sit down," Will ordered as he came in. He took his place and looked around the table as the guests slowly began to take their seats. Poppy sat down, but Dorothea said she forgot the orange juice and hurried back into the kitchen.

"Where's Kirk?" Will asked as he glanced around the table.

Poppy realized that the place where the snowboarder always sat was vacant. She felt her heart drop. He wasn't fool enough to try to get out of here on his own, was he?

There was no answer for a moment. Then Allison spoke up. "He left."

"Left?" Will echoed. "How?"

"He took the skis he found and planned to ski down the road. At least, that's what he said."

Will started to get to his feet.

"He left more than an hour ago," Allison said. "I saw him leave, but you're welcome to try to catch him. He planned to ski down to the bunkhouse and take Slim's truck with the plow on it. He said he'd seen that the keys were in it."

Will swore and sat back down. He turned his attention to Allison. "You didn't go with him." Poppy could tell what he wanted to demand was why she hadn't come to him before Kirk had left.

She let out a laugh that sounded close to a sob. "I'm not crazy. If he's that desperate to leave here..."

"Maybe he's just scared," Channing said. "It doesn't mean he's the killer." She glanced around the table, smiling. "Any one of you could have killed Big Jack."

"Channing," Lamar warned.

Will was thinking about the pickup Kirk had taken. Slim always parked on the other side of the bunkhouse closest to the road out. It had a small plow on the front, but nothing that could bust a road through this storm or Will would have taken it himself into Whitefish for the sheriff.

He looked around the table and saw relief on most of the faces that Kirk had left. They were convinced the killer was gone. All of them except maybe Channing. With her, he didn't know if she just enjoyed stirring up trouble or what. Apparently most of them were willing to believe that Kirk had killed Big Jack.

"Eat," Will ordered and the platters began to make their way around the table.

"He'll die," Lexi said, staring down at her plate. Will was surprised by what he heard in her voice. He noticed that a smile was playing at her lips. "He is going to get what he deserves."

"Shut up," Allison snapped. "You don't know he's responsible for Big Jack."

"At least we aren't with him," Dean said.

"Like you would be brave enough to try to leave," Channing said and laughed.

"Please just eat," Will prompted and looked down the table at Poppy. She saw the worry on his face. The pain, the disappointment and the concern that this was far from over. She was just glad that he hadn't decided to go after Kirk. Let the sheriff deal with it. On the radio, she'd heard that the worst of the storm would be tonight. By tomorrow afternoon, it would be moving out. If they could just hold it together until then…

Lamar ate, but he didn't taste a bite. He kept thinking about his father and worrying about his brother. At breakfast, Mick had kept his head down, moving his food around his plate, but eating little.

He couldn't believe that idiot Kirk. The damned fool was going to either go off the road or freeze to death if he didn't die of carbon monoxide poisoning after he got stuck and had to run the pickup's engine to stay warm.

Kirk had been another one of his father's hires. As he looked around the table, he realized that Ruby had been his father's hire, as well. Which was also proof that his father didn't have a head for business.

He met Allison's gaze across the table. She looked even more frightened than she had last night. If someone had dropped a utensil, they all would have jumped a foot. He feared that someone would spill the salt again. He could tell that the older woman, Dorothea, wanted nothing to do with any of them. She'd made every excuse possible not to sit with them this morning.

But none of that was what concerned him. He kept playing back last night in the barn. Had his brother seen Ruby go into the barn? Or Allison? And, if Allison, what would happen when Mick learned that Allison had been there to meet Lamar?

Because it would come out as soon as the sheriff reached the ranch.

It would put him at the scene of the crime.

Right now, he just wanted breakfast over. There was something he had to do.

The moment the meal was finished, he excused himself and, grabbing his coat, headed toward his cabin. But he didn't stop at it. He kept going. At one point, he looked back through the driving snow, but could see no one.

Will was right. If he got too far from the row of cabins, he couldn't see a thing but freezing white flakes whirling around him. It would be easy to get lost just feet away from the cabins. He thought of Kirk again and shook his head. The damned fool could already be dead.

At his father's cabin, he realized he might not be able to get in. Would his father have locked the door when he'd left to go to the barn last night? Would Will have come down and locked it in case there was evidence inside?

He couldn't shake the feeling that his father had been meeting someone—just as Lamar had met Allison last night. What if it had been Ruby Mick had seen? Which made him wonder if the person Lexi had seen was even his father. With the temperature up here in the mountains what it was at night, whoever had been out last night would have been wearing their On the Fly matching coats and hats. No one could be sure who'd they seen coming and going in the dark.

So many questions and no answers. He hoped he'd find an answer inside his father's cabin as he grabbed the door handle. To his surprise, it turned in his hand. He quickly stepped in out of the cold and snow. For a moment, he stood just inside looking around. The cabin was a mess. He couldn't tell if this was the way his father had left it or if someone had searched it. That thought sent a chill through him. What would someone have been looking for? Maybe the same thing he was: answers.

He stepped deeper into the room, more convinced that the room had been ransacked. His father had never been neat, but it was clear that Big Jack's belongings had been dumped out and gone through. Had the person found what he or she had been looking for?

After checking the entire cabin, he stopped in the bathroom doorway to look at the larger room. If his father had something he didn't want found, where would he hide it?

His gaze circled the room, coming to a stop on the large chest of drawers in the corner. He moved to it. The top drawer was ajar. Someone had already gone through it. He pulled out the drawer, then the next, piling each on the bed until he got to the bottom one.

He jerked it out a few inches before it stuck. He could see

that the drawer was empty. His father wasn't one to unpack his suitcase and put his belongings away even if he had planned to stay longer than four days.

Whoever had searched the room had probably tried the drawer, just as he had, seen that there was nothing inside and, when it stuck, had shut it again.

Lamar worked the drawer out. He could feel that there was something under the drawer that was keeping it from opening. He thought he heard paper tear as he yanked it the last of the way out and flipped it over.

Someone had taped a thick manila envelope to the bottom of the drawer. There was a small tear in the envelope.

He laid the drawer on the bed and ripped the tape off and started to open the envelope when he heard a sound at the door. Moving quickly, he tucked the envelope under his coat and stepped back into the bathroom.

In the mirror over the sink, he could see the front door. It opened slowly. He pressed himself against the bathroom wall as he watched a bundled-up figure in an On the Fly jacket and hat step in, along with a gust of wind and snow.

CHAPTER FOURTEEN

Will went out to see Slim in the barn, to tell him about his pickup and make sure he got some breakfast.

"I'm so sorry," Slim said. "I didn't realize what had happened until I rushed out of the barn and saw him driving away in my pickup. I would have come and told you, but I didn't want to leave the body."

"It's all right. I should have thought of it. I've checked to make sure that none of the keys are in the other rigs. I don't want another fool taking off in this." He glanced toward the body. He'd wanted to cover Big Jack but didn't want to contaminate the murder scene.

"Go up to the kitchen," he told Slim. "Poppy put some breakfast aside for you. I'm going to lock up the barn. I can't ask you to stay down here and watch the body. Huck hasn't come back. There's a good chance he won't be able to for a day or more. We'll all keep an eye out in case someone tries to get in, okay? But I think the damage is done. Can't imagine anyone would want to get back in here, anyway."

Slim quickly agreed. "I stayed warm enough cleaning out

the stalls, but I can feel the temperature dropping. It actually looks worse out there," he said, glancing toward the door.

"It is. I'm wishing now that I hadn't sent Huck," Will said. "I'm worried about him."

"You have enough to worry about. You know Huck. He'll be fine. He loves this. Brings out the adventurer in him."

Will smiled, knowing it was true. But this storm was bad. Would Huck have enough sense to turn back if it looked like he couldn't go any farther?

Slim headed up to the lodge, while Will locked up. He could barely make out the roofline of the lodge through the falling snow. He thought about his guests, his wranglers, Dorothea and Poppy. His brothers were twenty miles away at the cattle ranch down in the valley so they wouldn't be able to help. Will was on his own up here on the mountain. He had to get them all through this.

Yesterday, looking for Lexi and again this morning when he'd heard screaming, he'd strapped on his sidearm. He just hoped he wasn't going to have to use it as he locked up the barn and headed for the lodge.

He hadn't gone but a few steps when he saw Poppy come out the door of the lodge and head in the direction of the cabins. He swore. Didn't she know one of these guests was a killer?

Lamar relaxed as the figure framed in the doorway lifted his head. Mick.

He started to step out of his hiding place, but stopped himself as he watched his brother close the cabin door. What was he doing here?

For a few moments, Mick didn't move. He was taking in the mess, including the bureau drawers piled on the bed.

His brother let out a curse and began to cry in huge, heart-wrenching sobs. Lamar wanted to go to him, but had waited too long. The sobs ended as quickly as they had begun. Mick wiped his eyes with the sleeve of his coat, then seemed to attack the mess on the bed, throwing the clothes, then the bureau drawers, against the wall.

The antique bureau drawers splintered as they hit and fell. Mick kept throwing them and the clothes until there was nothing on the bed but the bedding. His brother was breathing hard as he looked around the room.

For a moment Lamar feared he could come in the bathroom. He had no explanation for why he'd stayed hidden. He was relieved as Mick caught his breath, considered the disaster he'd made and turned to leave. But right before he reached the door, he put his fist through the mirror on the wall.

The glass shattered but stayed in the frame. His brother stared at his jumbled reflection for a long while. "Burn in hell, you bastard," he said before he threw open the door and stumbled out into the storm.

Lamar stayed where he was, his heart breaking for his brother, but shaken by what he'd witnessed. Grief for the father Mick had lost? Or something much darker and more sinister?

CHAPTER FIFTEEN

Poppy was covered with snow by the time she reached Lexi's cabin. She knocked on the door and, getting no answer, knocked harder before calling the woman's name and trying again.

When the door opened, it was only a crack. Lexi peered out. "I was taking a nap." She didn't look like she had been asleep, but she did look scared.

"Can I come in? Please."

Lexi hesitated but finally stepped back to let her in.

Poppy wasn't surprised to find the young woman's cabin neat and clean. The bed was made. Not even an indentation in the comforter. Lexi hadn't been sleeping. The small light over the desk was on and the chair pulled out.

Lexi went to it now and closed a notebook she'd obviously been writing in. It piqued Poppy's interest to know what the woman had been writing down. A diary of the events that had befallen her here? Something to do with work? A letter? It could be anything.

But whatever it was, Lexi didn't want her to see it.

"I'm fine," the young woman said, standing back and cross-

ing her arms as she waited for Poppy to leave. "You shouldn't
have bothered to walk all the way down here in the storm."

She looked around the room, her gaze settling on Lexi.
"We need to talk about yesterday."

"There is nothing to talk about. I fell, you found me."

Poppy thought about sitting on the edge of the bed, but
given the way this room looked, she knew that it might make
the superneat Lexi even more nervous. The only other option
was the chair in front of the desk. As she reached for it, Lexi
grabbed up the notebook and held it to her chest.

"I was busy," she said defensively.

"I can see that," Poppy said, pulling the chair away from
the desk and sitting down in it. "Tell me what's going on,
Lexi. You're in some kind of trouble. Why else would you
have been running yesterday? Who were you running from?"

The young woman looked around as if trying to find a
way to escape. She clutched the notebook even harder to her
chest and looked as if she might cry.

"I want to help you," Poppy said.

"Help me? Help me by leaving me alone."

"Please, I know you're scared."

"Big Jack was *murdered*," Lexi cried. "I found him with his
head caved in. I looked into his dead eyes." Her face was filled
with horror. She slumped onto the foot of the bed, hugging
the notebook to her.

"Why did you follow him?"

Her gaze was on the cabin wall, but it shifted slowly to
Poppy. "I already told Will."

"That you just saw him go by and followed him in the
middle of the night because you thought he was sleepwalking? Lexi, the sheriff isn't going to believe that. Please talk to
me. Maybe I can help."

"You can't." She got to her feet again. "You should leave.

Leave." Her voice was shrill. She sounded like she might start screaming at any moment.

Poppy rose. As she did she saw that there was something written on the back of the notebook Lexi had crushed to her chest. It was a name and what appeared to be an amount of money, followed by what appeared to be dates. The name was Kirk. The amount was just under twelve thousand dollars.

"If you change your mind—"

"I won't," Lexi said.

Poppy turned toward the door. She saw the trail of salt at the edge, but feared whatever trouble the young woman was in, salt wasn't going to save her.

Will was waiting for Poppy when she returned. He felt a wave of relief to see her. He couldn't help but worry about anyone who left the safety of the lodge, but especially Poppy. He was responsible for getting her involved in this.

But even as he thought it, he couldn't be sorry. Having her here these past few days… It had to have been fate. If Buckshot hadn't broken his leg, if Garrett hadn't told him about Poppy's catering business, if he hadn't gotten up the courage to call… Well, she wouldn't be trapped here on the ranch with a killer, he thought with a shake of his head.

If this was fate, then it had a dark sense of humor.

Poppy entered the building, shook off the snow from her coat and hung it up by the door. When she saw him, she gave him a smile that went straight to his heart.

"Can we talk?" he asked and led her to his office behind the kitchen. After offering her a chair, he closed the door and took a chair opposite her. "I saw you leave to go down to the cabins. Poppy—"

"I'm sorry if I worried you. I went down to Lexi's cabin to question her about yesterday."

"I wish you hadn't done that. You know how dangerous this is."

She nodded. "I had to talk to her. She lied about what happened off the trail to the waterfalls."

"I know." He raked a hand through his hair. "The running tracks on the hillside before she fell. She was running from something."

"More like *someone*. Maybe they even pushed her. When I called for her yesterday she didn't answer until I told her it was me."

"Did she tell you anything today?" he asked.

She shook her head. "I didn't get anywhere with her. She was scared even before Big Jack was killed. Now, she's terrified. When I interrupted her at her cabin, she was busy writing in a notebook. She grabbed it up when I came in and held it the entire time I was there. I don't know what's inside it, but written on the outside was the name Kirk followed by what looked like a monetary amount of almost twelve thousand dollars and what appeared to be a list of dates."

Will frowned. "You have any idea what that might mean?"

"No, but it seems clear that something is going on with these employees. The owner is dead and none of them seem to trust each other."

He couldn't agree more. "I don't like any of this. We already have one person dead. This storm couldn't have come at a worse time."

"Unless the killer was planning on the storm," she said.

He met her gaze. "Big Jack was the one who set up the retreat. Lamar said it had come out of the blue. It was definitely last-minute."

She seemed to consider that. "Maybe he knew about the storm and had planned to use it to his advantage but someone was onto him."

Will shook his head. "There is no doubt that more was

going on with this bunch before they even got here. We never open this early, but Big Jack was so insistent…" He looked at her. She sometimes took his breath away. Her hair sparkled with melting snowflakes and those eyes… He wanted to drown himself in them.

"But even if Big Jack had known about the storm ahead of time, he couldn't have known it would be this bad, though, or that it would hit early. No one did," she said.

"Last night, he'd agreed to leave today before the storm hit," Will said. "If he'd known about it, he'd changed his mind." He couldn't help staring at her, remembering the girl she'd been—and the horrible teen he'd been. But here they were now. He felt his heart beat faster. No woman had ever made him feel like this. It terrified him. And after that kiss last night? He was completely enamored by her.

"Still no word from Huck?" she asked.

He shook his head as he got to his feet. She rose, too, no doubt thinking their "meeting" was over. He closed the distance between them. "I have a killer loose on the ranch and all I can think about is kissing you again and so much more."

Poppy smiled as Will cupped her cheek in his large hand. In his dark eyes, she saw flecks of gold. Such kind eyes. So caring. So trusting. "I have a confession," she said as she broke eye contact and stepped away from him. She couldn't think clearly when he was touching her.

"A confession? If it's murder—"

"It's almost as bad," she said, turning to face him. "Dorothea's right. I did take the job so I could come back here to get even with you for breaking my heart all those years ago."

His gaze softened. "I don't blame you. If I could go back…" He looked miserable. "Dorothea said your plan was to put a spell on me with your bewitching cuisine."

She couldn't help but smile. "That was the plan."

"Well, like I told you, it worked like a charm," he said, taking a step toward her. "I'm completely taken with your cooking. But I suspect there's more to your plan."

"I was going to get you to fall in love with me. I wanted you to know what it felt like to have your heart ripped out of your chest." He grimaced. "You were the first boy I fell for. I saw you as this adorable cowboy. All I wanted was for you to look at me like you did some of the girl guests who were closer to your age or older."

"I know this won't help, but those girls wanted nothing to do with me. I knew how you felt. Worse, my brothers knew. They teased me and I regret that I was embarrassed and didn't know how to handle it. I handled it by pushing you away when anyone was around but you."

Tears welled in her eyes. She remembered the heartbroken girl she'd been and that awful ache she'd felt not just in her chest, but in the pit of her stomach. One tear broke loose and cascaded down her cheek. Will closed the distance between them, catching the tear with the rough pad of his thumb. His voice dropped in a way that turned her center molten.

"That last day when you told me you were moving?" he said, his voice soft and low. "I'm sorry, but I was relieved. I wasn't ready for you. I'm not sure I even am as a grown man. Poppy, you're a force to be reckoned with. You always have been. You put yourself out there at twelve. You were so brave, wearing your heart on your sleeve. You terrified me. You still do."

She shook her head as he pulled her closer.

"When you cried that day…" He looked away for a moment as if struggling with his emotions before meeting her gaze again. "It broke my heart, too. I felt so bad. I wanted to take it all back but it was too late. I was such a jerk at fifteen. So immature. Why didn't you just slug me in the mouth and make yourself feel better?"

Her laugh came out more like a sob. "Oh, I thought about it."

"It's not too late," he said and let go of her to tilt his head to the side. He pointed at his strong square jaw. "Just give me a good one, right there. Come on. A girl who tried to ride a wild stallion must have had quite a right hook. Bet you still do. Let me have it."

She wiped her tears. "That's just it. I no longer want to slug you." Rising on her tiptoes, she kissed the handsome cowboy. It felt as if the two—the fifteen-year-old boy and the thirty-five-year-old cowboy—had melded together into the man standing before her.

He took her in his arms and held her tight as the kiss deepened. When they finally parted, he said, "I'm crazy about you, Poppy Carmichael. That's what terrifies me. My heart is wide open to you. So if you want to rip it out and stomp on it, there is nothing I can do. Your plan worked."

She shook her head. "No, it didn't. It backfired. I never wanted to fall for you again, but it's happening."

Will laughed. "Our timing is terrible, but at this moment, I've never been happier. Or more worried about keeping you safe. When you're out of my arms…"

"I guess I'll have to spend as much time as I can in them," she said and kissed him again.

They jerked apart at the sound of pounding feet approaching and someone calling Will's name. A moment later the office door flew open. Dorothea burst in, wide-eyed with fear.

"There's been another murder."

CHAPTER SIXTEEN

Lamar returned to his cabin to find it empty. He had no idea where his brother had gone, but he was glad for a few minutes of privacy. He took the large manila envelope from beneath his coat and carried it over to the small desk.

There had to be a reason his father had hidden it. Also a reason why someone had turned his cabin upside down searching for it. He pulled out the contents and frowned as he thumbed through the papers.

It appeared to be nothing more than employee files. Not the originals because someone would have noticed they were missing. No, these were copies. He glanced in the envelope, thinking there had to be more. There was.

As he tilted the envelope, his father's cell phone slid out with a bang on top of the desk. He picked it up and tried to open it, only to find it was passcode-protected. He tried a few dates. His father's birthday, his brother's, his own. Nothing worked. Maybe Mick would know it.

He pocketed the phone and began to go through the employee files, wondering what he was looking for. Why would his father have hidden this envelope the way he had unless there was something in here...?

Lamar heard someone try to open the door, then the scrape of a key. He quickly put the files back into the envelope and shoved them into the only handy place—the top drawer of the desk. He'd barely gotten the drawer closed when his brother came in out of the storm. Mick looked fearful and he seemed to be breathing hard.

"What is it?" Lamar asked, immediately concerned that something else had happened.

"Nothing. It's just cold out there. If you haven't noticed, it's storming."

"You sound out of breath," he said, getting up. His brother seemed to be sweating as he jerked off his stocking cap and his gloves.

"If you must know, I ran up the hill from Allison's cabin, all right?" Mick said, removing his coat as he headed for the bathroom.

"Is that blood?" Lamar asked, remembering his brother smashing the mirror and hoping for an explanation.

Mick turned and looked down at his right hand. His knuckles were scraped and bleeding. "Kind of looks like it, doesn't it?"

"What the hell?"

"I don't want to talk about it." With that he threw down his coat on his pile of clothes on top of his open suitcase in the second bedroom and went into the bathroom and slammed the door.

Lamar only had a moment to wonder what was going on with his brother when he saw Will wading through the drifting snow outside the cabin window, followed quickly behind by Poppy and Dorothea. Oh, hell, he thought as his pulse jumped. Something *had* happened.

He glanced toward the closed bathroom door and murmured under his breath, "Please don't let this be about Mick."

CHAPTER SEVENTEEN

Will trudged as quickly as he could through the falling snow, Poppy and Dorothea at his heels. He'd wanted them to stay in the lodge, but they weren't having it. Not that he could blame them. They wouldn't be safer there alone, so he'd let them come with him.

He stopped at the entrance to the cabin. Poppy and Dorothea caught up as he put his gloved hand on the doorknob, took a breath and opened the door. The smell hit him first. That coppery odor of blood that he knew only too well growing up on a ranch. They stepped just inside the door.

"Don't touch anything," he said, although he was sure that both women already knew that. He motioned for them to stay by the door. He could see Dorothea's snowy tracks melting on the rug that covered the hardwood floor from when she'd entered the cabin only minutes ago after knocking at the door and not getting an answer. She'd come in with fresh towels, planning to pick up the soiled ones after she'd found a message that had been left for her at the lodge.

He stepped deeper into the room, following the tracks. As he came around the end of the bed, he saw a leg. It was bent at an odd angle. He took another step, saw the second leg and then the fully dressed body lying dead on the floor.

Lexi lay, staring sightlessly up at the ceiling. A pool of blood had formed around her head like a halo.

Careful not to touch anything more than he had to, Will checked for a pulse, knowing he wasn't going to find one. He didn't. It was hard to know how long she'd been dead. He knew that rigor mortis usually set in from ten minutes to several hours after death. That was quite a window of time to try to track down where everyone had been.

He noticed that the lamp that had been on her desk lay beside her on the floor. There was blood on the lamp base. Like Big Jack, it appeared she'd been bludgeoned to death.

"Is she…?" Poppy said from just inside the door.

"She's dead," Dorothea said, her voice breaking. "Stone cold dead. Don't you think I know dead when I see dead? Why would she leave me a message on the board at the lodge?"

Will rose and turned to them. "Clearly she didn't. Someone wanted you to find her." He shook his head. "Looks much like the way Big Jack died."

"You think it was the same person, then?" Poppy asked.

Will shrugged. "Who knows? I would hope so. I would hate to think we have two separate killers on the ranch with us." He moved to the thermostat on the wall and turned it off. In the bathroom, he turned up the heat and closed the door so the pipes didn't freeze. With the storm and the temperature continuing to drop, it shouldn't take long for the cabin to cool down and keep the body as best as was possible under the circumstances. He didn't know what else to do.

"Do you see the notebook?" Poppy asked.

He frowned as he looked around. "No." He moved to the desk. He was still wearing his gloves as he opened the top drawer and then checked the rest of the drawers. "Nothing."

"So the killer must have taken it," she said.

Will didn't want to search the cabin further. He figured it would be difficult enough for the sheriff once he was able to get here.

"You're going to have to tell the others," Dorothea said. "You have to warn them."

Will nodded. The other guests already knew that there was a killer among them. But she was right. There was no way to keep this a secret. "I will. But I don't want either of you leaving the lodge again. Let's go." He locked the door behind him and they made their way toward the lodge through the driving snow. The huge flakes whipped through the air, sticking to everything they touched, and continued to pile up.

The wind had blown the snow into drifts that looked like ocean waves cresting next to the buildings. It had been a losing battle to keep a path from the cabins to the lodge with a good two feet of snow on the ground, the wind forming drifts that were even higher, and more snow was coming down. It could be days before help could get to them. He tried not to think about that. Or about how many more would die before this was over.

As they passed cabin one, Lamar opened his door and looked out at them. He looked worried. He should be, Will thought. They all should be.

Lamar heard the shower come on in the bathroom as he shut the door. He'd seen Will's solemn face. Something bad had happened. He turned to look at the closed bathroom door. His brother was taking a shower? He thought about Mick's skinned knuckles and swore under his breath. Could this get any worse?

Unfortunately, he knew it could. He glanced toward the desk drawer where he'd put the manila envelope, anxious to study the employee files further. There had to be something in there of interest to his father. Something worth hiding. A clue as to who might be stealing from the company? Who might be running drugs out the back door? Who might be a killer?

Stepping to the bathroom door, he tried it. Locked. He shook his head. His brother was acting guilty as hell. "Mick?" he called through the door. "Mick!"

"What? I'm taking a shower," his brother called back irritably.

"Do you know Dad's passcode for his phone?"

No answer. "Did you hear me?"

"No, why would I know it?"

He heard the shower curtain draw closed again. A heartbeat later, the lodge dinner bell began to ring. Lamar glanced at the clock on the wall. It was too early for lunch. He'd been right. Something had happened.

"There's a problem. Will's ringing the bell," he called through the door. "I'm going up to the lodge." He picked up his coat, heard the shower shut off and hurriedly stepped to the desk to withdraw the envelope. Stepping into his bedroom, he slipped it under the mattress on his bed. As he shrugged on his coat, his brother came out wearing nothing but a towel.

Lamar couldn't miss the deep scratch on his brother's neck that went down almost to his chest.

The bell was still ringing.

"I think we're wanted at the lodge," he told his brother as fear nipped at him. "You should hurry and change."

"I'm not going anywhere. I'm tired. Whatever it is, you can come back and tell me." He stepped into his bedroom, pulled back the covers and started to climb into his bed.

"You're scaring me."

Mick made a face. "I'm tired, all right? I just want to be left alone."

"How did you skin up your hand and get that scratch on your neck?"

His brother touched the gouge on his neck and grimaced. "I told you, I don't want to talk about it."

"Mick, there's a murderer loose up here on this mountain. If you—"

"I got in a fight with Allison, all right? She scratched me, and before you ask, I didn't touch her. I slugged the wall. It hurt like hell. Happy?" He rolled over, pulling the down comforter up. All Lamar could see was his brother's wet curly hair, dark against the pillow.

He thought about what his brother had told him, wondering if any of it was true. "You know if you're in trouble, I'll do what I can to help you," he said.

There was no response from the bed.

Poppy stood with her back to the fireplace, but the heat did little to warm her.

Will was out in the storm ringing the dinner bell. Dorothea was busy lighting green candles and waving sage around. She'd already emptied two saltshakers along the threshold of the front door and another one along the back door that was kept locked except when there was a dance.

"You're wasting salt," Poppy said without much enthusiasm. "Lexi had salt by her door threshold. It didn't help."

The older woman mugged a face at her. "Better to do nothing like you?"

"You have a point. But what would you like me to do?"

Dorothea came over to her. "What's this about a notebook?"

"When I dropped by to see Lexi earlier, she was busy writing in a notebook. It was something she didn't want me to see."

"She was alive when you left?"

Poppy gave her a disbelieving look. "Of course."

"Why would you visit her?" Dorothea asked, but they were interrupted as the guests began to stream in. Ruby was the first one in, followed by Dean, Lamar, Channing and Alli-

son. They all seemed confused and worried. Allison looked
as if she'd been crying. Her eyes were red and her mascara
was smeared.

Will quit ringing the bell and followed them in. He looked
around the room and asked, "Where is Mick?"

"He's taking a nap," his brother said.

For a moment, Will seemed as if he was going to send
Lamar back to his cabin to get him, but apparently he changed
his mind.

"If you would all please sit down," he said. "I have some
bad news."

They sat hesitantly, none of them acting chummy, Poppy
noted.

"There's been another murder," Will said. "It's Lexi."

"What?" Dean demanded and looked around at the others
as if he wanted to run out of the room. Allison had let out a
cry, more like a whimper, before hugging herself.

Channing sighed and said, "I guess Kirk was the smart one
leaving when he did."

Ruby remained quiet, but she leaned forward to put her
face in her hands.

"I'm going to need to know where you have all been since
breakfast," Will said as he motioned to the notepaper and pens
still on the large square coffee table.

"This is getting ridiculous," Dean said. "I was in my cabin
with the door locked." He looked around the table. "What
about Mick?"

"I'll talk to him when he wakes up," Will said.

Dean snatched up a piece of paper and pen and began to
write on it, mumbling, "This is a waste of time."

"Don't forget to sign and date your alibis," Will said and
stood watching as each finally did as he'd asked, but with
obvious reluctance.

"What about them?" Dean demanded, jabbing a finger in

Poppy's and Dorothea's direction as he tossed his paper into the basket.

"Don't worry," Will assured him. "We'll all fill them out."

"Yes, what if it isn't one of us?" Channing said. "What if it's one of you?" Her gaze settled on Poppy. "I saw you coming out of Lexi's cabin earlier."

She felt her mouth go dry. "I went to visit her. I've already told Will."

Dean's laugh sounded brittle. "He'd believe anything you told him. But how do we know that you didn't kill her? Come on, why would you visit Lexi? Had you met her before this retreat?"

"You don't have to say anything," Will instructed her. "This is a murder investigation. We're all suspects. The sheriff will be asking the questions when he arrives. He'll want to talk to all of you."

"Only the ones of us who are still alive," Dean said. "If we're that lucky."

They all turned at the sound of a vehicle busting through the fallen snow and coming to a stop right outside.

A huge sigh of relief blew like a breeze through the room as everyone jumped up to see who it was.

"Thank God," Dean said. "It's the sheriff. Finally, we can get out of here."

But the person who came through the door was Huck, followed behind by a limping Kirk. All the air felt as if it had been sucked from the room.

Will seemed to take one look at his wrangler and knew. "Huck, you didn't get through," Will said, sounding as depressed about that as the rest of them, Poppy thought.

Huck shook his head. "I had to turn back. I barely made it. And look what I found on my way back." He motioned toward Kirk. "He was damned near frozen to death. If I hadn't come along when I did…"

Kirk walked in, head down. As he passed Channing, who was sitting on the end of the couch, her hand resting on the arm, Poppy would have sworn that Kirk either passed her something or took something from her hand. A note? She blinked, telling herself she'd imagined it since Channing jerked back her hand as if the devil had just touched it and glared after Kirk.

Still, it certainly had looked like the two had passed some sort of message between them. As Kirk moved to stand in front of the fire, Poppy noticed that both of his hands were now thrust deep into his pockets.

She moved over to give him room on the hearth. He was shivering, but he didn't look like a man who'd been lost for hours in a snowstorm.

CHAPTER EIGHTEEN

After everyone tossed their alibis into the basket, they left, seeming anxious to get back to their cabins and lock themselves inside. Will hoped they all stayed that way until lunchtime. But Lexi had been locked in. Who had she opened her door for? Someone she thought she could trust.

Dorothea had gone up to her room no doubt to try to cast more protective spells. He hoped one of them worked because at this point he didn't know what to think. There was no clear motive for what was happening. All he knew was that he had two dead guests. He told himself it had to be about the thief Big Jack had suspected. But still that felt wrong.

As he looked around the deserted room, he saw Poppy was sitting on the hearth as if cold. He threw more logs on the fire and then joined her. The soft crackle and pop, the scent of burning pine, and the heat on his back had a familiar comfort to it that he needed right now.

This guest ranch was his home. There'd been accidents over the years and trouble with guests, but nothing like this. He felt as if he'd been set up. Big Jack had suspected he had a crook in the company. Was that the purpose of this retreat?

He'd brought his troubles here thinking he would get to the bottom of them?

Obviously he hadn't known he would end up dead or that another employee would die. But he'd known something.

Will knew he had to talk to Lamar. But right now, he just wanted to sit here with Poppy. "Are you all right?"

She looked up seeming surprised, as if her mind had been a million miles away. Or maybe just as far as Whitefish. Had she been wishing she'd never come here? Like she'd said earlier, her plan had backfired.

"I was trying to figure out a connection between the murders," she said.

He let out a laugh. "I thought you were wishing you'd never laid eyes on me and this ranch again."

She shook her head as she smiled over at him. "Admittedly, this is not how I planned these four days, but then again my plan went awry a long time ago. No, I was thinking. The only things connecting the murders are that Lexi worked for Big Jack and they were both killed in much the same manner."

He nodded. "It seems to be about whatever was going on at On the Fly."

Poppy agreed. "Whoever chased Lexi that day at the waterfalls, it couldn't have been Big Jack. He was with Ruby."

"I can't see the two of them being in on it. Why harass Lexi?"

"Exactly. Wasn't Lexi the head of the sewing department? That doesn't seem like a job that would put her in danger."

"Unless she discovered something about one of the others," he said.

"Or about the fly-fishing vest company. When I went down to see Lexi, she was scared. I think she was writing down what she knew."

"About Kirk Austin?"

"Maybe," Poppy said thoughtfully. "The name on the note-

book that has now disappeared from Lexi's room *was* his."
She turned to look at Will. "Did Kirk seem like he'd been
lost in a winter storm for hours?"

He shook his head. "According to what Huck told me,
Kirk's story is that he went off the road and got the pickup
stuck. But Huck said he didn't see it on his way back here."

"How far did Huck get?"

"Not far. He said the roads were drifted in worse the closer
he got to the valley. He was smart enough to turn around and
come back before the roads closed behind him."

"Where was Kirk all that time? In Slim's truck?"

"What are you suggesting?" Will asked. He could see that
she wasn't sure.

"That maybe he didn't go very far at all? That maybe he
was only trying to establish an alibi for himself?"

"But he would have had to have hidden somewhere until
he showed up on the road and Huck found him," Will said.
"He couldn't sneak into the bunkhouse or his own cabin
without fearing he'd get caught. The barn was locked up. I
suppose he could have stayed with one of the others, but then
that would mean that they were in on it with him."

He saw her eyes widen. "What about cabin nine? You said
it had a water leak and wasn't ready for guests. But it still had
heat, right?"

Will got to his feet. "I suppose you're going with me."

She smiled. "I'll get my coat."

Lamar wasn't all that surprised to return to his cabin and
find Mick gone. He swore. So much for taking a nap. He
looked outside at the storm. His brother wasn't fool enough
to try to leave, was he?

Stepping into the bathroom, he caught the scent of his
brother's favorite aftershave and shook his head. Nothing
seemed to be missing from his brother's things he'd left be-

hind. Which meant that Mick had gotten up as soon as he'd left, shaved, dressed and gone courting.

He told himself that whatever had happened earlier with Lexi, it couldn't have had anything to do with his brother. But it could have had something to do with Allison. She'd looked as if she'd been crying.

Lamar raked a hand through his hair and told himself he'd deal with it when they all returned to California and On the Fly. His brother breaking the no-dating rule was nothing compared to two murders involving the company. More than ever, he needed to know what was going on before anyone else died.

Locking the cabin door, he went to his bedroom and pulled out the envelope. Sitting down on the bed, he began to go through each file. He hadn't gone very far when he found a loose sheet of paper that his father had made notes on in his chicken scrawl. He frowned as he tried to read them.

No vacation. Works late.
New supplier. Falsified documents?
Card reader logs time, place, and employees in and out.
Cameras in key locations.

The last note his father had written read: *Talk to Lamar.*

He stared at the words, knowing now that Big Jack had definitely thought someone was stealing from them. Someone who never took a vacation? Who worked late? He frowned as he studied the list his father had made. They did have a new supplier for some of the fabric. Did his father think there was something questionable about the supplier? The rest of the notes were things his father thought they should be implementing at the company. Except for the last one. Big Jack had been trying to narrow down the suspects. Had he been getting too close to the truth?

Still, Lamar couldn't believe that whoever was stealing from the company had resorted to murder to keep from being discovered. As Will had said, it seemed a long shot since, once Lamar got back, he should be able to figure out what was going on. His father was right. He hadn't been paying close enough attention to the day-to-day operation. He'd trusted his employees.

And it had gotten his father killed. And now one of their employees.

He closed his eyes for a moment, leaning back against the headboard. What he'd told his brother was right. It hadn't set in yet that Big Jack was gone. *Murdered.* He could hear the roar of the wind and the storm outside the small cabin but that wasn't what chilled him to the bone. The killer had realized that Big Jack was getting close to exposing him—or her.

But how had his father known something was going on at the company? He spent so little time there. It came to him like a shot. Ruby. If his father was seeing her away from On the Fly, then she might have told him about her suspicions.

He put the papers back into the envelope, stuffed it back under his mattress again and, dressing for the storm raging outside, headed for Ruby's cabin.

Cabin nine was a good walk from the lodge under normal conditions. But as Poppy stepped out she was hit by a blast of wind and snow. She ducked her head and followed behind Will as he broke a trail through the drifting snow.

There was already somewhat of a trail that Will had shoveled and the guests had made along the front of the cabins. But still the snow was up to her knees. She caught glimpses of the cabins as they passed, but often could see nothing but Will's back ahead of her through the snow.

She'd been in one whiteout since returning to Montana. That time, she'd been driving and suddenly she couldn't see

the road. There was nothing but white. She recalled that
panicked feeling. That's what made whiteouts so dangerous.
She couldn't help but think of Kirk's story about going off
the road. If she was right and he was lying, then he could be
the killer. His leaving was about establishing an alibi—a ruse.

The snow got considerably deeper once they passed cabin
eight. Will pushed through a drift that was up to his thighs
to the last cabin. He tried the door and it groaned open, snow
blowing inside. Will reached back for her, practically dragging her through the deep snow and inside out of the blizzard. He closed the door behind them.

It was surprisingly warm in the cabin. She saw that Will
had noticed it, as well.

"The heat had been turned off, along with the water," he
said as he moved to the thermostat on the wall. "Someone
turned it back on."

"I feel like mama bear," she said. "And someone has been
sleeping in the bed." There was an indentation in the comforter.

Will checked the bathroom before turning back to her.
"Someone definitely stayed here."

"Kirk."

"It certainly looks that way. Unless some of the others have
been using it as a clandestine cabin so no one could see what
they were up to." Will shook his head. "If it was Kirk, then
he lied about how far he went." He sighed. "I need to talk to
Lamar. I'll walk you back to the lodge."

"Wouldn't you like a woman's perspective when you talk
to a suspect?"

"I was going to say that I don't want you any more involved in all this than you already are," Will said. "But realizing how ridiculous that is..." He met her gaze. "You're
saying that women see things that men miss?"

She raised a brow and smiled. "Maybe we just see different things than men."

He still hesitated for a moment, then said, "None of us are safe until we figure out who is behind the murders. Okay. Let's start with Kirk."

"Lead the way."

Lamar knocked at Ruby's cabin door and waited, huddling against the storm as he did. He knocked again.

"Who is it?" she asked through the door.

"Lamar." He waited, not sure she was going to let him in. But a moment later, the door opened a crack.

"What do you want?" She looked upset, which surprised him. She'd kept her cool when the others had been falling apart.

"I need to ask you about my father."

She hesitated but only for a moment before she opened the door and he stepped in. Her cabin felt overly warm after he'd been outside. He stood just inside the door as she moved into the center of the cabin. "What about Jack?"

"Do you mind?" he asked as he took off his jacket and stomped snow off his boots. She motioned to the chair from the desk but he shook his head. He was too keyed up to sit down.

She waited, looking as if she'd been expecting him to question her at some point.

"How long have the two of you—"

"Six months."

He raised a brow. "That long?" He did a quick calculation in his head. "So before you went to work at On the Fly. I assume that was why my father insisted on hiring you."

Her smile had sharp teeth. "He hired me because I'm good at my job."

Lamar couldn't argue that. "You were the one who told

him something was wrong inside the company. Why didn't
you come to me?"

She said nothing, just met his gaze and held it.

"You can't think I have anything to do with…" His words
died off in a curse. "If there is money missing—"

"There *is* money missing."

"How do you know that? You're the design and market-
ing person, not the bookkeeper."

"I have eyes and ears."

So did he, but apparently he hadn't been using them. He
grabbed the chair and pulled it over to drop into and sat for
a moment with his head in his hands as it all seemed to hit
him. There was a thief at On the Fly. Maybe even a drug deal
going on, and he'd missed it and it had cost his father and
Lexi their lives. Ruby seemed angry about it and he couldn't
blame her. While his father owned the company, Lamar had
been the boss who should have known.

When he finally pulled himself together, he raised his head
and asked, "So you told my father your suspicions." When
she said nothing, he said, "Did you have someone in mind at
the company besides me?"

With a start, Dorothea realized she was all alone in the
lodge. "Hello?" she called as she came down the stairs to find
everyone gone. Her voice seemed to echo. She passed through
the dining room into the kitchen, convinced Poppy would
be hard at work preparing for lunch.

But the kitchen was also empty and when she went back
into the main lounge she saw that Poppy's coat was gone. So
was Will's. She felt a chill. Where had they gone? Had there
been another murder?

She was considering what to do when the front door blew
open on a gust of wind and snow. She jumped and spun

around as Dean Donovan came in. He managed to retrieve the door, slamming it, before he began brushing snow off himself.

"Where is everyone?" he asked, glancing around.

"Will should be back at any minute," she lied, surprised how uncomfortable she felt alone with the young man. He seemed weak. She told herself she could take him in a fair fight. But she wasn't about to turn her back on him.

She watched him remove his glasses and wipe off the moisture with the tail of his shirt before putting them back on and pushing them up his nose.

"I don't smell food," he said, glancing toward the kitchen.

"It's still too early for lunch. Poppy hasn't started cooking yet." That alone was very strange. What if something had happened to her and Will had gone out to look for her?

"I'm hungry." He started for the kitchen and Dorothea followed, annoyed that the young man thought he could just help himself. He opened the refrigerator and looked inside, then closed it.

"There's fruit and brownies," she said, pointing to where they were left out for guests.

He shook his head. "I was going stir-crazy in my room. I'm not sure how much more of this I can take." She knew the feeling. "When is this storm supposed to finally stop?"

"I don't know. Last I heard late tomorrow."

Dean swore and headed out through the dining room.

Dorothea put on her apron, remembering the knife she'd left wrapped up in the pocket and, taking the plate of brownies, followed him.

"You must have a theory about what's going on," she said as she put down the plate before going to stand nearer the fire. Dean plopped down into one of the large leather chairs and put his feet up on the coffee table. He hadn't even taken off his snowy boots.

She started to say something about that, but held her tongue.

He saw her eyeing his boots, though, and slowly removed them from the table with an angry grunt. "How would *I* know what's going on?" he demanded. "No one ever tells me anything. Or asks what I think."

She knew the feeling, but said, "You work with these people so you must have a pretty good idea who is doing this."

With a huff, he said, "I'm just the stockroom guy. Like they pay any attention to me. I'm like a piece of furniture around there. Did you know that I was almost killed a few weeks ago? That's right, a crate of boxed vests fell from the forklift. If I hadn't moved when I did..." He shook his head.

"Who was driving the forklift?"

"Mick. Said it was an accident." Dean scoffed at that. "He wanted to scare me."

"Why would he want to scare you?"

He shook his head. "He's weird. Spoiled. Had everything handed to him. He doesn't do squat at the plant but flirt with the girls and take money out of petty cash. He's supposed to be in charge of inventory." Dean laughed. "I could walk out with a forklift of vests and no one would even know it. Not that I would."

"What did Lexi do there?" she asked as Dean took a big bite out of one of the brownies. She knew, but she wanted his take on it.

"She was in charge of the sewing department," he said around the brownie. "Most of the sewing is done off-site. She has a few women who come in and sew with her. Or she did have." He quit chewing for a moment as if only then remembering that she was dead, then continued and swallowed as if he'd lost his appetite.

"Why would someone kill her?"

Dean shook his head. "How would I know?"

"You're smart and you notice things," she said. "That's the great thing about people not paying any attention to you. You become invisible. You can walk through a room and no one even sees you."

He nodded and smiled. "I do notice things." He met her eyes. "My guess is that Lexi saw the killer since she was the one who found Big Jack."

"Why wouldn't she tell?"

He shrugged. "Maybe she had something to hide, like what she was doing up at that hour. I didn't buy her story about seeing Big Jack go by and following him, worried he was sleepwalking." Neither did Dorothea. "I think she was already in the barn."

"Doing what?"

Dean raised a brow. "What do you think?" He made an obscene gesture.

She groaned inwardly. "With whom?"

"That is the question, isn't it? Wasn't me. Not even Lexi would go out with me."

Dorothea looked up then to see Mick stop in front of the lodge. He turned to look back through the blowing and drifting snow. A moment later Channing walked past him as if he was invisible. He hurried to open the door for her, saying something. Was Mick now hitting on Channing? If so, she didn't seem to be interested considering the expression on her face.

But as Channing walked through the door Mick held open for her, she seemed to brush against him. Their hands touched and Dorothea saw her pass something to him. A cabin key? A love note? She'd thought the same thing had happened between Channing and Kirk. Maybe she'd imagined it just as she had during what had looked like this last exchange.

She shook her head. Every group came with its own unique intrigue, but this was the worst of the worst. They had two murders and now these two were hooking up? "Maybe they will all kill each other," she said under her breath.

But it wasn't long before she realized she must have been mistaken. As everyone wandered into the lodge before lunch, Mick was flirting with Allison again and Channing was ignoring them both as if she had no interest at all.

CHAPTER NINETEEN

Cabin six's curtains moved. Kirk peered out the window after Will's second knock. He glanced from Will to Poppy, then back again. The curtain fell back into place and a moment later the door opened wide.

"To what do I owe this visit? Or is it to whom?" Kirk asked and grinned. He had a glass in his hand and it was clear that he'd been drinking.

Will kept the liquor locked up during the day in the lodge so he assumed Kirk had brought his own. "I need to ask you a few questions."

"You going to ask me questions, too?" Kirk said to Poppy, his grin widening. He gave her a wink. "You sure can cook for a woman who looks like you do."

"Maybe this isn't the best time," Will said.

"Why not?" the former snowboarder snapped. "I haven't had that much to drink."

They stepped in. Kirk offered them some from his flask. They declined.

"I'm going to get right to it," Will said. "I know you didn't get far in the storm and that you came back and hid in cabin nine."

Kirk looked for a moment as if he was going to deny it, but then he laughed and said, "I should have known someone would figure it out. So what if I did?"

"Where is Slim's truck?"

"Not far from here. You were right about that, too. I didn't go far before I got stuck. I hiked back, stayed in the cabin before heading down the road to make it look like I'd returned from there. That's when Huck picked me up."

"Why didn't you just admit what you'd done?" Will asked. "Why lie?"

"To save face," Poppy said.

Kirk shot her a grin. "All that big talk about me skiing out of here? I couldn't even drive a damned truck out. If you must know, I was embarrassed. You want more truth, huh? I didn't quit the snowboard circuit. I got hurt and then I got scared. I just couldn't face it anymore. So there. You know everything. All my dirty secrets." He took another drink from the flask. "So go tell them. Give them all a good laugh."

"This sounds as if it is more about you losing Allison," Poppy said. Both men looked at her in surprise.

Then Kirk pointed his finger at her and said, "You should try to hang on to this one, Will. A girl with brains, too."

"Hardly a girl," Poppy corrected.

Kirk flushed and then gave her an awkward bow. "My apologies."

"That means you don't have an alibi for when Lexi was murdered," Will said.

Kirk's eyes widened. "Wait, I had nothing to do with that. I didn't even know she was dead until I came into the lodge with Huck. Seriously, you can't pin that on me. Why would I want to kill her?"

"That's a good question," Will said. "Why would you?"

Kirk shrugged. "Hell, I'm still blown away by Big Jack being dead. What is it about this place?"

"I don't think it's the place," Poppy said. "You all seemed...
tense when you got here, like something was going on."

"Hell, yes. This trip was sprung on us at the last minute,"
Kirk said. "I had other plans but Big Jack said screw my other
plans, all of us had to come on this damned retreat, something about bonding or some such shit." He shook his head.
"It made no sense. I could tell that his sons were just as surprised as the rest of us. Mick was pissed."

"Who were the others who didn't want to come along?"
she asked.

"Dean, for one. He's terrified of planes and horses and,
hell, just about everything. And Allison lives for her job. But
Big Jack told them to buck up. He even bought us all special coats and hats for the trip. Free advertising for him. And
he told us we had to wear them, something about unity or
some such bull."

Will looked to Poppy as if waiting for the next question.

"Anything...strange going on at the company?" she asked.

Kirk shrugged. "Big Jack wasn't around a lot. We could
all see that Lamar was trying to push him out. Mick wasn't
happy working there, not that he did much work. He was
too busy flirting and fighting with Allison. I could tell that's
why he came in early and stayed late. He liked getting her
alone and, like I said, she lived for her job so she was always
there even after-hours."

"They have a stormy relationship?" Will asked.

"You could say that," Kirk said with a laugh. "She flirts,
but she doesn't back it up. Not with Mick, anyway." He shook
his head. Then he stopped to look at each of them. "I swear
to you, I had nothing to do with Lexi's death or Big Jack's."
He sat down heavily on the end of his bed. "I'm not even sure
I have a job when this is over." He was shaking his head, lost
in his flask and his thoughts as they left his cabin.

They didn't speak until they reached the lodge. As they

came in the front door, Poppy saw Dean and Dorothea sitting around the fire talking. Now there was an odd mix if there ever was one, she thought.

Mick and Channing were sitting at opposite ends of the couch. Allison had taken a chair across from him. Ruby seemed to be watching Dean and Dorothea. There was an empty brownie plate on the coffee table. Apparently some of them had come down to the lodge hoping for an early lunch.

Dorothea started to rise, but Will motioned her to stay put as he followed Poppy into the kitchen.

"I have to get lunch started," she said, looking at the time.

Will leaned against the counter. "What do you think?"

"About Kirk?" She shrugged. "It just feels like there is so much we don't know."

"That's why I need to talk to Lamar. Maybe I'll go do that. Do you need help with lunch?"

She shook her head. "I'm going to keep it simple."

He chuckled. "I doubt that." Then he stepped to her and gave her a quick kiss. "Be safe, okay? I won't be long." And he left.

Poppy, true to her word, kept lunch simple. But since cooking was the way she thought through things, she took the leftover roast beef and made burritos with black beans, rice, avocado and a fresh mango salsa. She had just put two coconut custard pies in the oven when Will returned.

"I couldn't find Lamar," he said. "I shoveled the path to the cabins, but it was filling in right behind me." Will looked worried.

"Did you try the other cabins?"

He shook his head. "I figure they'll all surface at lunch. At least, I hope so."

"Your timing is perfect. You can ring the bell. Everything is ready except for dessert and it will be ready by the time we eat," she said.

"I know I keep saying this, but you're amazing." As if embarrassed, he turned on his boot heel and headed for the front of the lodge and the dinner bell. A few moments later, Poppy heard it ringing. By then Dean was already seated in the dining room complaining he was starving.

"I see you and Dean are now friends?" she whispered to Dorothea and grinned.

"Actually, I feel sorry for him. Apparently no one at On the Fly was very nice to him."

Poppy lifted a brow. "Sounds like a motive for murder to me."

The older woman looked uncertain. "He did mention that not even Lexi would go out with him."

They both glanced toward the dining room where Dean was playing with the salt and pepper shakers as if they were toy soldiers and they were in hand-to-hand combat.

"Uh-huh, he looks like a real killer," Dorothea said and went to work.

Poppy was glad when everyone still alive showed up for lunch, including Lamar. Will insisted Mick put his alibi in the basket before letting him take a seat at the table.

"I think it would be a good idea for all of you to stay in your cabins with the doors locked except for meals," Will said as the food was passed around. He'd suggested that before but it didn't seem to be happening, Poppy thought.

"When is the storm going to stop?" Allison asked, sounding close to tears.

"From what I heard on the radio? Tomorrow afternoon," Will said. "It will take a while for the roads to open, though. Once our landline is up and working again, we'll call the sheriff."

"So maybe we'll get out of here tomorrow," Dean said, sounding pleased. "We'll miss our flight—"

"If the airport is even open," Channing said impatiently.

"Personally, since Big Jack isn't here to tell us what we have to do, I'm going to rent a car and drive home," Kirk said. "I figure On the Fly should pick up the bill." The room fell silent. He seemed to realize he'd said something wrong. "No offense to Big Jack." He raised his water glass. "May he rest in peace."

"I hate to break it to you," Will said, "but I don't think anyone will be leaving tomorrow. Once the sheriff gets here—"

"How could you have all forgotten that there have been two murders?" Ruby asked as she glanced around the table. "And it isn't like you didn't know the deceased," she said, sounding disgusted with all of them.

"She's right," Channing agreed. "You all suck. But look at it this way. You think you're just going to walk away from here?" She shook her head. "At least one of you will be handcuffed and riding in the back of a patrol SUV by tomorrow."

Kirk dropped his fork, the sound like a gunshot. Everyone jumped and looked embarrassed. The room fell silent again as heads dropped and people became interested in only eating. It was clear that none of them wanted to spend any more time than they had to together, Poppy thought.

She saw Kirk push back his plate as the timer went off in the kitchen. "There's dessert," she said.

But Kirk shook his head. "I've had enough. Enough of all of this," he said, getting to his feet. With that he left.

In the kitchen, Poppy pulled her two custard pies out of the oven. She carried one back into the dining room. Then went back for plates and a knife to cut it. The smell of warm custard covered with the toasted coconut filled the dining room. She sliced through the coconut to the rich creamy custard to the crust. This was one of her favorite, easy recipes. She put a piece on a plate and started to hand them around the table.

Ruby took a piece and so did Mick, but the rest of the guests passed. Poppy cut a piece for Will, Dorothea and herself. The tension around the table felt so fragile that if anyone knocked over a glass, let alone dropped another utensil, she feared what would happen.

One by one, the guests excused themselves to go back to their cabins. Will acted as if he didn't notice the strain as he finished his pie, telling her it was delicious. Dorothea ate hers without comment. When finished, Will took plates out to the bunkhouse for Huck and Slim. She knew he had them keeping an eye on things as best they could with the storm.

It wasn't until Poppy got up to clear the table that she noticed the knife she'd used to cut the pie was missing.

CHAPTER TWENTY

Poppy was in the kitchen finishing up when Will returned. Seeing her did more than brighten a bad day. He no longer felt only a stirring in him. Just the sight of her had turned into an aching need, a hunger that her luscious dishes only made worse. One bite and he was enchanted not just by the sexy, irresistible woman who'd concocted it, but fascinated by her mind. All this even knowing that every bite could still be a ploy to punish him for being such a fool at fifteen.

He didn't care. Maybe it was having a murderer on the mountain with him. Or maybe he just didn't have the energy to resist her anymore. He knew how dangerous it was. But compared to sharing a table with a killer...

"Everything all right at the bunkhouse?" she asked as he walked in.

He nodded, relishing the heat of the kitchen and the tantalizing smells coming from it since Poppy had arrived. Outside the storm still raged. He felt as if the snow would never stop. But he was born and raised here and knew how quickly everything could change. It *would* stop snowing, the sun *would* come out and the snow *would* begin to melt rapidly this time of year, causing flooding.

That all seemed so minor compared to the situation he found himself in with the people he was responsible for protecting. He thought about his father. Would he have handled things differently? He felt as if he'd let himself down, not to mention his family and the people he cared about.

He watched Poppy fill a large pot of braised beef with vegetables and stir in spiced flour before adding broth. The woman could make the act of making gravy erotic.

"Beef stew," she said as if sensing him watching her. "I thought that and fresh rolls with butter would suffice for dinner since eating is the last thing on anyone's mind."

"I'm so sorry," he said as he leaned against the counter. Sorry for so many things going back twenty years.

"This is not your fault. None of it."

He shook his head. Suddenly he wanted more than anything to be the man this woman needed. The man he'd been too young and foolish to be at fifteen.

She met his gaze. He could stay for days in her green eyes.

"There's something I need to tell you," she said. "The knife I used to cut the custard pie? Someone took it. I asked Dorothea, but she already snatched one that she carries around in her apron pocket."

"So one of the guests is now armed with a large knife," Will said and swore under his breath. "I know they're scared. If this storm doesn't move on soon…"

She stepped to him and cupped his jaw in her warm hand. "We're going to get through this. The storm will move on. The sheriff will come and sort this all out."

He smiled at her as he took her hand and kissed the warm palm. He wished he had her faith. Right now, with Poppy this close, all he wanted to do was take her in his arms and kiss her senseless—and then carry her upstairs to his bed. He caught a whiff of her unique scent, something citrusy that he knew was as delicious as her cooking. With her hand still in his, he drew her to him, needing to feel her in his arms.

Earlier, he'd told her that he was falling for her. True as it was, he knew it was a mistake to admit it. He'd resolved to keep her at arm's length because she wasn't like the other women he'd known. Add to that their history. If he let this go any further, he knew where they were headed. Once in his big bed, the two of them naked... He swore. He'd rather cut off his right arm than hurt her again.

He had enough trouble without getting in any deeper with this woman. Tell that to the overpowering desire that arced between them. Just the thought that they might not get out of this alive... He drew her closer, brushed his lips over hers and heard her release a contented sigh. He knew he was playing right into her hands—just as Dorothea had warned him.

The shoe was on the other foot. If she wanted, she *could* break his heart. He was a man cursed with a passion for this woman. He knew he should be scared. Hell, terrified. What this woman could do to him, if she wanted to...

Her lips parted. As her gaze locked with his, he dragged her against him and kissed her with the passion that had been building up inside him for days. He'd never wanted anyone the way he wanted her. He felt like a man who'd been lost in the desert and now found cool, fresh water. He wanted to drown himself in her.

The front door burst open on a gust of wind and snow.

"Will? Will!" Lamar's voice carried through the lodge, along with the sound of his boots on the hardwood floor as he headed in their direction.

Will groaned as they were forced apart. Poppy groaned silently. She'd waited twenty years for this only to have it interrupted. That had been the kiss she'd been waiting for. She'd felt him begin to truly surrender to her.

She stepped away, straightening her apron and turning to her stew as Lamar rushed into the kitchen. She needed a moment, she told herself as she opened the oven door and slid the large pot inside, closing the oven before turning back to Will and Lamar. She knew her face was flushed from the kiss. But Lamar didn't seem to notice. Clearly he was worked up.

"We need to talk," the man said, glancing from Will to her.

"Whatever you have to say, Poppy can hear it."

Lamar hesitated for a moment. "Is there somewhere we can go to discuss this, the three of us, in private?" Poppy saw that he had a large manila envelope in his gloved hand.

"Let's go up to my apartment," Will said and glanced at her. Poppy nodded and took off her apron as she followed them upstairs.

She'd never been in Will's apartment over the lodge. It was at the front of the structure, at the opposite end from her room and Dorothea's. In the summer months when the guest ranch was at its maximum occupancy, both the men's and women's bunkhouses would be full of staff. From what she'd gathered, Dorothea and the cook stayed in the rooms upstairs. Will's brothers worked the cattle ranch in the valley, leaving the guest ranch business to him.

As she stepped into his apartment, she had to smile to herself. It was all cowboy and all male from the paintings on the walls and the rugs on the floors to the antique spurs on the mantel over the fireplace and the leather furniture. There were books everywhere, which also made her smile. One book was open on the small table next to what was obviously his chair.

Through a doorway, she caught a glimpse of his log bed draped with a homemade quilt and more books on the end table next to it. She imagined the two of them snuggled up in that bed and had to turn away. Just being in his space made her heart beat faster. That old ache was a new, much stronger one after that kiss downstairs. Her blood ran hot. She had yearned for this man for so long…

She'd thought that once he admitted that he was crazy about her that would be all she needed. But now she realized she wanted much more. All the kisses had done was start a fire inside her that only this cowboy could put out.

Poppy moved to the window overlooking the ranch. She could barely make out the barn through the falling snow. Pressing her forehead against the cool glass, she tried to regain control of herself. What about her plan to break Will's heart? If she made love to him, would she be able to walk away? Because no matter how Will felt right now, once this was over…

Will had said he was falling for her, that he loved her cooking, and clearly he wanted her. But for how long? She knew his history and she warned herself to tread lightly. He'd said he didn't want to hurt her. Did she need to remind herself that he hadn't purposely hurt her when they were young? He just hadn't wanted her when she'd wanted him. What if that happened again?

Or vice versa, she reminded herself. Maybe she was right and all she had to do was make love with him and the spell would be broken. She could get on with her life—

"I found something my father had hidden in his cabin," Lamar said as Will closed his apartment door. "It's all of the employee records from the company."

Poppy turned as Will went to the fireplace, threw on another log and closed the grate before offering her and Lamar a seat. She took the couch, leaving the chairs for the two men.

Lamar was clearly upset. He seemed to take a breath as he tried to calm down. "My father believed that someone was stealing from the company. I'm sure that's why he brought these documents with him. He'd made notes about tightening security." He looked from Poppy to Will for a moment.

"But I have since learned that someone might have been running a drug business through On the Fly. I think he had a crazy idea that by bringing the suspects on this retreat, he was going to find the culprit."

"You think he got too close to the truth," Will said. Lamar nodded. "Well, that could certainly shed some light on what's been happening up here. But how do you explain Lexi's death?"

The man shook his head. "I can't. Unless she saw more than she said the night she found my father in the barn."

Will seemed to think for a moment. "Poppy and I have reason to believe that someone in your company was threatening Lexi. The day on the hike to the waterfalls, Lexi got hurt running from someone who was either after her or she thought was after her."

Lamar took off his On the Fly stocking cap and raked a hand through his hair. "I have no idea what was going on at my own company." Poppy heard the guilt in his voice. "My father and I were involved in a power struggle. He wasn't good with business. On the Fly is relatively new. He'd already bankrupted several other businesses. He was great with ideas, but terrible at actually running a business, and yet he was the one who realized something was wrong."

"You can't blame yourself," Will said. "Someone took advantage of you. Do you have any idea who?"

Lamar shook his head as he looked at the manila envelope balancing on the arm of his chair. "I went through these employee records. There must have been something in them that my father saw that I'm missing. When I went to his room to look for some clue to what was going on, I realized that someone had been there before me. I don't know what the intruder was looking for, but I suspect it might have been these papers. My father had hidden them well."

"If you didn't find anything in them," Will said, "I really doubt I would."

"I agree. I doubt the sheriff will be able to make heads or tails of them, either. I took some notes on what I found, but I was hoping you could keep the papers somewhere safe. I've had them hidden in my cabin but…"

He didn't need to say more, Poppy thought. He was sharing the cabin with his brother. At this point, he probably didn't trust anyone with the information.

"I would be happy to," Will said. Poppy could tell that Lamar had come here for another reason.

"When you say drug business…" Will said.

"It's possible my father had found out that the company was being used to distribute heroin."

He let out a curse. "So we aren't talking petty theft," Will said.

"Possibly not," Lamar agreed as he got to his feet. "It might explain why someone is willing to kill to keep the secret."

Poppy couldn't help being surprised. She could see that Will was, too. This changed things. She wondered where Lamar had gotten his information, but figured that was for the sheriff to ask.

"I appreciate you coming to me with this," Will said as he rose, as well, to take the large envelope the man handed him. "I'll put this in my safe." He walked Lamar to the door, told him to be careful and, closing the door, turned to face Poppy.

His gaze locked with hers. "Poppy." He said it all in that one word, his voice raw with emotion. She knew he could see all the yearning in her gaze just as she could see desire firing his brown eyes.

But the way he said her name, it was also a question. Was she all in even knowing what was at stake?

She rose on trembling legs as he locked his apartment door and moved toward her. She didn't have to tell him that she wanted this as much as he did. He closed the distance between them and took her in his arms again.

The kiss was as hot as the blaze crackling in the fireplace.

His tongue probed her mouth, finding the sensitive places that made her weak. She parted her lips, surrendering to his kisses as heat burned at her center.

With a moan, he pulled away from her mouth to trail kisses down her throat.

"You are so beautiful," he whispered, his lips setting her skin to blaze.

Slowly he began to free each button of her shirt as his lips and tongue caressed more accessible bare hot flesh. She shuddered against him, burying her fingers in his hair.

As he reached the swell of her breast, he freed the last button and slipped her shirt off one shoulder to get to the hard, aching nipple straining against the fabric of her bra.

She moaned in pleasure as his mouth suckled her breast through her bra before he slowly slipped her bra strap off her shoulder. Her breast spilled from the bra, her nipple hard and large and hot and damp from the wet heat of his mouth.

He dropped his head to her breast and sucked hard at her nipple. She arched against his mouth as he lathed her breast with his tongue until she cried out with need. Will freed the other breast, cupping them in his large, rough hands to kiss and caress the tender flesh. Molten fire raced to her core.

She buried her fingers deeper in his hair as his lips made their way down her rib cage, then her stomach. She felt his nimble fingers release the first button on her jeans. Achingly slow, he released another button and another. When his fingers found her center, she was hot and wet with throbbing need for him.

She thought she would die if he stopped as he touched her softly, slowly. Her legs went weak and she would have collapsed if he hadn't lifted her onto the arm of his leather chair. She grabbed the back of the chair, needing to hang on as his fingers worked their magic to the point that she was about to erupt.

An explosion filled the air, making them both jump.

CHAPTER TWENTY-ONE

Will let out a curse as light flashed orange at the large window overlooking the ranch. "What the hell?" He released her to rush to the window in time to see someone running along the side of the barn. Kirk Austin. Kirk ran through the snow toward the cabins, disappearing in the storm as the barn was quickly engulfed in flames.

Poppy joined him at the window, pulling her shirt around her nakedness as she did. "The horses!" she cried an instant before Will saw Huck and Slim racing to the corrals to open the gates so the horses could go into the pasture and away from the flames.

He looked at her, torn between his need for her and finishing what they'd started, and rushing to the burning barn.

She must have seen the pain in his face. "Go!"

He nodded and headed for the door.

"What can I do?" she asked behind him.

"Stay here." He stopped for a moment to look back at her. She smiled and nodded. And he was out the door, racing down the stairs toward the burning barn, his mind racing, as well. What the hell had happened? A barn didn't suddenly explode into flames. Someone had done this. Done this to hide the evidence since Big Jack's body was still inside.

He thought of Kirk running away from the scene of the crime.

Grabbing his coat by the front door, he burst out into the storm. Snowflakes whirled around him in a flurry of white, icy cold. He could feel the heat before he was even close to the barn.

Huck came out of the smoke against the blazing back-ground. "We can't get near it."

"The horses?"

"Slim has them all moved into the far fenced pasture."

"There's nothing we can do," Huck said. "We have no way to put it out."

He was saying what Will already knew. The barn was going to burn to the ground. They couldn't get near it as hot as it was burning. Fortunately, it was far enough from the bunk-houses that they should be fine.

A few guests had come out of their cabins to see what was going on.

"What do you think happened?" Huck asked over the roar of the blaze and the storm. Will met his gaze. They both knew what had happened. One of his guests had caused the explo-sion, although he could only guess how. What he thought he knew was who. While the rest of them had run toward the burning barn, Kirk had been running away.

Will was just thankful that Kirk had turned the horses out first. They'd been in the stalls, but when he'd looked out, they were all out in the corral. Destroying evidence, what-ever evidence against him might have been in the barn, Kirk had at least not stooped to killing the horses.

He wasn't too worried about finding Kirk. The man couldn't get far, and the last Will had seen of him, Kirk had been running toward his cabin. He wouldn't know that he'd been seen so Will figured that was where they would find him.

A thought struck him at the same time it did Huck.

"The other body—" Huck barely got the words out before they both turned and ran toward Lexi's cabin.

Poppy couldn't just sit inside. She told herself that there must be something she could do. After Will left she'd stood in his apartment trembling all over. They'd come so close to making love. She could still feel his mouth on her skin, his fingers inside her. She shuddered with both longing and disappointment in herself.

She had wanted Will Sterling to make love to her. But at what price? Caught up in her desire for him, she hadn't cared when his hands and mouth were on her. Now she was coming to her senses. She'd reeled him in with her cooking—just as she'd planned. She had more than his attention. She had him where she wanted him. She'd seen the burning desire in his eyes, felt it in his kisses and caresses.

He wanted her. But, she thought with a groan, she'd wanted him just as badly. Unfortunately, now that she'd calmed down, she also realized that she wanted more than a one-night stand with him. She knew the man's reputation. He was a confirmed bachelor. They wanted two different things.

Standing in his apartment with the male scent of him still filling her nostrils, she warned herself. If she wasn't careful she was going to let him break her heart again. Only this time, she would have only herself to blame.

Straightening her clothing, she headed downstairs, sickened by what she'd seen from the window. Also she couldn't help worrying that Will might do something foolish like rush into the barn to get Big Jack's body out. Surely he wouldn't do that. The body! That had to be why someone had set the barn on fire. Barns didn't just explode, did they?

As she looked out, she caught a glimpse of Huck and Will running through the deep snow toward the cabins. Grabbing her coat and pulling on her boots, hat and gloves, she rushed out after them. Running was next to impossible in the deep snow. She lumbered through it even though she'd lost sight of the two men.

Cabin doors opened. She heard someone yell, "What's going on?" She kept going, reminding herself belatedly that one of the guests had a butcher knife. All the cabins were a good distance apart. Each set back in the pines.

She could see Huck and Will rushing toward Lexi's cabin.

The explosion drove them both back. Smaller than the one that had set the barn aflame, this one blew out the windows in a shower of glass that fell darkly on the fresh white snow. She heard the glass sizzle and realized she'd stopped in her tracks and stared dumbly at the burning cabin. The killer had managed to destroy any evidence left behind with the bodies of Big Jack and Lexi.

Poppy turned away, unable to watch as flames licked through the cabin as the wind whipped both snow and smoke around her.

Lamar had been in his cabin when he heard the explosion. It had hardly registered with him, he'd been so shocked from his own discovery.

After he'd taken the manila envelope to Will and told him everything he knew about what was going on, he'd gone back to his cabin. Earlier, he'd taken notes on all the employee files his father had hidden.

He looked at the information so many times that he was ready to give up when one of them struck him as odd. It was one of the employee's birth dates. Why did it seem familiar? He knew he'd seen it written down somewhere before. Closing his eyes, he tried to remember. Not in the files. Before they'd flown up here for the retreat? Yes, on his father's plane ticket. It hadn't meant anything but now he recalled Big Jack telling him that he'd had to get a new cell phone.

4-11-1990.

He felt the weight of his father's phone in his pocket at the same time he felt a chill move through him. Slowly, he took out the phone, telling himself it was just a coincidence. He had to be wrong. He turned on the phone, and when he couldn't open it again, he put in 4111990.

The passcode didn't work. He let out the breath he'd been holding, relieved. He told himself that all the crazy thoughts that had been going through his head were just that: crazy.

Then he looked back down at the phone and typed in 041190.

Bingo.

His heart dropped as the passcode opened his father's phone. For a moment his heart was beating so hard that he did nothing.

But after a moment he checked his father's messages. There were numerous ones from Ruby. He scrolled down them until he found the one he was looking for. He stared at it, shock making him numb. So many secrets. So damned many secrets.

At the sound of voices outside his cabin, he stepped to the window and saw Will and Huck. Both were wearing side-arms as they started past.

Will and Huck were headed down to Kirk's cabin when Lamar came out of his.

"I don't know what's going on, but I want to help," he said as he quickly pulled on his boots and grabbed his coat.

Will didn't argue. Right now he'd take all the help he could get. He had no idea what kind of fight Kirk might put up. Nor did he know if the man would be armed. As they reached cabin number six, Will motioned for Huck and Lamar to hang back. He stepped to the side of the door to knock. He knocked again louder.

Earlier, he'd been convinced that Kirk wouldn't make a run for it—not after he'd already tried it once and failed. But if he thought he'd been seen—

The curtain moved.

"Kirk, it's Will. Open up." He waited, still standing to the side of the door in case the man did have a weapon.

The door slowly opened. Kirk looked from Will to Lamar and Huck. "What's going on?"

Will could see that the man wasn't armed. He pushed into the cabin, driving Kirk back. The others rushed in, as well.

Kirk stepped back as they all entered and went on the defensive. "Hey, what's this about? You can't just come busting in here like—"

"I saw you running from the side of the barn," Will said.

Kirk's expression changed in an instant from belligerent to conciliatory. "I didn't do it. I swear to you." He held up his hands in surrender.

"What were you doing by the barn?" Will demanded.

"I was headed down to the lodge. I heard noises and I was getting spooked. I just had this feeling..." He shook his head. "As I neared the lodge, I saw someone with a crowbar breaking into the barn."

"Someone?" Lamar said. It was the first time he'd spoken.

"*Someone*. I couldn't tell. Whoever it was they were wearing an On the Fly coat and hat. They slipped inside and I went to see what was going on."

"You didn't think to come up to the lodge and tell me?" Will asked.

Kirk shook his head, looking embarrassed. "I wanted to be the one to catch the killer." He instantly turned belligerent again. "Hey, there is nothing wrong with wanting to be the hero for a change, all right?"

"So you went after the person," Will prodded.

"By the time I reached the barn and looked inside, I couldn't see anyone. It was creepy. I knew Big Jack was still in there." He shuddered. "I could hear someone moving around so I decided to wait them out, but then I got cold."

Lamar groaned. Will didn't blame him. "Then what?"

"I decided to come tell you what I'd seen. But as I started to walk away there was an explosion. The next thing I knew the barn was on fire, so I ran."

"You didn't see the person who you saw go in come out?" Will asked.

Kirk shook his head. "They must have gone out another way." He shrugged. "So I hightailed it back to my cabin thinking that if anyone saw me they would think…" He looked at Will and then the others. "I swear it's the truth."

Lamar grabbed the sleeve of Kirk's coat by the door and took a whiff. "Your coat smells like a gas fire."

"I told you I was right next to the barn when it went up," Kirk cried.

Will looked to Lamar and then Huck. He wasn't sure he believed the man's story. He could see that his companions weren't buying it, either.

He turned back to Kirk. "We're going to have to lock you in your cabin and keep you here until the sheriff arrives." Kirk started to argue. "I'll make sure you're fed, but other than that, you'll have no contact with the others."

"Are you kidding me?" the man demanded. "You leave me down here in this cabin and I'll be a sitting duck. The killer will get me."

"The killer would have to break in to get you," Will pointed out.

"Like the way the killer broke into the barn and set it on fire," Kirk argued.

Will turned to Huck. "Make sure both doors are barred and he can't get out the windows."

Kirk slumped down on the end of the bed. "You're making a terrible mistake."

"I hope not. But you made a terrible mistake when you decided to play hero rather than come to me when you saw someone break into the barn," Will said. "Now we're both paying for it."

With that he and Lamar left and headed back toward the lodge.

Poppy felt as if she was going stir-crazy. She had a case of cabin fever but the idea of going outside had no appeal—even if Will hadn't told her and Dorothea to stay put. He'd strapped on his gun before he and Huck had left the second time. He'd told them nothing, but it was clear they had a suspect in mind.

Dorothea sat staring outside as if waiting for the evil they all feared to come roaring in looking like something from a horror movie. Poppy suspected that the killer would have a face like anyone else. That's what made it so hard to tell the good guys from the bad.

Unable to sit still any longer, she thought of the basket of alibis Will had put in his office. At the time, she'd wondered why Will had bothered to collect them. The killer wasn't going to admit anything. Everyone else might lie, as well. But she guessed that at least the sheriff would have somewhere to start when—and if—he finally got there. He could check what they'd originally said against what they were telling him later to see if there were any discrepancies.

She began sorting through the basket. There'd been two murders so there were two sets of alibis for each guest. It didn't take long to form the two stacks, reading them as she went. Lexi, she saw, hadn't done one after Big Jack's murder. Almost all of them said that the person was in his or her cabin alone.

She was almost finished when she noticed an extra piece of paper at the bottom of the basket.

One side of it was torn unevenly as if someone had ripped off a piece from their notepaper. The letters were almost illegible as if scrawled in a hurry—or scrawled so their handwriting wouldn't be recognized.

As she reached for it, she caught only a glimpse of what was written on the scrap before she was startled to hear Will ringing the bell out front.

She hurriedly put the other alibis back into the basket on top of the extra one as the front door opened and Will and Lamar came in on a gust of snow and wind.

The only words she'd seen on the scrap of paper were the words *two killers*.

CHAPTER TWENTY-TWO

"You all know the drill," Will said once everyone was gathered in the lodge and he'd told them that Kirk had been seen near the barn and he was now in protective custody, locked in his cabin.

Outside, the wind whipped snow past the windows. Beyond the snow piling up, the sky had darkened as the sun set. "Write down where you were and if you saw anything suspicious," Will continued.

"What's the point?" Allison demanded. "You caught Kirk. You already know who did it."

"We're holding him until the sheriff can get here because he was in the area when the barn was set on fire," Will said. "But we have no proof that he did it."

"No proof?" she cried. "The rest of us were in our cabins."

"Not according to Kirk. He swears that he saw one of you with a crowbar breaking into the side door of the barn."

"So it's his word against ours?" Channing said with a sigh. "And his word is so *trustworthy*."

"He's been lying since we got here," Mick said.

"Lying about what?" Lamar demanded of his brother, but Mick only shook his head. "If you know something—"

"Please," Will interrupted. "Just fill out the paperwork." A few of them started to comply, the others dragging their feet. He wanted to lock them all up.

With no way to put out either of the fires, all he'd been able to do was watch the structures burn—with the bodies inside. He felt helpless and that made him angry. Someone had killed two of his guests and was now systematically destroying the ranch his grandfather had built. He wasn't just angry. He was also scared for the people trapped here.

He'd rung the dinner bell to get everyone together, hoping there wouldn't be anyone missing—and that someone hadn't gotten caught inside one of the burning buildings. But apparently everyone had survived since the only person missing was Kirk.

They had another twenty-four hours to live through before there was much chance of getting word out to the sheriff. He hated to think what could happen in all that time.

"Once you're finished, Poppy made beef stew and rolls for dinner. There is leftover coconut custard pie for anyone who wants it. You can take it back to your cabins and heat it in your microwaves or eat it here. Your choice. But then everyone is on lockdown. You aren't to leave your cabins until morning when you hear the breakfast bell."

"Do you really think you can enforce that?" Dean asked with a nervous laugh. "What's to keep us from being murdered in our sleep?"

"If your door is locked—"

"Like Lexi's cabin was?" Channing asked with a snicker. "Let's face it. If one of these people wants to kill you, Dean, nothing is going to stop him." She shifted her gaze to Allison, then Ruby. "Or her."

"That's enough, Channing. You, too, Dean," Lamar said.

"Will is trying to keep us all safe under horrendous circum-stances. A little cooperation would be appreciated."

"This wasn't our idea to come up here," Allison cried. "We were forced to make this trip and look how it's turning out."

"Yes," Lamar agreed. "It was my father's idea and I believe he's paid the price for it, wouldn't you agree?"

The room went silent.

Will broke the silence. "We're all upset. All we can do is wait out the storm. I know it's hard. It's hard on all of us."

"No one is trying to kill *you*," Allison snapped.

"No, they're just burning down parts of my ranch to cover up any evidence they might have left behind," Will said. The room fell silent again for a long moment. "If you've all written down where you were before the barn exploded and Lexi's cabin after it, and signed and dated it and put your informa-tion in the basket, then Poppy has the food boxed up for each of you. Like I said, stay in your cabins tonight until you hear me ring the breakfast bell in the morning."

They all left except for Lamar. He waited until everyone was gone before he said, "I'm so sorry about your ranch. I can't tell you how much I regret my father bringing us all here. I don't know what he was thinking."

Will could see how all this had taken a toll on the man. He'd lost his father and one of his employees and he blamed himself for not seeing it coming. "You can't blame yourself. I'm sure your father had no idea it could get this dangerous."

Lamar shook his head. "My father was a gambler, but I know you're right. He thought he was dealing with a thief, a drug runner. He couldn't have known the person would kill. Not that I blame him. I know these people. I don't want to believe it is any of them. You really think it's Kirk?"

Will no longer knew what to think. "I have my doubts. But I feel better with him under lock and key because if he isn't responsible, then the killer might be afraid Kirk can identify him or her."

"So Kirk really could be in danger himself."

"We're all in danger at this point," Will said. "Hopefully we can keep everyone alive for the next twenty-four hours. Usually after the storm moves on, the phones are back up working within hours. Crews will be plowing the roads to get them open…"

"I can't help wondering why I didn't see any of this," Lamar said with a shake of the head. "These are my employees. You'd think I would know which one is capable of murder. This trip has certainly opened my eyes to a lot of things."

"Just be careful," Will said. "If the killer thinks you might be getting close, that you've figured it out…"

Lamar nodded. "That thought did cross my mind, thanks. I'm watching my back." He looked toward the windows and the storm. Was he worried that the killer might be waiting for him between the lodge and his cabin? "I should get to my cabin." The man turned to where there were three boxed-up meals waiting, one for him and two for Slim and Huck.

"I'll take these to the wranglers on my way," he said as he picked them up. "Unless you'd rather do it." He looked back at Will.

"Thanks," he said as Lamar left.

In the silence that followed, Dorothea huffed as she got to her feet. "He's awfully smooth-talking and accommodating, don't you think? What makes you think Lamar isn't our killer?"

Poppy wasn't hungry but she knew they had to eat. They filed into the dining room, sitting at one end of a long table. She served the stew as Dorothea continued her train of thought, ticking off the suspects one by one and offering her take on each.

She shot a look at Will. Was he wishing they could go up-stairs and finish what they'd started? She tried to concentrate on what Dorothea was saying, realizing that Will seemed al-most happy for the distraction. Was he having second thoughts about what had happened between them before the explo-sion? That thought made her heart ache.

Dorothea had her own unique view of the world, one that went against all common sense, she realized as she tried to focus on what was being said.

"First there's Big Jack," Dorothea was saying. "You think he's not a suspect because he's dead, right?" She laughed. "He set this whole thing up. I would put him at the top of my list.

"Then there's his girlfriend, Ruby." She sniffed in distaste. "I wouldn't trust her as far as I can throw her. Says she's a graphic designer." Dorothea shook her head. "But have you seen her handwriting?" She glanced at Will. "Don't give me that look. I glanced over her shoulder when she was writing her supposed alibi. The woman is a fraud. Mark my words."

Will shook his head. "Your take on people is always…il-luminating."

"Dean," she continued as if he hadn't spoken. "He's scared of his shadow. An average guy working in the stockroom of a fly-fishing shop. Looks harmless. Made me feel sorry for him. But there is something odd about him. He said he doesn't fish."

Poppy helped herself to a roll. Will joined her and Doro-thea moved her recitation to in front of the fire.

"And that is relevant how?" Will asked after they were settled again. His gaze went to Poppy and lingered just long enough to warm her cheeks.

"Strange he got a job working at a company that makes fly-fishing vests," Dorothea said and moved on. "Now take Lexi. There was an odd one. And another one afraid of her shadow. She was scared from the moment she got here, so clearly she knew before Big Jack was killed that something was going to happen. She's at the top of my suspect list since she was the one who said she found Big Jack murdered. A meek woman like her wandering around in the dark of the night following her boss? I don't think so."

Dorothea took a breath before continuing. "Then there is—"

"Wait a minute," Will said. "You think Lexi killed Big Jack?"

"Why not?" Dorothea shrugged. "She was capable. Dean told me that he'd seen her lift the huge industrial sewing machines that they use with one arm. She was strong enough to bludgeon someone to death. Also Big Jack was the kind of man who wouldn't hesitate to turn his back on a woman."

Poppy thought she made a good point and said as much. It only seemed to encourage Dorothea, which hadn't been her intent.

"So who does that leave? Channing. Now there's a snide, cunning one. She likes to stir the pot, keep everyone at odds. Is she just unhappy? Or is there more to her brand of meanness?

"Then there is Allison. Uses her sweet, baby-doll looks to get what she wants, plays Mick against Kirk and vice versa. Don't believe for a minute that she's innocent in any way. Which brings me to Kirk."

Will cut the coconut custard pie, handing a piece to each of them. Dorothea took hers as if he hadn't interrupted her strange train of thought.

"Kirk. He's another one who has gotten by on his looks. He's not so easy to figure out." The woman frowned. "He wants to please, wants to be liked, wants everyone to think he's cool. He's needy and, at least on this retreat, he hasn't succeeded in getting any of the recognition he yearns for. A man like that...he must be very frustrated and desperate. I would definitely keep him at the top of my suspect list. Needy men like that often don't get along with their bosses—or anyone else for that matter. I think there is deep-seated anger in him. Especially since Dean told me that it wasn't an injury that keeps Kirk off the slopes. He chickened out. That's how he crashed and hurt himself. Dean thinks he's afraid and it torments him."

"Interesting," Poppy said, since she'd heard Kirk actually admit to some of that. "Sounds like Dean was a wealth of information, but what if he was just telling you these things to draw your attention away from him as the killer?"

Dorothea gave her a look that said she was far too smart for that and continued. "Then there is Mick, the youngest son living in both his father's and his older brother's shadows. Another unhappy man who isn't living up to his abilities and doesn't really care. But don't think that he's not ambitious, he is. But he just wants the money. He'd sell the business in a heartbeat and become a beach bum if he got the chance. Big Jack was standing in his way."

"Mick?" Will said. "You think Mick killed his father to get rid of him so he could have the business? That still leaves Lamar in his way."

With the arch of an eyebrow, Dorothea said, "This retreat is far from over."

Poppy felt a shudder at her words. Was it possible Lamar was in danger from his cabinmate? If his brother really had killed their father...

"Which leaves Lamar, the smooth talker," Dorothea continued. "The one everyone trusts. But should they? Wouldn't the man running the business know what was going on better than anyone else? And clearly he wasn't getting along with his father. Now there is no one standing in his way."

"So your theory is that he killed Big Jack so he could take

over the company?" Will said. "Where does Lexi fit into this theory?"

"The shy, timid, nonthreatening woman?" Dorothea asked with a smile. "She was like the wallpaper that no one noticed. Because of that I'll bet she knew all of their secrets and once someone realized that…"

"Interesting, your take on the guests," Poppy said. Will agreed.

She noticed that he seemed subdued. Was he sorry about what had almost happened in his apartment earlier? Maybe he was like her. He'd had time to realize what was at risk if it went any further. But it was a risk that Poppy feared she was willing to take.

For a few moments, all that could be heard was the wind in the eaves outside and the soft popping of the logs in the fireplace. Poppy thought about the scrawled words on the scrap of paper she'd seen in the basket on the coffee table. She told herself that maybe she should mention it to Will, but didn't want to in front of Dorothea.

"Thank you, Dorothea. That was wonderfully enlightening," Will said, getting to his feet. He glanced at Poppy, but quickly looked away. "I have some things I need to take care of. I have Huck and Slim patrolling the area. I'm going to be relieving them during the night. In the meantime, if either of you need me, ring the bell."

With that he grabbed his coat and left on a gust of cold wind and snow that blew across the floor.

"I need to do some prep work for breakfast," Poppy said, standing, as well. Dorothea had been watching the two of them closely, she realized with a silent groan. Poppy was in no mood for more recriminations from the woman.

But all she got from Dorothea seemed to be a sympathetic look as if the woman had seen how cool Will had been with Poppy. Did she think Will had dodged a bullet?

Going into the kitchen, Poppy was surprised to realize that she was in no mood to cook. She'd always turned to cooking when she was upset. But who wouldn't be upset? There'd been two murders. The barn and one of the cabins had been torched. And they still had twenty-four hours at least before help would arrive.

But she knew that what had her despondent was Will and the feeling that the connection between them had been cut. They'd come so close to making love. If the barn hadn't exploded they would have been curled up in his bed upstairs.

Instead, he was out patrolling the ranch while she was standing in the kitchen feeling like crying. She felt off balance and her heart was aching. All she'd done was make things worse. She'd thought that coming here, tempting Will and seducing him to give him some of his own medicine would let her finally forget him. Instead, she was standing in the ranch kitchen, knowing there was nothing she could cook that would make her feel better and feeling foolishly close to tears.

"You only have yourself to blame," Dorothea said as she came into the kitchen.

Poppy groaned inwardly. True as her words were, she couldn't bear this right now. "Dorothea—"

"Let me guess. You got caught in your own spell." Surprisingly, the woman didn't sound that happy about it. "You ended up falling in love with him all over again, didn't you?"

CHAPTER TWENTY-THREE

Poppy woke with a start after a restless night. Most of the night she'd listened for the sound of Will's boot heels out in the hall. But she had finally fallen asleep, her heart aching.

Now she listened, not sure what she might have heard that had awakened her. Not Will. That was just it. She heard nothing. No wind ripping at the eaves. No storm howling late into the night. No icy snowflakes tapping at the window.

She threw back the covers and moved to the window. The storm had stopped as quickly as it had begun. The sun had come out as the blizzard passed, turning the fallen snow into a blanket of crystals. She stared out at it, awestruck. The wind and snow had turned the landscape into a sculpture that was both blinding and beautiful. It was so pure and white that it was hard to believe it could be so deadly.

Help would be coming. The landline could already be working. She felt a wave of relief, followed quickly by a sharp pain of sadness. It was over. The plows would be out opening the roads. Will would be able to contact the sheriff. Soon the sun would begin melting the snow and the freezing water would run like a raging river along ditches and creeks. Flooding would be the next big problem, but by then she would be back in Whitefish getting ready for the upcoming luncheon on her schedule.

That world seemed a faint memory. So much had happened. She no longer felt like that Poppy Carmichael and wondered if she ever would again.

That deep well of sadness also filled her with concern. Everyone would be questioned, but there would be little that the sheriff could do. As hard as Will had tried to contain the crime scenes, the killer had destroyed both. No one had thought the person would go to that extreme.

Once they were all questioned, everyone would be free to leave. The sheriff couldn't keep them here without evidence against them, could he? And any evidence had been destroyed. The killer had seen to that.

Life would go back to the way it was just a few short days ago. She thought about Will and felt sick at heart. She'd come here for retribution and instead she was the one who'd gotten caught in her own deceitful web, just as Dorothea had said.

"That's what you get," she told herself as she headed for the shower. For now, she still had a job. Everyone would still need to be fed while they waited for the sheriff. After showering, she was getting dressed when she heard the sound of Will's boots in the hallway. She froze as she heard him slow. He was just outside her door.

Poppy waited for him to knock, willing it to happen. But after a moment, he continued on down the hall until she could no longer hear him. Her heart dropped. She'd wanted desperately for him to knock on her door.

She stood for a moment listening, hoping he'd come back. When he didn't, she feared there had been more trouble. Will had lost more than a barn and one of the cabins. Worse, two people had died violent deaths here at the guest ranch. Her heart went out to him. She could walk away, but he would be living here with the memory.

But *could* she walk away? Heartbroken again? She let out a bitter laugh. This time she wasn't twelve. And this time she only had herself to blame. Will had warned her, but she hadn't listened. She told herself that she was lucky they hadn't ended up in that big log bed of his. But that was a lie.

Downstairs, she realized that she was alone. She spotted the basket just inside the office's open doorway and frowned. With everything that had happened, she'd forgotten about the extra note she'd found at the bottom. Moving to the basket, she quickly dug through. Not finding it the first time, she took out all the notes and went through them only to realize the scrap of paper that warned there were two killers was gone.

Lamar woke to find his brother's bedroom empty. He swore as he got up to look out the window. To his shock, the storm had quit. He looked down at the porch and the steps and saw his brother's tracks partially filled with snow. So Mick had left last night, no doubt after Lamar had dozed off.

"I need to know what's going on with you, Mick," he'd pressed when they'd returned to their cabin after the meeting at the lodge yesterday evening.

His brother hadn't been hungry, but he was definitely morose as he'd collapsed on the bed. "Nothing's going on. Cut me some slack. My father just died."

"Died? He was murdered."

"Your point?"

Lamar didn't believe that was all that was bothering his brother. "What is going on with you and Allison and don't tell me nothing."

Mick had shaken his head. "Maybe I'm interested in her. Maybe it's more than that."

"What does that mean?"

His brother had sat up angrily. "What if I was in love with her and your stupid no-dating employee rule was ruining my life?"

Lamar had been tempted to point out that the rule had been established by their father. But Lamar had enforced it after their father had spent less and less time at the company. "If you really love her…"

"Why do you say it like that?" Mick had demanded. "Do you think I'm incapable of loving someone? You think I'm the one who was most like Dad." He'd let out a huff of a laugh. "You're exactly like him. You just don't have as much fun as Dad always did. When was the last time you even had a date?"

He'd said nothing, knowing that if he let his brother goad him into it, he'd set his brother straight on a lot of things, especially Allison Landon. "I'm just worried about you."

"Well, stop, because I'm not a kid anymore," Mick had said. "I can take care of myself, big brother. Butt out." He had lain back down in his bedroom to stare up at the ceiling. "Anyway, Allison was just stringing me along. She's a tease, comes on hot, turns ice cold and pushes you away." He'd seen the anger in his brother's expression. "I love her but I hate her, something I doubt you could ever understand."

"You might be surprised." He'd thought of his father and pushed that thought away. As for Allison… He couldn't help thinking about the other night in the barn and what Allison had told him. If true to her word, she would be leaving town as soon as they returned. He thought it was the best thing, especially for his brother, but like a lot of things, he would keep that to himself.

"What do you think about Ruby?" Mick had asked.

The question took Lamar by surprise. "She seems to be good enough at her job, why?"

"Just curious." With that his brother had rolled over and, closing his eyes, went to sleep.

Or at least Lamar had thought he'd gone to sleep. So where was Mick?

He raked a hand through his hair and caught his reflection in the mirror on the wall. It seemed to mock him. Why hadn't he told his brother about what he'd discovered, the confirmation on his father's phone that there was a lot more going on at this retreat than any of them had suspected?

Will came in from outside to find Poppy doing what she did so well, cooking in the guest ranch's large sunny kitchen. She had the radio on and must not have heard him approach. He took advantage of that to watch her unnoticed for a few moments. Last night during his watch over the ranch, he'd had plenty of time to think about everything, but especially what had almost happened yesterday in his apartment.

Just the thought made him ache. He'd promised himself that he would keep her at arm's length, because he couldn't trust himself not to hurt her again. He'd warned Poppy. He knew how he was with women. A few dates and he got bored. It's why he really had thought he was a confirmed bachelor. No woman had ever made him want to make that walk down the aisle.

But then he'd never met the now-all-grown-up Poppy Carmichael. She made him crazy. That's why he'd backed off after what had almost happened yesterday. He didn't know how to deal with his feelings. If he had made love to her…

With a curse, he realized he'd done the one thing he'd promised himself he wouldn't. He'd hurt her again. He'd seen it in her expression. He wanted to rip out his heart at the pain he'd seen in her eyes last night when he'd turned away from her.

He'd told himself there was no other way. Had he gone to

her last night after his patrol shift, if he'd kissed her again, nothing could have stopped him from making love to her. And once that happened...

She turned as if sensing him and started to smile, but then sobered. "What's wrong?"

"We need to talk." He'd barely gotten the words out when the landline rang. They both started at the sound. He turned and rushed to it. He'd tried it in the middle of last night and the first thing this morning, but there still hadn't been a dial tone.

Snatching up the receiver, he said, "Hello?"

The line crackled with static. "Will?"

He'd never been so glad to hear his brother Garrett's voice even though the connection was terrible. Afraid he might lose him and the line might go dead again, he said, "Call the sheriff. We've had two murders up here." He waited for Garrett to say something, but all he heard was static. "Garrett, are you there? Did you hear me?" Nothing.

After a few moments, he disconnected and tried to place a call to his brother, but he couldn't get a dial tone. With a curse of frustration, he put the receiver back in the cradle and turned to find Poppy standing behind him.

"Did Garrett get the message?" she asked hopefully.

Will shook his head. "I don't know."

"There's something I need to tell you."

He listened while she told him about the scrap of paper she found in the basket. "*Two* killers?" He shook his head. "And now the note is gone?"

"It might have been someone's idea of a joke," she said.

Will also questioned whether it meant anything at this point. "Poppy—" Dorothea came down the stairs as the timer went off on the oven. "Can we talk later?"

She nodded and turned back to breakfast. "We can eat in about fifteen minutes," she told him over her shoulder.

Will started to go out to ring the breakfast bell, but Dorothea stopped him. "I need to talk to you." He groaned. Everyone needed to talk this morning, but this was one conversation he could do without.

"Dorothea—"

"It can't wait a minute longer," she insisted and pointed toward his office.

He realized it was probably best to get it over with, anyway, and let her lead the way.

"I've never been one to offer advice..." Dorothea began the moment the door was closed behind them.

He pretended to choke on her words and remained standing, wanting this over as quickly as possible.

She ignored the gibe and continued. "But this time, I have to say something. I've watched you boys grow up. All three of you were raised like wild horses that had to be broken by your father. I know he was hard on you boys, hardest on you."

"Dorothea, are you going to dig up ancient history? Because I have to call everyone in to breakfast."

She was not deterred. "I remember only too well that year when Poppy was hanging around and you were being...fifteen and so full of yourself. That girl was crazy about you—"

"*This* is what you want to talk about? Dorothea! Where are you going with this? I was there, remember? I know."

"You don't know squat!" she snapped. "What the devil is wrong with you?"

He raked a hand through his already messy hair. "I'm not sure how to answer that or even where to begin."

"Will, you're crazy about her, she's crazy about you—"

He started to argue, but she cut him off.

"Oh, don't even bother to deny it. You think I haven't seen the way you look at her? The way she looks at you? Even when you were fifteen and she was twelve, when it was just the two of you, you were best friends. It was when some of those snooty girl guests started flitting around that you threw her over as if you were embarrassed by her."

He groaned, remembering what a heartless fool he'd been. "I can't change the past."

"What about your future? It's as clear as the nose on your face. So what is holding you back?"

"I don't want to hurt her again," he blurted out. "I promised myself I'd keep my distance and I haven't. You were right. She's definitely put a spell on me. But it's one I have to break because you know how I am with women."

Dorothea made a disgusted sound and pointed her finger in his face. "Keep telling yourself that. I've never thought of you as a coward. Maybe Poppy will break your heart and you'll just have to tough it out if that is the case. But I say she's fallen in love with you all over again and she isn't happy about it because she thinks you don't feel the same way. Now here you are crazy about her but afraid to take a chance." She shook her head. "If you let her get away, you will never forgive yourself—and neither will I. Can you look me in the face and tell me that you aren't crazy about her?"

He shook his head. He couldn't deny it and clearly she knew it. "I can't promise her marriage, a family, anything."

"Why?"

Glancing around the office as if the answer was there, he said, "Because I live in an apartment upstairs. I run a guest ranch. That was the deal I made with my brothers. I thought once my father wasn't micromanaging everything I did... But look how one first guest stay without him has gone."

"Are you serious? None of this is your fault. You think your father could have handled it any better?"

He shook his head. He didn't know. Worse, he didn't know what he wanted anymore. Since Poppy, he realized. "Now after this latest fiasco with two guests murdered? I'm not sure I can do this. I doubt either Garrett or Shade want the job, either. Which means I have no idea what will happen to the guest ranch. But you're right. I want more. Poppy has made me realize I definitely want more."

"Have you told your brothers?"

He shook his head. He hadn't even admitted it to himself until this moment.

"Well, figure it out and soon. So help me if you let that woman get away..."

He stared at her for a moment before he burst out laughing. "Wait a minute. You were the one who warned me about her. You said she was a kitchen witch and she was whipping up potions that were going to make me fall for her so she could break my heart. What makes you think that isn't exactly what she still plans to do?"

Dorothea narrowed her dark eyes at him. "Maybe that is exactly what she will do. Laugh in your face and walk away. But you'll never know if you let her leave here without tell-ing her how you feel. Mark my words, let Poppy get away and you will regret it to your dying day. Take a chance, Will Sterling. Poppy did."

She turned on her heel, threw open the door and stormed out. He stared after her, realizing he'd just admitted to himself how he felt about not just Poppy but running the guest ranch. His father had loved it and left it to his sons to continue the legacy. Will had grown up with guests coming and going. The only break they had from guests was in the winter when there were chores to do down at the valley part of the ranch.

Just the thought of walking away scared him and excited him. Just as the thought of Poppy did. Her coming here had triggered his discontent with his life more than even all the death and destruction.

But what was he going to do now? He felt as if he had the rest of his life stretched out before him with more options than he'd ever considered. Was he really ready to bail on the guest ranch after having his first and only guests and running it alone? The thought made him laugh. Who wouldn't after everything that had happened?

He wondered if this wasn't really just about Poppy and it was the thought of going back to the way it was—without her.

Fortunately, he didn't have to make the decision right now. Instead, he had guests that needed to be fed. And there was still a killer at the guest ranch. Hopefully his brother had gotten the message and the sheriff was on his way. Otherwise... they would wait it out until the phone line was up again.

As Will stepped out into the main room of the lodge, Huck came charging in. "It's Kirk. Someone broke him out. He's gone."

CHAPTER TWENTY-FOUR

Will couldn't believe what he was hearing. He'd been the last one on watch over the camp. Just before daylight, he'd come back to the lodge to get a few hours' sleep. Also he'd remembered that he hadn't put the envelope Lamar had left with him in the safe. He'd left it lying out and had been worried that someone might have taken it.

Fortunately, when he reached his room, it was right where it had been before the barn exploded. Before he and Poppy had almost made love. That thought had brought it all back in HD clarity. He'd ached with a desire that felt more than sexual.

He'd put the envelope in the safe and collapsed on his bed, too tired to even dream. And yet sleep hadn't come quickly. Instead, he'd thought about Poppy just down the hall until exhausted, he'd let sleep take him.

Will swore now. This just kept getting worse. "Anyone else missing?"

"I have no idea," Huck said. "Do you want me to start going from cabin to cabin? I could get Slim to help."

"No," he said, stepping past him and outside to ring the

dinner bell. It was time to find out what was going on. He couldn't imagine why anyone would break Kirk out—unless that person knew he was innocent. Or unless that scrap of paper Poppy had found in the basket was true. There were two people in on this. But why break him out and call attention not just to Kirk—but to themselves? Unless Kirk knew too much and they broke him out to silence him. Which meant they would be finding another body before the day was out.

He rang the bell again and then stepped back inside where it was warm to wait and see who showed up. As he did, he went through the dining room to the kitchen to let Poppy know what was going on. Dorothea was there with her. He realized he'd interrupted something, but didn't have the time to even worry about what they might have been talking about. Probably him.

He met Dorothea's I-told-you-so look across the room when he told her about someone breaking Kirk out of his cabin. Well, she'd certainly hit the nail on the head this time. This retreat was cursed. Bad luck had come in spades.

"I rang the bell to get them all up here to see who else might be missing."

Poppy looked worried. "Breakfast is almost ready. Dorothea was just about to let you know."

He nodded, hating that there felt like a wall between not only him and Poppy. Dorothea wasn't a fan of his right now, either, he could see. His fault, but that, too, was something he didn't have time to think about right now. He had to find out what was going on with his guests. While he seldom listened to Dorothea, she'd been right about one thing. He just hoped she was wrong about how much bad luck they still had coming their way.

At the sound of someone coming in the front door, he headed back into the main lounge.

★ ★ ★

As Lamar entered the lodge, he saw that Allison and Dean were already seated in front of the fire. Channing came in behind him a few moments later.

"Has anyone seen Mick?" Lamar asked and glanced around at all of them before he turned to Will. "I woke up this morning and he was gone." He saw Will exchange a look with Huck, who was standing by the door.

"Someone broke Kirk out close to daylight this morning," Will said. "If it was your brother, why would he do that?"

Lamar let out a curse. "I have no idea." He frowned. "They couldn't go far, even though it's finally quit storming."

"Where's Ruby?" Dorothea said. "Appears Mick's not the only one missing."

Will hadn't even noticed since Ruby caused the least amount of problems. "Good question," he said as he went to ring the bell again before returning.

Allison began to cry. "When are we going to get out of here?"

"Oh, turn off the waterworks," Channing groaned. "You aren't the only one going through this. Give the rest of us a break."

"The landline was working earlier," Will cut in. "My brother called. I asked him to call the sheriff, but then the line went dead again. I don't know if he got the message or not, but if he did, help is on the way."

"And if he didn't?" Dean demanded.

"My brothers will probably head this way, anyway, to check on us," Will said. "I'm sure Garrett's worried, that's why he called. So within the next few hours, help should be arriving. That's why I want you all to stay in the lodge from now until then."

"What about my brother?" Lamar asked.

"If he and Kirk took off, then they're on their own until

help arrives," Will said. "I'm sure the sheriff will organize a search party if they haven't returned by then. I don't want any one of you going looking for them. Two people missing are enough."

"Three people," Dorothea reminded him. "You don't think Ruby went with them, do you?"

"She's probably the one who broke him out," Channing said. "Not Mick."

"In case anyone is hungry," Poppy said from the edge of the dining room, "breakfast is—" Further words were lost at the sight of Ruby as she stumbled in holding a bloody towel to the side of her head.

Will raced to the woman, who was clearly unstable on her feet. He helped her over to the couch. "Get the first aid kit," he ordered Dorothea, who was already on her way, mumbling about how she was expected to be a nurse, too.

"What happened?" Will asked her as he helped her out of her wet coat and boots and Poppy brought a throw from the back of a chair to put over her. Had she fallen down? Surely someone hadn't tried to kill her, as well.

"I was attacked," Ruby said in a weak whisper.

"Did you see who did it?"

"From behind. Dark." She pulled Will down. Poppy could see the woman's lips moving but couldn't hear any better than anyone else in the room. But she did see Ruby press something into Will's hand, which he pocketed furtively. Then the woman's eyes closed.

Will left Dorothea to bandage Ruby's head as the others stood around looking pale and scared. Poppy had been standing at the edge of the lounge after getting the throw, but as Will approached her, he motioned for them to go back into the kitchen.

He looked scared and upset as he pulled what Ruby had given him from his jacket pocket and held it out.

Poppy stared in shock. "Is that what I think it is?" she asked, keeping her voice down.

"Ruby wasn't able to tell me much except that she's an agent with the DEA and…" He seemed to hesitate as he pocketed the badge again. "After she was struck, she found that her gun was gone."

As if this couldn't be more dangerous. Now, whoever had attacked Ruby had her gun. "Maybe it was Mick or Kirk and they took it and left the ranch and won't be coming back."

Will looked skeptical. She couldn't blame him. Her theory was all hope and little substance. "They can't get far. All of the vehicles are still here except for Slim's pickup, which according to Kirk is stuck somewhere down the mountain. Maybe between the two of them they can get it out—if Kirk really did get it stuck to begin with. He could have been lying about everything, just as Mick had said."

"If so, why would Mick help him?" she asked.

"It seems a lot was going on at On the Fly. Ruby's been undercover at the company."

Will stepped to the kitchen landline and tried the phone. No dial tone. "Ruby has a concussion. She needs an ambulance and we need—" Whatever he planned to say, he didn't get a chance as a disturbance broke out in the other room.

"I'm going to get the food on the table," she said. "Maybe…" But Will was already headed for the raised voices in the lounge.

"What the hell?" Lamar cried as he jumped back from Dean as a collective gasp filled the room.

"What's going on?" Will demanded as he came into the large lounge to find Dean brandishing a familiar-looking blade—clearly the one that Poppy had said disappeared from the table.

"He had the knife in his jacket pocket!" Allison cried. "He's the killer!"

"Stay back, all of you!" Dean yelled as Dorothea finished bandaging Ruby and got to her feet. She hurriedly moved away from the man.

"Settle down!" Will ordered. Everyone had moved back away from Dean and the deadly looking blade. "Give me that knife," he said more patiently.

Allison began to scream. Lamar told her to shush. "But he's the killer," she cried.

"No one was stabbed," Lamar said. "But they could be, if you don't shut up."

"Dean, you can trust me," Will said.

The man shook his head, holding the knife threateningly as he took a step to the side. "I don't trust any of you. I'm going to leave here and none of you are going to follow me."

"You're probably only going to manage to cut yourself, Dean," Channing said with obvious amusement. "I've seen the way you cut your meat at dinner." She made a sawing motion and laughed. "You're not going to slice anyone open."

Lamar shot her a disapproving look. "Not helpful, Channing."

She rolled her eyes. "Look, let him go. I don't know why you're trying to keep anyone here. The more who want to leave, the better. Anyway, the sheriff is probably on his way. If Dean doesn't want to face him, then I guess Allison is finally right about something. Dean's the killer."

Will took a step toward Dean and the knife. "You don't want to leave," he said as the man worked his way toward the front door. "Poppy made breakfast. You need to eat. You don't want to go outside. It's still cold and there is too much snow to go anywhere. The plows will be working. If you just wait—"

"Wait and *die*." Dean sounded close to tears. "Whoever is doing this is picking us off one at a time. There are only five of us left, which means one of you has to be the killer."

"Unless Kirk and Mick are the killers," Channing said, studying her fingernails as if all of this bored her. "Then you'll be going out there into the snow where they might be just waiting for you to come along. Easy pickings."

"Channing, stop it," Lamar ordered.

She looked up, her eyes narrowing in anger and fear, Will thought, as she said, "Lamar, your days of telling me what to do are over. I say let Dean go. *He pulled a knife on us.* We don't want him here."

Allison began to cry loudly. Lamar snapped at her to quit.

"I don't have to do anything you say anymore, either," Allison said through her tears. "I quit. I never want to see any of you ever again." She began to cry harder, but more quietly.

Having reached the door, Dean hesitated as he glanced outside, clearly no longer sure of what to do.

Will took a step toward him. "Give me the knife, Dean. It's part of a set. Poppy noticed it was missing. She needs the whole set to cook in our kitchen." He took another step. "Poppy, what are we having this morning?"

He could see her out of the corner of his eye standing at the edge of the dining room, watching and practically wringing her hands with worry.

Her voice broke when she first began to speak, but she quickly checked herself. "Biscuits and sausage gravy with eggs Florentine and home fries, along with a fruit salad." She sounded almost apologetic that the meal wasn't one of her usual works of art.

Will took another step. "Biscuits and gravy, Dean. Something to stick to your ribs. At least eat before you leave." He was so close he knew the man could stab him before he could move away quickly enough. "Come on, Dean. You have to eat. You're safe here with Dorothea and Poppy and me. Give me the knife." He held his hand out, willing it not to tremble.

Dean's face suddenly folded. His face contorted. He scrubbed at his eyes with his free hand. "I don't want to die."

"I don't, either," Will said.

Slowly, Dean handed over the knife. A collective sigh came up from the lounge with a few murmurings from Channing about what a chicken Dean was.

"Okay," Will said as he took the knife, feeling a little shaky. "Let's eat." He shot Poppy a look of appreciation. Her eyes were bright with tears, which she quickly blinked away and took a breath as if she'd been holding hers. She gave him a shake of her head and a small, relieved smile that seemed more full of admiration than he deserved. "Breakfast now and no arguing."

"You expect us to eat with Dean?" Allison cried.

"We just won't let him have anything more than a butter knife," Channing said and laughed. "Dean, you're so scary."

He put his head down as he took a seat, his lower lip trembling. Will couldn't help feeling sorry for him. This group was never going to cut him any slack. He could certainly see how Dean might want to get back at them all, starting with Big Jack.

They all sat down, some of them still squabbling as Dorothea and Poppy brought out the food. Will thought this must be what it would be like to have teenagers. Just the thought of having his own children sitting at this table surprised him. He'd never thought of his own children—until Poppy.

He looked down the table at her. He'd never thought of a lot of things before her. Not that she didn't still terrify him on so many levels. A woman like her needed a man worthy of her courage and strength. He wasn't sure he was that man even if he wanted to be.

Everyone ate in a wary silence. Dean kept his head down, clearly embarrassed. Channing seemed to be in her own world as usual. Allison barely touched her food. She appeared worn out, as if she had no more tears to cry. Lamar kept glancing out the window as if looking for his brother and Kirk. Partway through the meal, Will went to check on Ruby. She was fine, confused and weak from her concussion. He tried the phone again. No dial tone. He prayed that she could hang on just a little longer.

Poppy was finishing up in the kitchen when Will came in after breakfast.

"Thank you for earlier," he said, keeping his voice down.

She shook her head. "You scared me," she said. "I was afraid he would stab you."

His smile was self-deprecating. "You weren't the only one. But I couldn't let him go out there and try to leave. We would only have another body on our hands."

"How's Ruby?"

"Better. The others are resting. At least they seem to have quit squabbling. Earlier, I thought I heard a plow down in the valley."

"So maybe it won't be too long," she said.

"How are you holding up?" he asked, his gaze locking with hers.

"I'm okay. I don't want you worrying about me."

He chuckled. "Too late for that. When this is over—"

She put a finger to his lips. "Let's not go there yet."

Will took her hand before she could remove her finger from his lips and turned it to kiss her fingertips. "We're going to get out of this."

Poppy nodded as he let go of her hand. She'd felt his kiss rush from her fingertips all the way to her center. Coming here had been a mistake in so many ways, she thought as her heart ached. She met his gaze, wishing he would take her in his arms and hold her and tell her he couldn't ever let her go.

"I should get back in there," he said. "Don't want them killing each other." He grimaced at his bad joke and left.

Poppy watched the handsome cowboy leave, her heart breaking, and had to look away. Sunlight poured in through the window. She could hear dripping as snow and ice began to melt from the eaves outside. The air smelled of spring. The cold and darkness of the storm was gone. But the beautiful March day outside felt so wrong for the mood inside the lodge. So wrong for the way she and the others were feeling.

At the sound of the front door bursting open, she jumped and quickly looked to see who had come in. Her heart dropped as she saw Mick Hanson standing in the doorway. He was covered in snow—and blood.

CHAPTER TWENTY-FIVE

Cries came up from the lounge as Will and Lamar rushed to Mick. The man staggered in, looking both exhausted and injured.

"Are you badly hurt?" Will asked, and Mick shook his head. There was a gash on his cheek that was still bleeding and blood on his coat and gloves.

"Where have you been?" Lamar demanded, but Mick pushed him away to stagger toward the fire and drop to the hearth.

Will saw him glance toward Ruby.

"What happened to her?" Mick asked.

"She was attacked. Do you know anything about that?" Will asked.

Mick shook his head.

Will studied the man, afraid to ask. "Where is Kirk?"

Mick shook his head. "He's dead."

The room went deathly quiet for a moment. "Why in God's name did you break him out? Mick, what were you thinking?" Lamar cried.

Mick raised his head only a fraction of an inch to look at

his brother. "I didn't want him to go to prison for something he didn't do."

"That wasn't your decision to make," Will said. "Why is Kirk dead?"

Mick let out a soft chuckle. "Turns out I was wrong. He wasn't innocent. I knew he was a liar and a lot of other things, but… He confessed everything. Before he tried to kill me." He let out a snort. "He planned to let me take the blame for all of it." He put his head in his hands for a moment. "The bucking horses? Kirk. A rubber snake. Said he was trying to scare Lexi because he feared she was onto him."

"Why?" Will asked.

"Kirk was using On the Fly to distribute cocaine."

"What else did he confess to?" Lamar asked, sounding suspicious.

Mick took a breath, avoiding his brother's gaze, and said, "He killed Dad and Lexi," his voice breaking. "Dad had figured it out. Either Lexi told him or he just found out somehow. Lexi had been keeping track of the shipments apparently. She was gathering evidence against him."

Lamar sat down on the edge of one of the leather chairs facing the fireplace. "Someone ransacked Dad's cabin."

His brother nodded. "Kirk thought Lexi had turned her evidence over to Dad, but he couldn't find it. That's why he burned the barn and the cabin. Said he couldn't take any chances."

"Why did he tell you all of this?" Will asked.

"He wanted my help to get him out of the country. He really thought I would help him after everything he did."

"Why did he try to kill you?" Will asked.

"When he told me all that, I went for his throat." His next words came out on a sob. *"He killed my father!"* He dropped his head in his hands again and began to cry.

Lamar got up and went to him and put an arm around him,

but Mick shrugged it off and quit crying. "I just want to be left alone." He looked around the room and said, "Could I please have a drink of water?"

"I'll get it," Poppy said from the edge of the dining room.

Will saw Mick look again to the couch in front of the fireplace where Ruby lay. Had she moved? Is that what caught the man's eye? Stepping to the couch, Will squatted down next to her to check her pulse. As he did, he was surprised when her eyes opened. She tried to speak but her voice came out a whisper. He leaned closer.

Behind him, he heard Mick thank Poppy for the water. Closer, Ruby grabbed his hand and squeezed it as she whispered, "He's lying," and closed her eyes. He felt his back stiffen as he slowly got to his feet.

When Will turned, he saw that Mick was watching him closely. Lamar had moved off the hearth, giving his brother the room he seemed to need. But Poppy was still standing next to Mick after bringing the glass of water.

Will took it all in in a horrifying instant. That was all the time he had before Mick met his gaze and shot to his feet from the hearth to grab Poppy in a headlock. From his coat pocket, he pulled a gun. Ruby's gun, Will thought before terror seized him.

"Let her go, Mick!" he said in a voice that belied the terror he felt. *Not Poppy. No, please, not Poppy.* "There's no place to run. You don't want to kill any more people."

Lamar had jumped to his feet but Will signaled him and the others to stay back. "Everyone just stay calm," Will ordered.

He heard Allison begin to cry and Dean murmur, "I told you. Now we're all going to die." Dorothea hadn't said a word, but out of the corner of his eye he could see that all the color had drained from her face.

He met Poppy's gaze. Her green eyes were wide with fear, but he could see her trying to remain calm just as he was. He wanted to tell her that everything was going to be all right, but he couldn't promise that. He couldn't promise her anything.

"Just let her go," Will said, his heart pounding so hard he feared it would burst from his chest. "The sheriff is on his way. You don't want to hurt anyone else."

Mick let out a bitter laugh. "I'm in so deep now, what's one more murder or a half dozen?"

"No," Lamar said. "You couldn't have been the one to kill Dad and Lexi. It was Kirk."

His brother laughed. "Kirk was up to his neck in it. But he didn't have what it took to kill. He whined and cried and wanted to turn himself in." Mick made a disgusted sound. "I knew once the sheriff got here that Kirk would sing like a canary. That's why I busted him out. He didn't want to go. I guess he knew what was coming. That is, if it wasn't for Ruby." He glared at the couch where she lay. "I thought she was dead. I was in a hurry so I didn't check her pulse..." He was shaking his head as if it was a mistake he wasn't apt to make again. "She tell you she's DEA?" He laughed as he met Will's gaze. "Of course she did."

"Ruby is DEA?" Allison said and began to cry harder. "Why didn't she arrest you?"

"Because she couldn't be sure who Kirk was working with," Mick said with a laugh. "All of you could have been involved. It isn't like you're all so squeaky clean."

"Mick," Lamar said in a heart-wrenching wail. "How could you kill your own father?"

"That bastard? He hired Ruby," Mick said. "Don't kid yourself. He knew it was me behind the dope and he put the DEA on me?" Mick sounded close to tears again. "Why couldn't he just come to me?"

"Because he's bailed you out so many times before," Lamar said. "Maybe he was done."

"Done?" Mick laughed at that. "You can't just be done with your son, your flesh and blood. No, you have to protect them. He let me down. He tried to make excuses for it, but in the end, he deserved what he got."

"Big Jack brought us all up here suspecting that Mick and Kirk were involved in the drug business?" Channing demanded. "If that's the case, then I think Mick's right. The old man got what he deserved."

Will knew he had to defuse this and quickly before they got Poppy killed. He could hear Dean muttering to himself about how they were all going to die.

"What's your next move, Mick?" he asked, trying hard to keep his voice as neutral as possible.

"What are my chances of getting out of this?" Mick asked, smiling. "You see any reason I shouldn't kill everyone in this room?"

As Allison let out a scream and started for the door, Will kept his eye on Mick. If he moved the gun barrel away from Poppy's head, he would go for him.

But Mick only laughed as Allison and then Dean practically killed each other fighting to get out the door first. Channing seemed to be amused by all of it as if she intended to stay and see how it all ended. Lamar hadn't moved and Will didn't like the look on the older brother's face. He didn't need Lamar playing hero.

"Stay out of this, Lamar," he warned him, praying he could contain this. Otherwise... He refused to let his mind go down that path. He had to do whatever was necessary to get Poppy away from Mick.

"Let me handle this," he told Lamar, his voice breaking with the tension he felt, the fear.

"He's my brother."

"Which is why you need to let me handle it."

Mick let out a curse. "Neither one of you are going to

'handle' me, all right? Just back off or I will put a bullet into the cook's head and then where will that leave us all?" He smirked. "Okay, here's what we're going to do. Will here is going to get his keys to that big old truck out there with the plow on it."

"I'm not even sure that truck will start," Will said.

Mick scoffed. "I'll take my chances since it's my best bet to get out of here. The snow is melting. Just not enough to leave in one of the SUVs sitting out there. Then Poppy and I are going to leave and none of you are going to try to stop us."

"I'm not letting you leave with her," Will said.

"I don't think you have much of a choice. I can shoot her right now, shoot you and my brother, and take your keys and leave. Up to you."

"You'd shoot me, too," Lamar said with a disbelieving shake of his head.

"In a heartbeat. You've been a pain in my ass all my life. I'm sick of being the little brother. You run On the Fly while I work at some menial job there?"

"That's just it," Lamar snapped. "You didn't work. You never have. Since you were a kid you always wanted someone to pay your way. You always took the easy way out. I'm not surprised you were selling dope out the back door of the plant. That's you. You never gave a shit about anyone but yourself."

Mick grinned. "And you're surprised I wouldn't hesitate to shoot you?"

"Take it easy," Will said, seeing how worked up both brothers were getting while there was a gun to Poppy's head. "I'll get the keys to the truck but take me instead of Poppy."

Poppy said, "No," and for the first time looked as if she might cry.

"I know the best way out of here," Will said. "I'm your best bet since I also know the truck."

Mick studied him for a moment. "Talked me into it. Get the keys."

Will started toward the office, but turned back to look at Lamar. "Can I trust you to keep your cool? You don't want Poppy's death on your hands."

Lamar's jaw muscle jumped but he nodded.

In his office, he quickly opened the safe with trembling fingers and took out the keys for his truck. He'd put them there because he'd been worried that another one of the guests would pull the same stunt that Kirk had.

As he stepped back out, he hoped Mick was good to his word and would let him drive them out of here. He held up the keys as he approached the man. "I'll take you off the mountain, give you the truck, but now you let Poppy go."

"Well," Mick said. "That's the thing. I'll let you drive, but Poppy's going with us. She's just a better insurance policy than you are."

"That wasn't the deal."

"That's because you aren't the one making the deals," Mick said.

"Don't do this." Lamar took a step toward his brother. "You need help. I will see that you get it and the best lawyer that money can buy."

Mick laughed. "My big brother." His expression darkened. "I'm leaving with Poppy and Will. If you try anything, I'll shoot her, then Will, then you. You can't save me any more than you can save them. So sit down and stay here until I'm gone and then I don't give a damn what you do." He began edging Poppy toward the door. "Will, you lead the way, and remember, anyone tries to stop me, she dies."

Poppy tried to breathe, but it was hard with a gun barrel pressed to her temple and Mick's arm tight around her neck. He'd grabbed her so quickly that she hadn't had a chance to move or scream or even think. Suddenly, he was threatening to kill her and she now knew that he'd already killed two people so his threat was real.

She'd looked at Will, seen the terror in his eyes and heard him tell everyone to remain calm. She was trying, but everything Mick had said only terrified her more. The man had killed his own father. He wouldn't hesitate to kill again—anyone who tried to stop him. And now Will was risking his life for her.

As they walked through the heavy snow, she could see how quickly it was melting. Rivers of water ran down the mountainside. With the sun working on it and the day warm, it wouldn't be long before the snow and the storm were nothing but a memory.

If she should live that long.

"Open the door," Mick ordered as they reached the passenger's side of the old truck with the plow on it.

She pulled the door open. It groaned in protest. Mick pushed her up and inside, the gun on her the whole time. He climbed in, put his arm around her and the barrel against her temple again. The inside of the truck smelled like a lot of old trucks, a combination of dust and age, oil and grease. The old brown leather on the cover was cracked and ripped in places. Will opened the driver's-side door and got in. He put the key in the ignition.

It took a few tries to get the engine running before he dropped the plow and gave the truck gas. She'd noticed that the tires on the rig were worn as they'd approached it. What would happen if they got stuck down the road? Would Mick just kill them both and take off on foot?

Poppy didn't want to die, but worse was the thought of Will dying. She was angry with him for putting himself in this position, but as he started to drive the truck down the road away from the guest ranch, she realized that Mick had needed him all along. She and Will were both part of his plan to escape.

"What was the real story between you and Allison?" Will asked as he drove.

Mick seemed surprised by the question. "I thought I was in love with her. Now I wish I'd shot her before she could get out the door." He sighed. "But at the time it was enough that she thought I was going to."

Poppy couldn't believe what a cold-blooded killer the man was. She remembered what Lamar said about him being spoiled. Apparently Mick got what he wanted or else. It was as if he'd been born without a heart.

"She kept playing me," Mick said almost to himself as he took his arm from around Poppy to rub a spot on his side. "I don't know what her story is, but she's lucky I didn't just take her."

"You mean rape her?" Poppy said, only to have the man grab her roughly and pull her against him again. The effort, though, made him groan as she pressed against his left side and he loosened his hold a little.

"It's not rape when she's been asking for it for months," Mick spat.

The truck lumbered slowly down the road, the V-shaped plow cutting through the heavy wet snow noisily. Poppy thought she'd couldn't despise the man more when he'd confessed to killing his father and Lexi, but she realized she'd been wrong. She cringed at his touch, wanting more than anything to get away from him. He smelled of blood and sweat and a foul darkness that seemed to ooze from his pores.

She turned her mind to how to escape. As she'd climbed into the truck, she'd seen a large wrench sticking partway out from under the seat, along with what appeared to be part of a jack. Both could be lethal weapons—if she had the chance to get her hands on either.

Will appeared intent on his driving, but she could see the tension in his face. His jaw muscle worked and when she furtively placed her hand on his thigh he glanced over at her. Their gazes locked for a moment and she felt a jolt as a signal passed between them. They would do whatever they had to do to get out of this.

Dorothea let out the breath she'd been holding. Like the others, she'd been afraid Mick would decide to turn the gun on all of them. He'd sounded crazy enough.

She rushed to the window in time to see Will, Poppy and Mick get into the old plow truck. What she didn't know was what to do.

Turning back to the room, she saw that Lamar was bent over in his chair as if in terrible pain. She imagined he was, given what he'd just learned.

Channing got up and walked toward the kitchen. "I suppose this means we're on our own for food," she said as she wandered into the kitchen. Dorothea heard her open the refrigerator and dig around. She wanted to tear the woman's hair out. Channing had been difficult since the beginning of this outing. But she told herself that maybe this was the way the woman handled trauma.

Lamar slowly sat up, pushed himself to his feet and headed for the door. He had a strange look on his face, like a man who had nothing to lose. Dorothea could see that the old plow truck was still in view.

"Don't go out there and risk their lives trying to play hero," she ordered. "Will knows what he's doing." She hoped Will did. She thought of Poppy with a gun to her head. Not exactly what the young woman had had in mind when she agreed to come up here and cook. No, Poppy came looking for retribution and got so much more than she'd bargained for. "I mean it, Lamar. You will only make matters worse."

He spun around to glare at her. "What do you suggest we do, then?"

"The only thing we can. Wait for help to arrive."

He scoffed at that. "We have no way of letting anyone know that we need help even if it could get to us. You saw that old truck. What are the chances Will can get through to the plowed roads in the valley?"

She had no idea. If Will got the truck stuck and couldn't go any farther... Well, then he would be of no use to Mick. And Poppy wouldn't, either.

Will was like a son to her...and Poppy... She guessed she'd fallen for her the same way Will had. The young woman *could* cook. She put love into each dish. She cared. Maybe that's why Dorothea had found herself liking the woman. Also she'd seen that Poppy was good for Will. She was strong and capable, just the kind of woman who would give Will a run for his money. They belonged together.

She swallowed the lump in her throat at their prospects right now.

Lamar sat down again and buried his face in his hands. "He's my *brother.*"

Channing came out of the kitchen after making herself a sandwich. The woman was on Dorothea's last nerve.

"Nice of you to offer to make everyone else one while you were at it," she snapped at Channing.

"You seem to think I'm happy about being here in this hell," Channing said. "I grew up in foster homes. I could write the book on dysfunctional families. I learned to make the best of a bad situation and keep my head down a long time ago." She plopped down in a chair and took a big bite out of her sandwich as she glared at Dorothea.

"I should at least check on Allison and Dean," Lamar said, rising again and shooting a look at Channing as if anywhere was better than in a room with her. She couldn't argue the point. "I have to do *something*," he said in a pleading tone that was meant for Dorothea, as if he thought she was going to argue with him.

She could see that the plow truck was no longer in sight. "Fine. See if you can get them to come back up here. We should all stay together." Though it had little appeal. She was nervous enough without having to reassure all of them.

"Don't bring that whiny bitch Allison back up here," Channing said. "You'll ruin my appetite." Lamar shot her a withering look as he pushed out the door.

Dorothea turned to Channing. "You don't seem to be a big fan of Allison's."

Channing chewed for a moment before she swallowed and said, "What is there to be a fan of?"

"You sure that's not jealousy talking?"

Channing threw down what little was left of her sandwich on the napkin she'd been using. "What is that supposed to mean?"

"Just that I saw the two of you in several heated discussions. I got the feeling that you were fighting over a man."

"What is this? Girl talk while we wait to see who lives and who dies?"

"Why not?" Dorothea asked. "You seem pretty complacent about what's going on."

"I told you, drama is nothing new for me. You want me to cry and get hysterical like Allison?" Channing shook her head. "That's not me."

"I'm trying to figure you out."

"Really?" The young woman smiled as if enjoying the attention. "Apparently you haven't yet."

"Oh, I don't know about that. Like earlier when Mick came back, I noticed something that I'd seen before but it didn't really register until today."

"Okay, I'll bite. What?"

"When Kirk showed up with Huck. You were the only one who didn't turn to see who was coming in the door."

"Maybe I didn't care."

"It happened again today when Mick came in. Everyone else turned to see who it could be. But not you," Dorothea said.

Channing said nothing for a moment. "So what? Have you noticed me caring about anything that's been happening here?"

"It makes me wonder. Either you really couldn't care less. Or you knew both times who would be showing up. Neither time were you surprised."

"I told you, I'm not the hysterical oh-gosh type."

"Maybe that's it," Dorothea conceded, but she frowned as she recalled something else. "Also I would have sworn that I saw you passing notes to Kirk and Mick."

"Notes?" Channing laughed. "Like in grade school? Really?" She shook her head. "I think all this has gotten to you more than it has me."

Dorothea started toward the fireplace to throw on another log when the phone rang. It startled her. It startled Channing, as well. This time the young woman turned to stare at the landline.

Rushing to the phone, Dorothea said, "Hello?" All she could think about was getting help for Will and Poppy.

"This is Sheriff Sid Anderson. Everyone all right up there? Got a call from Garrett worried—"

"No, we're not all right. Will just left here in the old truck with the plow. He's with Poppy Carmichael and the man with them has a gun. His name is—"

Dorothea realized that the line had gone dead. She swore, wondering how much he'd heard. As she looked up she frowned to see Channing had gotten up from where she'd been sitting. The woman now stood holding the other end

of the phone line in her hand from where she'd just disconnected it from the wall.

"What did you do?" she cried as she stared disbelievingly
at Channing.

"Oh, come on, Dorothea. Can't you guess? You said you
had me all figured out. Isn't that what all the questions were
about? Not girl talk. Just your insatiable curiosity. Clearly you
haven't heard what happens to the cat who got too curious."

It came to her in a flash. All the pieces falling into place.
The fights with Allison, the apparent disinterest in Kirk's return as well as Mick's. The passing of notes so no one knew
about the three of them. Channing had known exactly who
would be coming through the lodge door. "You and Mick."

"Not in the way you're thinking." Channing jerked hard
on the phone line. It came loose from the heavy old landline
phone, the cord shooting in her direction. She began to reel
it in, looping it into several thicknesses as she wrapped each
end around her hands.

Dorothea saw at once what the woman planned to do. She
felt her stomach drop to her feet. She could already feel the
cord wrapped around her neck as Channing started toward
her. Dorothea looked past her, gauging if she could reach the
front door fast enough.

"I locked it while you were on the phone," Channing said.
"I already locked the back door earlier. So no one is coming
to your rescue."

From the couch, Ruby groaned and tried to get up. Dorothea could see that the DEA agent was too dizzy to stand.
Ruby lay back with a moan and closed her eyes. Dorothea
leaned on the small table that held the phone for a moment,
her mind whirling, her heart a thunder in her chest, her mouth
going dry. Channing was right. There was no place to run.
No one to help her. She was on her own—just as Will and

Poppy were. Lamar wouldn't be coming back with the others. They would all be locked in their cabins. Lucky them.

Her hands began to sweat. She reached down to wipe them on her apron and realized she'd taken it off earlier and hung it over the chair at the desk where the landline had been plugged in only moments ago.

She stayed where she was—in reach of her apron. The woman seemed surprised and slowed when Dorothea didn't try to run. Channing had the cord coiled in her hands like a garrote.

Out of the corner of her eye, Dorothea could see a piece of the dishcloth she'd wrapped the knife in sticking out of the pocket of her apron—and within reach. Relief made her weak-kneed for a moment. If she could get the knife out before—

She turned a little to hide what she was doing as she pretended to wipe her sweating palms on the apron fabric. "You made another mistake," she said, surprised her voice sounded so calm as she tried to distract the woman. Reaching into the apron pocket as carefully as she could, she burrowed into the dishcloth feeling for the handle of the knife.

Channing laughed. "Do tell."

"You think I'm a foolish old woman."

The young woman's laugh rose higher. "Crazy, but not foolish."

Dorothea felt her eyes widen in alarm as she pushed the dishcloth still in the pocket of her apron aside. The knife was gone.

CHAPTER TWENTY-SIX

Poppy felt in a daze. She kept telling herself this wasn't happening and yet she could feel the cold, hard end of the barrel pressed against her temple and Mick's arm around her so she couldn't move.

Will seemed intent on his driving as the old plow truck labored through the drifts. Snow rose in the air to wash over them in hypnotizing waves. Her mind felt dull. She couldn't imagine any way out of this. She and Will were going to die. Mick was a cold-blooded killer and now they were at his mercy.

Just the thought angered her. This was not the way she wanted to end her life. At least she'd had a few days with Will. She thought of the kisses and wished that they had made love. Now time might have run out. Even if they couldn't be together, she wanted them both to survive. But how?

It was warm with the sun coming into the cab of the truck. Which was good because Mick hadn't let her put on a coat. Which meant she stood little chance away from the truck. Is that what Mick was thinking? He'd leave them beside the road and take the truck himself at some point.

Even as she thought it, she knew not having a coat was the least of her problems. Mick wasn't going to let either of them live.

Her heart broke at the thought. She needed to tell Will how she felt. He knew she'd come up to the ranch to seduce him with her cooking to try to get back at him for when they were young. He thought she wanted to break his heart. Which had been the plan. Now she wished she'd opened her heart to him and told him how she felt after being around the adult Will Sterling. Her cowboy had turned into an honorable man. He was so brave, so in control, even now when she was panicking inside.

As she glanced over at him, she knew he would do whatever he could to protect her—even at risk to himself. That was Will Sterling, the man she loved.

Will had no idea how far they could get down the road. Or what would happen when they couldn't go any farther. But he suspected it would be bad and that's what had him worried.

He had no plan. All of this had happened too fast. But if he got the chance, he would do whatever he had to do to get the gun away from Mick. Away from Poppy's head.

His heart had been in his throat since the moment Mick grabbed her and put the gun to her head. He had tried so hard not to panic. All the things he should have said to her… Some he hadn't even admitted to himself before that moment.

He tried to concentrate not on what could be lost this day, but how to get Poppy out of this.

Earlier, he'd seen that Mick had been favoring his left side. That told him that he was injured more than he wanted any of them to know. Apparently Kirk hadn't gone down easy. No doubt at some point Kirk had realized why his partner in crime had broken him out.

Will thought he might be able to use Mick's injury to their advantage.

"You all right, Mick?"

The man laughed. "A hell of a lot better than you."

"I saw that you seemed to be in pain earlier. On your left side."

"Mind your own business," the man snapped. "I'm fine. Can't you drive any faster?"

"I'm doing the best I can."

"Maybe you should try to do better."

Poppy let out a surprised cry as Mick grabbed her harder and jabbed her with the barrel of the gun.

"Drive and shut the hell up," the man ordered.

Will heard the pain in Mick's voice. He was definitely hurt more than he wanted anyone to know. He'd seen Mick grimace when the truck bounced over some hard-packed snow on the bumpy road out of the ranch.

Out of the corner of his eye, he saw Poppy looking at him. He was pretty sure she'd gotten the message.

Will looked ahead to where the road left the pines. He could see where Huck had broken through yesterday. But now the road had filled back in. There was little chance of getting through those drifts. He knew he had to make a decision.

He glanced over at Poppy. As if feeling his gaze, she turned to look at him. "Be ready," he mouthed.

Her eyes widened in alarm but she gave an almost indiscernible nod and bit down on her lower lip.

"I'm going to have to get some speed up," Will said. "Best hang on."

He stomped on the gas. The old truck reacted slowly, but since they were headed downhill, it didn't take much for it to speed up even before the engine caught up. The roar of the motor filled the cab of the pickup. Snow poured over the hood and up onto the windshield, the wipers doing little to clear it as the truck busted through the snow.

Will glanced at Poppy and gave her a slight nod, hoping she saw what was coming.

Poppy couldn't see how they could survive this, no matter what plan Will had, but she loved him for having one. She yearned to be in his arms. If only he could hold her one more time.

She glanced over at Will. He gripped the wheel, busting through the snow, the truck engine howling. What was in his heart? She didn't know. And that hurt more than anything. She didn't want to die before she told Will how she felt about him. Even if he didn't feel the same way—

"Will, there is something I need to tell you," she said, having to raise her voice to be heard over the roar.

"This might not be the time, Poppy."

Her laugh was strangled. "This might be all the time we have. So I have to tell you how I feel about you."

"Oh, give me a break," Mick said.

"I love you. I fell for you at twelve but I didn't know you like I do now. You're a good man, a kind, caring, loving man—"

"Enough," Mick said. "I can't take this sappy crap."

The truck was barreling toward the first of the huge drifts. Will was hanging on to the wheel, fighting it as the truck was buffeted by the fallen snow. She could see that he was fighting to keep it on the road, though she couldn't imagine how he could even see where the road was.

"This is not where I wanted to say this—"

"Now shut up and drive or so help me..." Mick tapped the barrel of the gun against Poppy's temple threateningly.

Will glanced over at her. She gave a small nod of her head,

telling him she hoped that it was all right. She could tell how he felt. It was all in the way he looked at her.

Sniffing, she lifted her arms to wipe her eyes, making the man groan. But it forced Mick to loosen his hold around her neck. He sat back a little, as if sitting too close to her hurt his left side. She had noticed even before Will had made a point of mentioning it. Mick was hurt. Not badly enough that he was apt to pass out, but enough that she could feel him grimacing with each bump in the road.

Ahead she could see nothing through the snow washing over the old truck. But before they'd started down this hill she'd seen the towering snowdrifts down in the flats. She was pretty sure that when the plow on the truck hit them, they were all going to go flying. She couldn't wait any longer.

She brought her right elbow down hard into Mick's side and shoved the barrel of the gun way. The deafening report of the gun filled the cab. The driver's-side window exploded a moment before Will forced open his door, grabbed Poppy and flung them both from the truck.

"Is there a problem?" Channing asked, chuckling as she took another step toward the older woman. "Suddenly you look a little pale. Are you ill?"

Dorothea glanced at the couch where Ruby seemed to be fading in and out from her concussion. She knew she wouldn't be getting any help from the DEA agent. She also knew in a footrace Channing would win. She had youth on her side. But Dorothea had cunning, she told herself as she tried to still her racing heart. A plan had come to her, but timing would be everything. She had to let the woman believe she'd won. That strangling her with the phone cord would be easy because Dorothea was running scared now.

But where was the knife Channing had taken from the apron pocket? That's what worried her. And yet, so far all the woman had for a weapon was that phone cord that she held in both hands as she approached.

"Don't run," Channing said. "You'll waste your time and mine. The thing is, if the sheriff is calling, then he's a long way off. Anything can happen before he gets here."

Dorothea thought of Allison, Dean and Lamar. They weren't coming back to save her. No one was. Channing thought she could get away with this. She and Mick both. Maybe they could. Channing could take the keys to Poppy's SUV. The keys were probably up in her room. The woman could simply follow the road that Will had plowed to where she would find Mick waiting for her.

Channing took another step toward her. Dorothea hadn't moved from the desk. She leaned against it as if she needed it to keep her legs from giving out under her while she waited, knowing it was risky. Channing was almost to her. Another step and the woman would raise her arms to reach behind Dorothea's neck with the phone cord wrapped tightly around both of her hands. It would be so easy to choke the life of a woman twice her age.

Dorothea waited until Channing took that step, made that move, lifting her arms and quickly bringing them down, en-circling her neck. She'd had to let the woman get close enough that her plan would work. It was imperative that she time it perfectly since Channing looked strong. If the young woman overpowered her—

For a moment, Dorothea was thrown off balance. She started to stumble toward the woman as Channing began to twist the cord and shut off her airflow. The cord bit into her neck as she reached for the ancient black landline phone from the desk. The base weighed ten pounds easily. Even the receiver was heavy. She picked up both, one in each hand, and swung.

Dorothea struck Channing first in the head with the re-

ceiver, catching her off guard. All it did was stun the young
woman, but it loosened the stranglehold Channing had on
her. Dorothea hit her again, this time with the solid base of
the phone. She heard bone crunch as she slammed the phone
base into the side of the woman's head as hard as she could.
She knew she had only one chance. If she failed— The cord
was tight around her neck, cutting off her air.

As the blow struck her, Channing fell backward. Dorothea had no choice but to fall with her because of the cord
around her neck still attached to the woman's hands. But as
she did, she hit Channing again for good measure with the
phone base, then pounded her on the other side of the head
with the receiver.

By the time they hit the floor, Dorothea landing on top of
the younger woman, Channing was unconscious.

Shaking and breathing hard, she feared the woman could
come to at any moment and finish the job she'd started. Dorothea put down her weapons and hurriedly unwrapped the
cord from one of Channing's hands and then the other, pulling it off her own throat. She gasped for breath as she was
freed of the cord choking her.

For a moment she just breathed, then taking the cord, she
flipped Channing over and quickly bound the woman's hands
behind her. As she finished, Channing came to and began to
fight her, trying to get up. Dorothea reached for her apron
and, sitting on Channing's legs to hold her down, used the
apron straps to bind her ankles together.

The moment she got off the woman, Channing rolled to
her side. She was screaming, yelling obscenities and trying to
get up. Blood ran down the side of her face from where the
phone base had cut into her scalp.

That's when Dorothea saw the knife on the floor right
next to Channing. She realized that Channing had set it on

the nearest chair—within reach. Had the woman been able to get to it earlier, Dorothea knew she would be dead now.

She leaned back against the side of the chair and tried to catch her breath as she thought she heard the sound of a motor in the distance.

Poppy felt Mick grab for her as a second shot pinged off the old metal door. The next thing she knew she was drowning in snow. She didn't know which way was up. When she opened her eyes there was nothing but icy white flakes that she could see filling her mouth and her throat. Panic crowded her and she began to flail, until she realized that Will still had hold of her.

He dragged her to the surface as he fought his own way from inside the towering drift. Then he pulled the two of them into the road the plow had just opened. Poppy fought to breathe as she frantically wiped the freezing crystals from her face and sucked in the air around her. The sun was high in the sky, its warmth reassuring her that she was alive.

She looked down the road and realized she no longer heard the sound of the plow truck's engine. Fifty yards away the truck was buried in snow. But she heard something, a thumping. She realized what she was hearing was Mick trying to break out of the truck.

Will got up, took off his coat and put it on her, zipping it up to her neck before he gave her a quick kiss. "Come on," he said. "We have to go."

He pulled her to her feet and they started back up the road. They hadn't gone far when they heard the gunfire. Turning, she saw that Mick had blown out the rear window of the truck and was now firing at them as he crawled out. He was coming after them, his intent clear.

Will knew they didn't stand much chance of getting away. Not when Mick had a gun and nothing to lose. "Try to run," he told Poppy as he took her hand. They began to run as best as they could through the snow that had packed down after the blade went through.

They still had some yards between them and Mick, but not so many between them and a bullet. But Will had seen the way Mick had climbed through the back window of the truck. He was hurt worse than he had been earlier. He'd hoped when the truck stopped in one of the drifts that it would throw him against the windshield. He thought it might have. Just not hard enough to stop the man.

As long as Mick tried to catch them and didn't stop to take aim with the gun, they had a chance. Ahead there was a curve in the road. Will told himself that if they could reach that…

He felt a burning in his left calf. It took him a moment to realize what had happened. Suddenly, he was falling head-long into the snowy road, dragging Poppy down with him since he was still holding her hand.

"Will?"

"I'm shot."

"No," she cried and turned to look back at where Mick was still coming.

"It's my leg," he said through gritted teeth. "Keep going up the road. Poppy, listen to me. You need to try to get away."

She shook her head as she checked to see how bad the wound was. "Do you think you can get up?"

He gave her an impatient look that was also filled with something so close to love that she clung to it for strength. She started to help him to his feet when she said, "What is that noise?" He listened for a moment before looking down the road. Mick had stopped to look back.

"It's the sheriff's department snowcat," Will said as he let out a relieved sigh as a huge large-truck-size vehicle with tracks rather than tires roared toward Mick.

Mick stood in the middle of the road, the gun in his hand, and he watched the snowcat headed toward him. Even from a distance, Poppy could make out the sheriff's department logo on the side.

Will pulled Poppy to him, as if he saw what was about to happen. He buried her face into his chest, holding her tightly. "I love you, Poppy," he said but doubted she heard him over the clack of the snowcat. Just as he doubted she heard the report of the gun.

In the distance, Will had seen Mick pull the trigger, the barrel of the gun against his temple—just as it had been against Poppy's. Will saw Mick's head snap back an instant before he dropped dead.

CHAPTER TWENTY-SEVEN

Will had never been so glad to see his brothers as they came running from the snowcat. They wrapped both him and Poppy into blankets in the warmth of the snowcat. He knew there would be a lot of questions. Mick was dead. So was his father, Kirk Austin and Lexi Raiser.

"I wish I had some answers for you," he told the sheriff on the way back to the lodge. He held Poppy close, both of them shivering uncontrollably, no doubt more from adrenaline and shock than actual cold. The EMT with them bound Will's leg wound to staunch the bleeding until they could get him to the hospital.

But Will had insisted on the snowcat taking him to the guest ranch first. "Ruby needs medical attention." If she was still alive. "I need to be sure everyone else is all right." He was worried as hell about Dorothea and the others he'd had to leave behind at the ranch. He couldn't explain it, but he'd been fighting the feeling that, even with Mick dead, it wasn't over. Not yet.

As they came over the rise and he saw the ranch, he was finally able to breathe. Dorothea was standing outside, safe.

Lamar was there, too, along with Dean and Allison. They all looked as happy to see the sheriff's department's snowcat as he'd been.

But with a start, he realized two of the guests were missing. He knew where Ruby was. But where was Channing?

Dorothea wasn't one to cry. She prided herself on being strong. But when she'd seen Will and Poppy she'd burst out crying. She rushed to Poppy, hugging her—something else she hadn't imagined herself doing—and then reaching for Will only to realize that he'd been shot.

"Get him inside," she ordered. "I'll fetch my first aid kit."

"It's just a flesh wound," Will assured her. "And the EMT already saw to it. But I'm worried about Ruby. She's inside the lodge on the couch," he told the EMT, who grabbed his kit and hurried inside.

"You should be on your way to the hospital," Dorothea said to Will.

Garrett shook his head. "You know my brother. He insisted on coming up to check on you first and get the EMT to Ruby."

Dorothea threw her arms around Will and then, sniffing back her tears, demanded to know why they were all standing out in the cold.

"Where is Channing?" Will asked as he limped toward the lodge, Poppy at his side.

"She's tied up," Dorothea said over her shoulder. "She and Mick were in on it together. I'm lucky to be alive. The bitch tried to kill me."

Poppy stopped inside the door of the lodge to stare at Channing bound and gagged on the floor.

"I gagged her when I couldn't take any more of her lip,"

Dorothea told the sheriff, who moved to the woman to remove the gag.

"Anything you say may be used—"

Channing cut off the sheriff. "Don't waste your Miranda rights on me," she snapped. "Untie me. This woman is crazy. I didn't do anything. Clearly she doesn't know what she's talking about."

"I saw the whole thing," Ruby said from the couch where the EMT was checking the wound on her head. "Dorothea's telling the truth. Channing and Mick were working together."

Channing spewed obscenities at the DEA agent for a moment before she took a breath and said, "Where's Mick?"

"He took his own life before we could arrest him," the sheriff said.

The young woman closed her eyes for a long moment. When she opened them, all the hatred inside her seemed to glow in them. "That's what I'm going to do the first chance I get. Unless I can take out the rest of you first."

The sheriff got to his feet, motioning for the deputy. "Cuff her and read her her rights."

Poppy heard the sound of a helicopter and a few moments later it put down out front in a blizzard of snow. With Garrett's help, the EMT got ready to transport Ruby and Will to the hospital.

"Are you going to be all right?" Will asked her as he drew her aside.

Poppy nodded. "Thanks to you, I'm alive."

"Only with your help." His gaze locked with hers for a moment before the EMT said it was time to leave.

She watched Will limp toward the helicopter. The blades whirred, throwing snow into the air as it took off. She felt as if her heart had just left with it.

"I have a lot of questions," the sheriff said. "The county

highway department is getting the roads open. I'll get you all transported down to the station."

Poppy remembered the basket filled with alibis. She went into the office and brought it back out. "Will had everyone write down where they said they were after each murder. I doubt they'll be all that helpful, knowing what we do now, but I will put them in a plastic zip bag for you."

"Thanks. Some uniforms should be here shortly," he said and smiled at her.

Dorothea seemed to hesitate as she met the sheriff's gaze. "Is there anything else I can get you, Sid?"

Poppy watched, unable not to be amused. About the same age, Dorothea and the sheriff were flirting with each other. *How long has this been going on?* she wondered and then shook herself mentally.

"I should make us all something to eat and drink," Poppy said and headed for the kitchen. A moment later, Dorothea joined her.

"Are you sure you're all right?" the older woman asked.

Poppy smiled at her. "Not yet, but I will be." She bit her lip and began to take food from the refrigerator as Dorothea brought the zip bag to the sheriff. "No hurry."

Dorothea blushed and called to her, "I'll be right back."

When the woman returned, her cheeks were flushed. Under other circumstances, Poppy might have teased her.

"What will you do now?" Dorothea asked as she began to help make sandwiches for everyone.

"I'll go back to my catering business," Poppy said, trying to hide her true feelings.

"You know he loves you."

She didn't have to ask whom. "He said he was crazy about me." Not the same thing as love, but it was definitely something to hold on to when it felt as if the earth under her was crumbling.

In the meantime, she had her cooking and she was thankful for that as she shoved a pan full of brownies into the oven and furtively wiped at her tears.

CHAPTER TWENTY-EIGHT

Will was rushed directly into surgery to remove the bullet. So much for Will thinking it was just a flesh wound. That was followed by several days of rest, doctor's orders, to let the gunshot wound heal.

Poppy came by the hospital, brought him flowers and food she'd cooked. They talked about everything but the two of them. They'd been through so much. He told himself that they needed time. What happened next would affect the rest of their lives. They both had to be sure.

"Ruby is doing fine," she said. "I didn't know if you'd heard."

He had, but he was still glad to hear that she would be released soon. He was anxious to get out of here, as well. Sunshine filled his room and he could hear birds singing outside in the trees. Spring had come to the valley but there was still a lot of snow in the mountains. Now with the warmer weather, there was flooding. It always seemed to be something with weather in Montana.

"You'll rebuild the cabin and the barn?" Poppy asked.

He nodded. "When we can get in there and do the work.

It's a mess up there according to Garrett and Shade. Also it's still a crime scene. It will be a while before we can get under construction." Not soon enough to open the guest ranch for the busiest season. It would be the first summer since his grandfather had started the guest ranch that it wouldn't be open.

Lately, he'd wondered if that wasn't a blessing. And there was the fact that he still didn't know what he wanted to do with the rest of his life. He'd been so anxious to take over the running of the guest ranch, but then everything had gone so wrong.

"But once you get the barn and cabin done, it will be as good as new," she said and laughed. "Because it will be new."

He smiled at her. He knew Poppy could tell how depressed he was over all of it, so he quickly changed the subject. "How is the catering business?"

"Busy. Dorothea came to see me the other day. She's staying at the valley ranch for a while, but I suppose you already knew that. She wanted to know if I would cater a tea."

"What?" He looked surprised. "A tea? Dorothea?"

"Seems she belongs to some women's group of—"

"If it involves cauldrons and black cats…"

Poppy laughed. It was a wonderful sound and one he'd missed. "No, she's taken up knitting."

He lay back on his pillow. "Seriously? I can't imagine her knitting."

"Apparently she's really enjoying it. She wants me to make sandwiches and cookies for a real English tea."

"I wish I could see that."

"When are you getting out of here? Maybe she'll invite you. You'll need something to do while your leg finishes healing. Knitting might be—"

"Right," he said and shook his head. "I haven't given it much thought about what I'll do until we can get up to the guest ranch and begin work." He didn't want to tell her that the wound had gotten infected and he couldn't leave until they got it under control and his fever went down. "I'll be out of here soon, though. There is always regular ranch work down here in the valley. My brothers wouldn't mind the help."

Their conversation lagged and Poppy rose from the chair next to his bed and said she had to get back. "Work calls. Is there anything special I could bring you?"

"No, but thank you. I could be out of here as early as tomorrow morning."

She nodded, getting the message. "Take care of yourself."

He grabbed her hand as she started to leave. "Thank you again. For everything." As he let go and she left, he mentally kicked himself. His heart was aching and the last thing he'd wanted was to let her go—let alone push her away.

But his whole life was up in the air right now. He didn't know if and when the guest ranch would be open again. He had no idea what he was going to do. And until he did, he couldn't, wouldn't, drag Poppy into it. He'd almost gotten her killed as it was.

That thought often woke him in the middle of the night. The fear that they hadn't been saved at all. That Mick had put a bullet in Poppy's head. That something like that could happen again.

He mentioned it later when his brother Garrett stopped by.

"You do realize that what you're saying is ridiculous. What are the chances of something like that ever happening again at the guest ranch?"

"That's just it, I don't know. But it isn't a chance I want to take with other people's lives ever again."

"Are we talking about Poppy? Dorothea told me that you two fell in love."

Will groaned and deflected. "Have you ever believed anything Dorothea says?"

"In this case, why would I not believe her? Poppy's gorgeous, smart, talented, has her own business. Hell, if you aren't interested in her, maybe I'll—"

"You stay away from her!"

Garrett laughed. "The look on your face right now says it all. So what are you waiting for?"

"I don't know what I'm going to do with my life."

"Whatever you want to," his brother said. "You want to sell the guest ranch? Shade and I are fine with that. You want to join us working the cattle ranch? We could use the help. But don't make any decisions for a while. Give it some time. And some thought. Just don't let Poppy get away. A woman like that doesn't come along every day."

Like he needed Garrett to tell him that.

Poppy knew she should be delighted. Her business had taken off as spring came to Montana. She was able to hire Kara full-time as they were getting more and more requests for catered events.

Working from early morning until late in the evening day after day was a blessing. By the time she got home, she was too tired to even fix herself something to eat. She would drop into bed, yearning for the oblivion of sleep. Unfortunately, she often woke in the middle of the night screaming from the nightmares.

"You need to talk to someone," Kara had said after Poppy had confessed about the nightmares. She'd only shared because she'd messed up a batch of cookies, something that wasn't like her. "How crazy was all that up there at the guest ranch?"

"Crazy."

"People just don't bounce back from that kind of trauma. So maybe you should see someone, you know, to talk to. I'm worried about you. Maybe if you talked to a professional," her friend insisted and gave her a name of a local psychologist. "You are getting too skinny—not to mention the bags under your eyes."

She'd hugged her friend and taken the psychologist's number. "I'm strong. I'll be all right. I just need to work."

Except that she was having trouble following the simplest of recipes. After completely spacing out at a catered event—Kara had caught the mistake and saved them—she'd burst into tears and finally made the call.

A few weeks ago, she'd gone to her first appointment. She hadn't thought talking about any of it would help, but was surprised when the nightmares became less frequent and finally stopped.

Cooking helped, just as it always had, but most days her heart wasn't in it. She tried not to think about Will, telling herself that he knew where to find her. If he wanted to. She'd heard that he was at the ranch in the valley recuperating and helping his brother with calving. She hadn't seen him and thought it was probably for the best. Seeing him would only make it hurt worse.

Poppy held on to the fact that she believed him when he'd said he was crazy about her.

"Sometimes love isn't enough," she'd told Kara. As much as it broke her heart.

Sheriff Sid Anderson stopped by Will's hospital room on the day he was being released. The investigation would take weeks. He'd gotten testimony from each of the guests and had questioned Will at length.

"Channing's had a change of heart," the sheriff told him. "She's decided to help in our investigation for clemency. Not that she'll walk. She was involved up to her neck in the drug distribution and is an accomplice in the murder of Kirk Austin. There's also the attempted murder of Dorothea Brand. So she'll be going to prison but maybe not for life. With good behavior she could see freedom again in fifteen to twenty years." Sid sounded tired. "I suppose you heard I'm not running for reelection this year."

"I'm sorry to hear that," Will said, meaning it. He liked Sid and thought he was a good, fair man. "Any idea who's going to run?"

The sheriff shook his head. "Couple of my deputies are threatening to." Sid got to his feet. "You take care of yourself. You can go back to your guest ranch whenever you can get back in there. We're all done. Sorry about your buildings that burned." He shook his head. "Bad business, drugs. The fly-fishing vest business made it pretty easy for them to distribute the cocaine. Mick and Channing were in the perfect jobs. All they needed was Kirk Austin. Sounds like he wanted out. He was worried about them getting caught."

"Channing didn't know about Ruby being DEA?"

The sheriff shook his head. "They were more worried about Allison. They were worried that she was onto them and going to talk. I'd say she is lucky to be alive."

"Big Jack and Lexi Raiser weren't so lucky."

"No, Big Jack apparently confronted his son." Sid shook his head. "I guess he never thought Mick would hurt him."

"And Lexi?"

"Channing said she'd overheard something at the plant where Lexi was the head of sewing. They didn't think she would talk. But that night, she'd followed Big Jack to the barn. Apparently she'd been worried about him, no doubt suspecting he was wising up to what was happening at his company. Channing said Mick thought Lexi saw him coming out of the barn after killing his father."

Will shook his head. "So Ruby knew Mick was involved?"

"Suspected. He was the boss's son. He had the run of the place so he and Lamar were the obvious suspects," the sheriff said. "Before the retreat, Ruby hadn't known who all was involved. Obviously a lot more people were involved than she first thought. And a lot more suspected what was going on but were afraid to say anything. Lamar told me that Allison was terrified for her life and planned to quit once they returned. She told him that she suspected drugs were going out the back door but refused to say who she thought might be involved or even knew."

"So Ruby suspected Lamar, as well, at first."

The sheriff nodded. "Lamar told us that Mick came back to their cabin right before he knew Lexi had been killed and his hand was skinned up and bleeding. He also had a long scratch on his neck, but Lamar didn't believe his brother was capable of murder. He thought it was from a fight with Kirk."

Sid picked up his Stetson from where he'd put it on the way in and started toward the door. "Well, it's all over now. If Channing doesn't decide to go to trial, all of it will die down. One thing is strange, though. Channing's lawyer? Lamar footed the bill."

"That is strange," Will said. "But you're sure Lamar wasn't involved?"

The sheriff shrugged. "Got to wonder why he'd pay for her lawyer, don't you?"

Poppy and Kara put on a true English tea for Dorothea in a room the woman had rented for the event. They'd made finger sandwiches and served real English tea, along with dainty scones and tiny cakes and bite-size buttery cookies that melt in the mouth.

To Poppy's surprise, the knitters were a varied bunch from a couple of wranglers and several grandmother types to some younger women and Sheriff Sid Anderson. It was hard to keep her face straight when she'd seen him nibbling at the sandwiches and drinking out of the china teacups.

"Don't you say a word," Dorothea instructed when she'd come into the kitchen to compliment them on the job they'd done.

Poppy shook her head. "I wouldn't dream of it. But it is a little amusing to see you using my cooking to lure the sheriff."

The woman shot her a warning look, but smiled. "You taught me well."

Not well enough, Poppy thought. She hadn't gotten her man but she hoped Dorothea did. The sheriff seemed like a nice man and it was obvious that he was interested in Dorothea.

"Will's going through something right now," the woman said as if Poppy had asked. "Just give him time." With that she'd handed Poppy a check and returned to her knitting group.

"She's the one who puts spells on people?" Kara asked, watching the woman go.

"I would imagine she's put a whammy on the sheriff," Poppy said and laughed. "The man looks as if he doesn't know what's hit him."

Lamar stopped by the ranch to see Will before preparing to fly out. "I'm sorry I haven't gotten by sooner," he said. "I've been taking care of funeral arrangements and everything else."

"Please don't apologize," Will said. "I'm the one who should be apologizing to you. I'm so sorry things turned out the way they did."

The man let out a snort. "You couldn't have done anything to change it. I'm just so thankful that you and Poppy are all right. Mick made his choices." He shook his head. "I'll never understand."

Will thought that was probably true. "What will you do now?"

"I have to go back to California and the company. The DEA busted the place while we were in Montana. Mick was so stupid. He left evidence all over the place. I'm not sure I can save the business but I have to try. For my father's memory and also for the employees who need the jobs."

"How are Allison and Dean?"

Lamar laughed. "Dean says he wants nothing to do with me or On the Fly ever again. Allison might stay now that Mick is…" He looked away. "She's dealing with knowing how close she came to becoming one of his victims. It's funny, but she said he really seemed to like her. I guess he told her that he wanted to run away with her when the retreat was over. She thinks he meant it."

"What about Channing? I thought she was in on it with Mick."

Lamar looked away for a moment. "Channing was involved in the drug distribution, as she's admitted to the sheriff." He turned back to Will and swallowed. "But she wasn't romantically involved with Mick. There's something I discovered during the retreat that I didn't tell you or anyone else. The reason my parents divorced was because my father had a lover. What we didn't know was that the woman he was having the affair with had a child."

"Channing," Will said and felt goose bumps ripple over him. "She's your half sister."

Lamar nodded, not looking all that pleased about it. "I'm not sure when my father realized it. When I found the manila envelope with the employee files in it, I found his new phone. I didn't know his passcode to open it. But then I remembered seeing a number he'd written down on his airline ticket. I'd seen it when I was going through the employee files. It was Channing's birth date."

"So he knew his former lover was pregnant years ago?"

The man shrugged. "If he did, he deserted Channing's mother."

"I'm sorry."

"It's funny," Lamar said. "Mick believed that because he and Dad shared the same blood, that our father should overlook every bad thing he did. He seemed truly disbelieving that Big Jack wasn't going to let him get away with distributing drugs out of On the Fly." He sighed. "But I think I understand it. Channing is… Channing. But while she is definitely damaged much like my brother, she's the last of my blood."

"Dorothea mentioned that Channing had told her she'd had a rough life."

"Apparently her mother was an addict and Channing ended up being taken away after my father moved on. She was tossed from one foster home to the next for years. That's no excuse," Lamar added quickly. "It just is what it is."

"The sheriff says Channing could get fifteen to twenty years," Will said. "Not that long before she's out again."

Lamar nodded. "Believe me, I've thought about that. I'm not sure my being there for her now will change anything. Mick told me during the retreat that I'm more like my father than he was. I don't think he meant that as a compliment."

"She may disappoint you," Will warned.

The man nodded. "Maybe it's in Mick's and Channing's genes. Something in our blood that made them the way they are. No respect for human life. No compassion. No empathy. Or maybe they needed something along the way that they didn't get. If so, isn't it possible that Channing could change?"

Will had no answer for him. But he could see that Lamar was going to try because Channing was his half sister. He also knew what Lamar was really asking. How could two sons of the same blood be so different? Not to mention, could there be something dark in him since he shared their same genes?

"What about you?" Lamar asked. "You'll rebuild, I hope."

Will nodded.

"I don't know about you, but while I'll try to save the company, I'm not going to make it my first priority anymore," the man said. "If this has taught me anything it's that life is short. I'm going to start living more. I never want to be like my father. Or my brother. I think I need to find out who I am and then start living."

Will understood only too well. He shook the man's hand and wished him the best.

Dorothea didn't mince words when she heard that Will had talked to a real estate agent. "What's this I hear about you wanting to sell the guest ranch?"

"My brother and his big mouth. I'm just testing the waters. I want to keep my options open."

"Are you serious?" she demanded.

"If we did sell it, you don't have to worry. I would make sure that you were taken care of," Will said.

She scoffed. "I'm not worried about me, you fool. I'll be just fine. I've put away all the money I've made over the years. With room and board taken care of, I'm worth a small fortune. Don't give me that look. You think I'm lying about that?"

"I'm thinking that rich or not you always have a home on one of the Sterling ranches no matter what I decide."

Dorothea shook her head, but he could tell that she was touched by his offer. "What makes you think I won't take some of my money and maybe take a trip around the world on one of those big ships?"

He laughed. "Because you would spend the whole time thinking about me and my brothers and worrying that we might be doing something you didn't know about."

She narrowed her gaze at him. "You mean like I am right now? What are you going to do about Poppy?"

He groaned. "How can I do anything about Poppy when I don't know how I'm going to be making a living, let alone where I'll even be living?"

Dorothea was shaking her head. "Don't give me that.

Why'd you buy that forest service cabin a few miles from the guest ranch? You bought it for her."

He wanted to argue but couldn't. "I just didn't want someone to buy it and move right next door and tear down a perfectly good cabin."

She laughed. "You are the one brother who usually doesn't lie to himself."

"Look, I can't even get back up to the guest ranch until the flooding stops. If I decide to keep the guest ranch, the destroyed barn and cabin have to be rebuilt. That will take a while. I don't see how we could open this summer. Maybe it's best if we don't. Let the news about the murders die down."

Dorothea was still shaking her head. "Do you think Poppy cares about any of that?"

"Well, I do, so that's what counts."

"Men," she said under her breath. "It's all about your male ego, isn't it? Well, keep this in mind, cowboy. You blew it with her when you were fifteen because of your ego and your immaturity. Hopefully you've matured. But don't let that ego of yours keep you from the woman you love or you will—"

"Regret it the rest of my life." He grinned at her. "Did I ever tell you that I love you?"

She blushed and dipped her head to avoid his gaze. "Now you're just talking crazy."

Will knew he had to go back up to the guest ranch. For a while, he made excuses for not going. But once the roads dried out and the flooding ended, there was nothing keeping him from driving up into the mountains to the isolated guest ranch.

He remembered how stark and bleak things had looked the day he'd been flown out by helicopter on his way to the hospital. His brothers had gone back in and closed everything up while he was recuperating. He suspected they knew he wasn't up to facing the place for a while.

Just the thought of the guest ranch reminded him of all of it—the blizzard, the murders, the feeling of being helpless against an evil he couldn't understand, let alone control. It still made him break out in a sweat to think about Mick with that gun at Poppy's head. She had been so brave. He could still see the two of them when he closed his eyes. Poppy in his arms and Mick coming after them.

Just the thought of her made his heart ache. He hadn't spoken to her since that day at the hospital when he'd let her know he didn't need her to come back. He yearned to see her, but needed time. Not that he knew yet what he wanted to say. He couldn't go to her until he did.

Telling himself he couldn't think about that now, he drove up the mountain. As he came up over the hill, the guest ranch came into view. He hit his brakes to stop and stare. All he'd seen in his memory was snow everywhere and cold and the blackened burned-out shell of the barn and one of the cabins. Now the aspens interspersed with the pines had begun to leaf out. Their leaves were a bright sunny green. The grass around the cabins had also begun to turn green.

It felt like a reawakening. Something rising from the ashes taking all the ugliness away. He stared at the lodge and felt his pulse slow. He'd thought he could never face this place again. It was as if everything good about it had been taken from him. But now he saw that it wasn't true.

He shook his head, smiling. He still loved this old lodge that his grandfather had started. He loved the history. It truly was special and only Sterling's Montana. He loved the few days he'd gotten to spend here with Poppy before they'd almost lost their lives.

As he stared at the lodge, he swallowed the lump in his throat. But did he want to keep running a guest ranch? That was the question he had to answer, wasn't it.

But that wasn't the big question in his heart as he drove the rest of the way up to the lodge.

Poppy smiled as she surveyed the beautiful pies she and Kara had made. "I think the chamber of commerce will be quite happy with these," she said, nodding her approval. "Now we just need to get them down to city hall."

"Maybe I could help with that," said an all-too-familiar voice behind her.

She spun around and couldn't help but smile at the sight of Will Sterling standing in her catering kitchen.

She'd wished for this dozens of times since returning to Whitefish. She'd worried about him and had picked up the phone to call, but always stopped herself. He'd called a few times right afterward to make sure she was all right, but their conversation had been stilted, neither of them knowing what to say after what they'd experienced. She'd told herself that they both needed time.

But that had been a lie. She had needed Will. Still needed him.

"I hope you don't mind," he said. "I let myself in."

Poppy had thought she might never see him again. She'd done her best to accept that. But her heart had never stopped hoping. "Are you in town for the chamber of commerce get-together?"

He shook his head. "But I'd be happy to help get the pies there."

"I have it covered," Kara said quickly as she began to box up the pies and put them on the cart they used to transport food in the downtown area. Their van was parked outside.

"This is my top assistant, Kara," she said, introducing them. "Will Sterling."

"I'm her only assistant," her friend said. "And I know who you are."

He grinned. "I wondered why my ears were burning."

Kara reddened. "No, it wasn't like..." She held up her hands in surrender. "I'll be leaving with those pies now."

Poppy smiled at her friend, who was obviously trying to get out of the way as quickly as possible. "I did make an extra pie. Field berry, if you're interested," she told Will as Kara left.

"I could never pass up anything you baked," he said as he removed his Stetson. "You sure I shouldn't help your top assistant?"

"Trust me, she has everything under control. I don't know what I'd do without her." Poppy stepped to the counter, took down a knife and began to cut the still-warm field berry pie. Behind her, she heard the scrape of a chair on the floor as Will took a seat at the small kitchen table. Her heart was pounding so hard she thought it might burst from her chest. She had to steady her hand to cut the pie and put a piece on each of the two plates she pulled down from the cupboard.

"So business has been good?" he asked.

"It's been crazy," she said. "But good." She turned with the two plates and forks and carried the pie over to the table to join him. "Kara is full-time now. When I started I'd hoped I could give her more than part-time." She smiled. "So it's worked out."

"I'm glad," he said as he looked down at the pie. When he looked up, his gaze locked with hers. "I had no doubt that you would succeed."

She drew away first. What had she seen in those warm brown eyes? Whatever it was it had her heart doing the jitterbug. "But it pales in comparison to those days I spent cooking at your guest ranch."

"I'll bet," he said with a laugh. "None of your clients have tried to kill you?"

"Not yet," she said and swallowed the lump in her throat as she picked up her fork and cut a bite of her pie. Not even field berry pie could tempt her right now. She doubted she could even taste it—let alone swallow it.

Will hadn't taken a bite of his pie. He picked up his fork, but then put it down again. "I feel like we left some things unfinished."

She glanced up in surprise, wondering if he was thinking the same thing she was, and realized as he reached into his pocket they weren't.

"Things got so crazy that I didn't even pay you."

"I never told you what my going rate was," she said, trying to hide her disappointment.

"I could have called and asked, but I decided to pay you based on the joy you brought to the ranch—plus a bonus, of course," he said with a small laugh. "Actually, there is no amount that could cover what I think you're worth."

He slid the check over to her.

She stared in disbelief. "Will, this is way too much."

"I don't think so."

Poppy stared at the check, fighting tears of anger, disappointment, frustration. She wanted to rip it up in front of him. Didn't he realize after everything they'd been through that she hadn't done it for the money? She couldn't even look at him for fear what she might say. Or worse, do.

Will mentally booted himself in the butt. This wasn't going anything like he'd planned. He thought she'd be happy about the check. Clearly she was not. He could see her fighting some strong emotions.

He rushed on before she threw him out. "Poppy, that's not the only reason I'm here," he said and cleared his throat. "I need your help."

She bit her lower lip as she looked up at him. Those green eyes were more like lasers than warm, calm tropical seas. "My help?"

"After what happened up at the guest ranch, I was going to quit." He saw her surprise. "I just didn't want to do it anymore for so many reasons. I wanted something...more. My brothers and I talked about selling it. I had even talked to a real estate agent. But when I went back up there, I realized that it wasn't the guest ranch that was the problem." He met her green gaze and held it. "It was you."

It took her a moment. "You realized *I* was the problem?" she asked, disbelieving.

He nodded. "You were what made me want more." Poppy looked confused. He couldn't blame her. "You changed everything. I thought I was happy. Well, at least content. But then, you... I'm not saying this very well."

"Oh, I think you're doing a fine job," she said sarcastically. "I came into your life—"

"With a plan to break my heart."

"But instead—"

"Oh, you did a number on my heart, as well," he interrupted.

She stared at him. Those green eyes weren't quite as laser hot now. "What are you saying, Will?"

"Something I've never told another woman," he said and cleared his voice. It had taken him weeks to come here. He couldn't do what he was about to do unless he was more than just sure of his feelings. So he'd waited, fighting his need to see her, to tell her.

"Poppy, you stole my heart. My whole heart. And not just for the few days you spent at the guest ranch. It started long before that. I have so many memories of you that first summer we met. I know I was acting like none of it mattered when I was fifteen, but, Poppy, I have never forgotten anything about that summer or you." He raked a hand through his hair. "What I'm trying to say is..." He met her gaze and plunged in. "I love you."

★ ★ ★

Poppy blinked. She wanted to pinch herself. Was this really happening? After all this time, Will Sterling had finally said the words she'd longed to hear.

"Will," she said, feeling as if the earth under her was finally solid.

He stood up and came around the table to pull her to her feet. Her legs felt rubbery, but in Will's strong arms, she never felt more safe. "I love you, Poppy Carmichael."

His kiss was pure sugar. She melted into it. Nothing she'd ever baked had tasted so sweet.

As he drew back, he looked into her eyes. "I can't tell you how scared I was coming here today. I thought you might throw me out, rip up my check, laugh in my face."

"I did almost rip up your check," she said, making him laugh.

"Yes, I saw that look in your eye and thought for sure that I'd blown it with you again. Poppy, I have no idea what our lives look like from here on out. I just know I want to spend it with you." He waited. "This is where you break my heart or—"

"Or tell you that I've loved you since I was twelve?" She laughed. "It feels like it's been that long. But all it took were a few days with you at the guest ranch and it was as if those years in between never happened. I couldn't forget you. I love you, Will Sterling, with all my heart, and I always will. I don't want to break your heart. I want to steal it."

"You already have." He laughed as he picked her up and spun her around, before setting her down and dropping to one knee. All around them was the smell of freshly baked pies. "Marry me?"

She looked into his warm-as-molasses brown eyes. Had she really wanted to break this man's big heart? "There is nothing I would love more."

He reached into his pocket and took out a small velvet box.

Her pulse took off like Lightning, the wild horse she'd tried to ride at twelve, as she looked down at the most exquisite emerald engagement ring she'd ever seen. The beautifully cut stone was surrounded by diamonds that shimmered.

"Oh, Will, it's beautiful."

"The stone is the color of your eyes. The moment I saw it, I knew I had to give it to you." He slipped it on her finger. "It fits perfectly." He seemed to be relieved.

"How did you know what size?" she asked, looking up at him in surprise as he got to his feet.

"Kara. I'd seen you take off that ring you wore when you were making rolls at the ranch. I asked for her help."

"Kara?" she asked in surprise. No wonder her friend had taken off like a shot when Will had arrived. "So you've been planning this for a while, have you?"

He nodded and smiled. "Not as long as you'd been planning to break my heart with your cooking, I would wager."

She studied him, her handsome cowboy. "You wouldn't be interested in seeing my apartment upstairs, would you?"

Will looked into the amazing sea-green eyes of his fiancée. He loved the sound of that word. He loved this woman. What she was suggesting made him ache with desire. She'd tantalized him with her cooking and her incredible body, starting a fire in him that nothing on this earth could put out but her.

"I suppose you have a bed?" he asked.

"Would it matter?"

He laughed. "Not in the least."

Sweeping her up in his arms, he carried her upstairs. The apartment was small and cute, the furnishings an extension of the woman he'd fallen in love with. Not that he'd taken the time to check the place out.

It took them a while to make it to the bed. The moment the apartment door closed behind them, he pulled her to him and kissed her. He loved her mouth, relishing in it, telling himself he planned to kiss this woman every day for the rest of his life.

As Poppy drew back, she looked into his eyes as if she still couldn't believe this was happening. He couldn't, either, but his thoughts went elsewhere as she slowly began to unbutton his shirt to place her warm palms against his chest. She bent to kiss his nipple. Desire rocketed through him.

After that, their clothes came off much faster. He drew her T-shirt over her head in anxious expectation of freeing her beautiful breasts. She was working at the buttons on his jeans as they began to stumble toward the bedroom. He couldn't wait to get this woman naked.

Poppy would have said their lovemaking was a heated blur of hands and mouths and whispered words of affection and appreciation. But in truth she remembered every touch, every kiss, every sweet, sweet breath of it.

By the time they reached the bed, Will had stripped her naked. He threw her on the bed, then just stood over her, looking, taking her in with his eyes in a way that made her already hard nipples ache.

He climbed onto the bed, leaning over to kiss that spot on her throat that made her moan with pleasure. His lips trailed down to her eagerly awaiting breasts where he suckled and nipped and licked until she felt a release deep inside her as he pulled her into his arms.

She wanted to touch him, but he whispered, "Not yet," as he waited for her to come down from the high where he'd taken her as he slowly explored every inch of her, building that growing need again with his lips, his tongue, his fingers. She arched against him, thinking she couldn't stand it a moment longer, when she cried out, her legs going weak with pleasure.

Finally, Will let her touch him, taking him in her hand, guiding him into her. He plunged into her depths and she clung to him, holding her breath for a moment, before he slowly began to move.

She thought he couldn't take her any higher. She thought she had no more response to the pleasures he was offering her.

But she was wrong. This cowboy knew his way around her body as if he'd been waiting to get her naked for a long time.

This time, when the release came, Will was right there with her. Wrapped in each other's arms they both cried out as they reached new heights locked together.

Breathless, Poppy lay back on the bed, Will's hand resting on her bare thigh, and tried to catch her breath. Had she ever in her life felt like this? Never.

She glanced over at Will. He had a look on his face as if he felt the same way. "Wow," she said.

"My sentiments exactly." He rolled onto his side to look at her. "Poppy, I never thought I could love you more. I feel like you and I could do anything together."

She knew the feeling. "Will, you aren't really going to sell the guest ranch, are you?"

Will didn't tell her what he'd seen after they'd made love. But he'd seen Poppy pregnant with their first child, her stomach round and hard, her breasts full to aching, her face glowing. He'd seen them with children and a dog and a house. He'd seen them curled up in bed together, content and happy and full of life and love in their old age.

He'd seen it all in that moment. He'd wanted to share it with her, but he felt like he would be spoiling the ending, like a book she hadn't read yet. So he'd only smiled over at her and said, "I have no idea what I'm going to do. I was hoping you might have some ideas."

Poppy, being Poppy, said, "Oh, I have lots of ideas," and

turned on her side to kiss him. "I wish we'd brought the pie upstairs."

He laughed and pulled her to him, hugging her. He could feel the steady beat of her heart against his. "Stay here," he said and got up to pull on his jeans before going downstairs. He returned with the two pieces of pie, which they ate in the bed.

"Do you want a big wedding?" Will asked after he returned from taking their pie plates back downstairs.

She shook her head. "My father is out in Oregon. But other than him, I don't have any family I need to invite. Just a few friends."

"So it wouldn't take that long for you to plan a wedding."

Poppy grinned at him. "Are you getting at what I think you are?"

He laughed. "I think we should get married soon. I don't want to spend any more time than I have to away from you."

She nodded and kissed him. He tasted the tang of blackberries, the sweetness of strawberries, and caught the scent of apple from their pie. As he lost himself in the kiss, he had a feeling that this woman would always taste like something delectable. He looked forward to watching her cook, knowing it would always seem sensual to him. He chuckled to himself. He could watch this woman melt butter the rest of his life, knowing he would never go hungry for anything or anyone else.

News of the wedding of Will Sterling and Poppy Carmichael spread like wildfire through the county. Poppy couldn't believe all the people she ran into in downtown Whitefish who would stop her and offer her best wishes.

"Some of them don't seem sincere," she admitted to Kara one day in her catering kitchen.

Her friend laughed. "A woman Will apparently dated a few times stopped in the other day asking for our prices for a little get-together she was thinking about having. She seemed disappointed to realize that you weren't here. I know she just wanted to check you out, see what you have that she didn't."

Poppy had stopped what she was doing. "That's just it. What do I have that made him fall in love with me?"

"Who cares? He did."

"I'm serious. The woman who came in looking for me, she was beautiful, wasn't she?"

"Gorgeous. Do you really not know how beautiful you are?" Kara demanded. "You're beautiful from the inside out. And you can cook."

Poppy laughed but thanked her. "I feel bad about dumping all of this on you," she said with a wave of her hand that took in the entire kitchen as well as the catering business.

"Seriously? You offered me a chance to be my own boss, make good money and do what I love. Yes, it's a terrible imposition."

She smiled at her friend, remembering Kara and Dorothea standing up with her at the wedding. It had been one of those amazing Montana spring days. They'd chosen to get married outside at the guest ranch with only a few friends and family and hadn't waited long after the engagement announcement.

She'd loved the expression on Dorothea's face when she'd asked her to be her bridesmaid. The woman had been surprised and then touched. Dorothea had actually cried.

Poppy looked around the kitchen, thinking of all the catering jobs that continued to come in the door. "You're going to need help. And soon."

"I put an ad in the local shopper. With luck, I'll find someone who loves to cook like we do. Don't worry about me. Enjoy your honeymoon. Are you packed?"

She nodded. "Three swimsuits." Poppy grinned. "What else could I possibly need in Hawaii?"

"Sunscreen," Kara said. "How are the renovations on the house coming along?"

Poppy thought of the large log cabin—her first home in Montana and soon to be her forever home. "It is so beautiful. What's amazing is that Will and I never discussed furnishings, design, anything, but we love the same things. The renovations have made the place even more warm and cozy. But wait until you see the new kitchen."

"I can't wait. But what about the guest ranch? Will you be cooking for guests?"

She didn't know and said as much. "We're talking about our future. For right now, Garrett is overseeing the reconstruction of the barn and cabin that burned down. The guest ranch couldn't open this coming summer, anyway. So we'll see how Will feels after that. It's giving us time to make the old forest service cabin our home. It will be close to finished when we get back from our honeymoon. We're both so excited."

"I'd be excited, too. Hawaii this time of year should be wonderful," Kara said. "Which reminds me, I've been thinking of making this pineapple-coconut cake I found a recipe for."

Poppy laughed as her friend went to get the recipe to show her. "We are such gastronomists," she said with a shake of her head.

Kara lifted her nose in the air. "Epicureans, that's us."

A young woman no more than eighteen or nineteen with dyed pink hair appeared in the kitchen doorway holding a copy of the shopper. "I thought this job was about cooking," she said, frowning at them.

Poppy and Kara burst out laughing.

Kara stepped to her and introduced herself, then handed her the recipe for the pineapple-coconut cake. "Could you make this?"

The young woman, who'd introduced herself as Molly Stevens, glanced at the recipe. "Sure, but I would use coconut cream instead of coconut milk to make the cake more moist." She shrugged. "I like moist cakes so I always use butter."

Kara smiled and said, "Molly, when can you start work?"

EPILOGUE

Poppy stood at the window, looking out at the deer getting a drink from the creek in front of the log cabin. Afternoon shadows played over the clear water as the waning sun still coated the surface with gold. A breeze stirred the pines.

The deer's ears twitched as if it had heard something. Its head came up and the young buck looked right at Poppy. Big brown eyes blinked. The deer turned back to the water and took another drink before disappearing back into the pines.

"I wondered where you'd gotten off to," Will said as he came up behind her and put his arms around her, pulling her close.

"Did you see the deer?" she asked.

"Hmm," he said as he nuzzled her neck.

Poppy leaned back against him. "It's so beautiful here. I can never thank you enough for saving this old house."

"I couldn't let it be torn down. Too many memories of you and that creek." He chuckled. She could feel the sound reverberating against her back, his words going straight to her heart. "I remember the first time I saw you wading in it," he said quietly as if seeing the twelve-year-old girl she'd been.

"It was before we even met. I'd heard that someone was living in this house, but you were the last person I expected to see.

"It had been one of those clear, sunny early-summer days when the creek was still running ice cold," he continued. "But there you were, this wraith of a girl. You had your jeans rolled up to your knees. I remember your hair. It looked like fire in the sunlight. You had it pulled up off your neck in a ponytail. But it was the expression on your face that intrigued me." He chuckled. "All those freckles and those eyes of yours. I'd never seen a color green like that before."

"What expression was that?" she asked.

"That intense determination of yours. You were going to cross that creek even though the current was strong and the water was freezing."

She turned a little to look back at him in surprise. "You never told me this."

"With good reason. I could see that you were headed right for a deep hole. I thought about warning you, but decided to just let you go under in that cold water and see how you liked it."

"You were all boy at fifteen."

He laughed. "Wasn't I, though. I wanted to see what you'd do. I figured you'd cry and half drown and I'd have to save your life."

She smiled and turned back to the window, seeing that day through his eyes. "Of course that fifteen-year-old thought you'd have to save me."

"I waited. You took another step and then another and down you went and, sure enough, you were swept up in the current. I started to race after you, but darned if you didn't save yourself. And instead of crying, you came out of that freezing water fighting mad."

She remembered that day. Being from the Midwest, she'd

never known water that cold. It had sucked away her breath, numbed her entire body and given her an ice cream headache.

"Once you got your footing again at the edge of the other side of the creek, though, you started laughing. I couldn't believe it. I stood in the pines and watched you, completely enchanted. You hadn't seen me. You had your face turned up to the sun and you laughed as if that was the best adventure ever."

They both grew silent for a few moments.

"That laugh of yours," he said. "It was music to my ears. Still is." He kissed her neck, nibbling at her earlobe and making her shiver with a need that only intensified with each day they shared together as a married couple. "Your laugh hasn't changed. I fell in love with that freckle-faced soaking-wet girl that day."

She turned in his arms and smiled up at him. "Took you long enough to admit it."

He chuckled. "You do realize that the moment I saw you again all those old feelings came rushing back. True, they were all tangled up with that last day we were together and the guilt and regret I felt for hurting you—and losing you since I thought I would never see you again."

Poppy squinted her eyes suspiciously at him. "Is that what you were thinking when you saw me that day standing in the kitchen of the guest ranch after all those years?"

"That and 'I sure hope this woman can cook.'"

Poppy swatted playfully at him. "Admit it, it was my cooking that got to you."

"Oh, your cooking could steal any man's heart, but for this cowboy? It's those freckles." He laughed and swung her up into his arms before she could swat him again.

"What do you think you're doing?" she demanded as he carried her toward their bedroom.

"I'm going to make love to you, woman."

"Now that is music to *my* ears," she said and smiled at her husband, the cowboy she'd fallen for at twelve, the man who'd made her dreams come true.

And in that moment, she saw the future so clearly that she felt she could almost reach out and touch it. Her belly swollen with child and Will fussing over her. In a blink of the eye, she saw more children. They filled up this large old log cabin with a cacophony of joyful sounds and had the run of the ranch. She saw Will teaching each of them how to ride, so young that their fat little legs were barely long enough to fit over the saddle.

In another blink, there were the two of them sitting out on the porch overlooking the creek, their hair streaked with gray, their faces wrinkled from laughter and the Montana weather. Their gazes soft with everything they'd shared.

She saw them, the two of them sitting out there watching deer come down to the creek for a drink. And Will reaching over to take her hand as the evening sun dipped behind the mountains.

"Oh, the memories," he whispered. "Oh, the memories."

★ ★ ★ ★ ★

Poppy's Oatmeal Cake with Brown Sugar Glaze

In a bowl, put 1½ cups hot water. Add 1 cup oatmeal. Set aside.

In mixing bowl, cream ½ cup butter, 1 cup brown sugar and 1 cup granulated sugar.

Add two eggs, mix. Add 1½ cups flour, 1 teaspoon salt, 1 teaspoon cinnamon and 1 teaspoon vanilla.

Add oats and water mixture.

Pour into a 9x13-inch greased cake pan.

Bake at 350°F for 30 to 35 minutes.

Brown sugar glaze:

Boil ½ cup butter, 1½ cups brown sugar and 4 tablespoons evaporated milk for 1 minute.

Serve over warm cake with ice cream or whipped cream.

Easy Coconut Pie

Mix together:

2 cups canned evaporated milk
1 cup granulated sugar
4 eggs, beaten
½ cup flour
6 tablespoons butter, melted
1 teaspoon vanilla
½ teaspoon salt
1 cup coconut

Pour into greased 10-inch pie plate. Bake at 350°F for 50 to 55 minutes or until a knife blade inserted in the center comes out clean. This pie makes its own crust.

Serve warm.

Poppy's Guest Ranch Brownies

½ cup butter
1 cup granulated sugar
2 eggs
2/3 cup flour
2/3 cup nuts, chopped
1 teaspoon vanilla
2 squares chocolate, melted, or ⅓ cup cocoa
½ teaspoon salt

Cream butter, sugar and eggs. Add flour, salt, vanilla, chocolate and nuts.

Bake in 8-inch square pan at 325°F for 20 to 25 minutes. Don't overbake.

Ready for more?
Read on for a taste of Luck of the Draw.

Garrett Sterling brought his horse up short as something across the deep ravine caught his eye. A fierce wind swayed the towering pines against the mountainside as he dug out his binoculars. He could almost smell the rain in the air. Dark clouds had gathered over the top of Whitefish Mountain. If he didn't turn back soon, he would get caught in the summer thunderstorm. Not that he minded it all that much, except the construction crew working at the guest ranch would be anxious for the weekend and their paychecks.

Even as the wind threatened to send his Stetson flying and he felt the first few drops of rain dampen his long-sleeved Western shirt, he couldn't help being curious about what he'd glimpsed. He'd seen something moving through the trees on the other side of the deep ravine.

He raised the binoculars to his eyes, waiting for them to focus. "What the hell?" When he'd caught movement, he'd been expecting elk or maybe a deer. If he was lucky, a bear. He hadn't seen a grizzly in this area in a long time, but it was always a good idea to know if one was around.

But what had caught his eye was human. He stared, too startled to breathe for a moment. A large man moved through the pines. He wasn't alone. He had hold of a woman's wrist in what appeared to be a death grip and was dragging her through the trees. She seemed to be struggling to stay on her feet. It was what he saw in the man's other hand that had stolen his breath. A pistol.

Garrett couldn't believe what he was seeing. Surely, he was wrong. Through the binoculars, he tried to keep track of the two. But he kept losing them as they moved through the thick pines. His pulse pounded as he considered what to do.

His options were limited. He was too far away to intervene and he had a steep, deep ravine between him and the man with the gun. Nor could he call for help—as if help could arrive in time. There was no cell phone coverage this far back in the mountains outside of Whitefish, Montana.

Through the binoculars, he saw the woman burst out of the trees as she broke away from the man. For a moment, Garrett thought she was going to get away. But the man was larger and faster and was on her quickly, catching her and jerking her around to face him as he put the gun to her head.

"No!" Garrett cried, the sound lost in the wind and crackle of thunder in the distance. Dropping the binoculars onto his saddle, he drew his sidearm from the holster at his hip and fired a shot into the air. It echoed across the mountaintop, startling his horse.

As he struggled to holster the gun again and grab the binoculars, a shot from across the ravine filled the air, echoing back at him. And then another and another and another. Four shots, all in quick succession. He winced at each one as he hurriedly grabbed up the binoculars again and lifted them to his eyes. His hands shook as he tried to locate the spot on the mountainside across the ravine where he'd last seen the two people.

With dread, he saw what appeared to be a leg sticking out of the tall grass on the ground where the two had been only moments ago. He quickly looked around for the man. In the dense trees, he caught the blur of someone headed back in the direction where he'd originally spotted the two.

He focused again on what he could see of the body on the ground. The leg hadn't moved.

In the distance, he heard the faint sound of a car engine roaring to life. He swung the binoculars to the end of the ridgeline and saw a dark blue SUV speeding away. It was too far away to get more than that.

Garrett swore. At moments like this, he wished he had cell phone coverage on the mountain. But his father had always argued that being off the grid was the appeal of the Sterling's Montana Guest Ranch. No cell phones, no TV, no internet. Nothing but wild country.

Reining his horse around, he took off down the trail back to the guest ranch lodge. It had begun to rain by the time he leaped off his horse and hurried inside.

He used the landline to call Sheriff Sid Anderson.

"I just witnessed a murder," he said when the sheriff came on the line. He quickly told him what he'd seen, including giving him what information he could about the SUV that he'd seen roaring away.

"You fired a shot into the air?" the sheriff asked. "So the killer saw you?"

He hadn't thought of that. "From across the ravine. I don't think the killer is concerned about me."

"Let's hope not," Sid said. "You think you can take me to the body?"

"I can meet you where Red Meadow Road connects with the forest service property."

"Twenty minutes. I'll be there. But be careful," the sheriff warned. "The killer might not have gone far. Or he might be on the way to your guest ranch."

Available June 2019
wherever HQN books are sold.